THE BELL JAR

The brilliant and moving first novel
by Sylvia Plath

"A special poignance . . . a special force, a humbling power, because it shows the vulnerability of people of hope and good will."

—Newsweek

"By turns funny, harrowing, crude, ardent and artless. Its most notable quality is an astonishing immediacy, like a series of snapshots taken at high noon. The story, scarcely disguised autobiography, covers six months in a young girl's life, beginning when she goes to New York to serve on a fashion magazine's college-editorial board. It ends when she emerges from a mental hospital after a breakdown."

—Martha Duffy, Time

"Sylvia Plath's only novel is a deceptively modest, uncommonly fine piece of work . . . A sharp and memorable poignancy. With her classical restraint and purity of form, Sylvia Plath is always refusing to break your heart, though in the end, she breaks it anyway."
—Lucy Rosenthal, **Saturday Review**

"On February 11, 1963, a 30-year-old American poet, separated from her husband and living with her children in a cold London flat, gassed herself and passed into myth. Eight months later ten of her last poems, written at a speed of two or three a day, 'written,' she said, 'at about four in the morning . . . that still blue, almost eternal hour before the baby's cry, before the glassy music of the milkman, settling his bottles,' appeared on two pages of **Encounter** magazine and caused a sensation. In 1965 her husband brought out a posthumous collection, **Ariel** . . . In the eight years since her death Sylvia Plath has become a major figure in contemporary literature."
—Richard Locke, **The New York Times Book Review**

A LARRY PEERCE/
ROBERT A. GOLDSTON FILM

THE BELL JAR

Starring
MARILYN HASSETT   ANNE JACKSON
JULIE HARRIS   BARBARA BARRIE
and ROBERT KLEIN as Lenny

Screenplay by
MARJORIE KELLOGG

Based on the novel by
SYLVIA PLATH

A BRANDT-TODD PRODUCTION
in Association with
LaMARCA PRODUCTIONS, LTD.
& BONIME PRODUCTIONS LTD.

Produced by
JERROLD BRANDT, JR. & MICHAEL TODD, JR.

Co-Produced by
LaMARCA PRODUCTIONS, LTD.
& BONIME PRODUCTIONS LTD.

Executive Producer
ROBERT A. GOLDSTON

Directed by
LARRY PEERCE

An AVCO EMBASSY PICTURES Release

THE BELL JAR
Sylvia Plath

Biographical Note by Lois Ames

Drawings by Sylvia Plath

BANTAM BOOKS

TORONTO · NEW YORK · LONDON

THE BELL JAR

*A Bantam Book / published by arrangement with
Harper & Row, Publishers*

PRINTING HISTORY

*Harper & Row edition published February 1971
8 printings through September 1971*
McCall *Magazine excerpt published April 1971*
Literary Guild of America edition published May 1971
COSMOPOLITAN *Magazine excerpt published September 1971*
*Bantam edition / April 1972
26 printings through July 1980*

*Bantam Books are published by Bantam Books, Inc. Its trade-
mark, consisting of the words "Bantam Books" and the por-
trayal of a bantam, is Registered in U.S. Patent and Trademark
Office and in other countries. Marca Registrada. Bantam
Books, Inc., 666 Fifth Avenue, New York, New York 10103.*

For ELIZABETH and DAVID

One

IT WAS A QUEER, sultry summer, the summer they electrocuted the Rosenbergs, and I didn't know what I was doing in New York. I'm stupid about executions. The idea of being electrocuted makes me sick, and that's all there was to read about in the papers—goggle-eyed headlines staring up at me on every street corner and at the fusty, peanut-smelling mouth of every subway. It had nothing to do with me, but I couldn't help wondering what it would be like, being burned alive all along your nerves.

I thought it must be the worst thing in the world.

New York was bad enough. By nine in the morning the fake, country-wet freshness that somehow seeped in overnight evaporated like the tail end of a sweet dream. Mirage-gray at the bottom of their granite canyons, the hot streets wavered in the sun, the car tops sizzled and glittered, and the dry, cindery dust blew into my eyes and down my throat.

I kept hearing about the Rosenbergs over the radio and at the office till I couldn't get them out of my mind. It was like the first time I saw a cadaver. For weeks afterward, the cadaver's head—or what there was left of it—floated up behind my eggs and bacon at breakfast and behind the face of Buddy Willard, who was responsible for my seeing it in the first place, and pretty soon I felt as though I were carrying that cadaver's head around with me on a string, like some black, noseless balloon stinking of vinegar.

I knew something was wrong with me that summer, because all I could think about was the Rosenbergs and how stupid I'd been to buy all those uncomfortable, expensive clothes, hanging limp as fish in my closet, and how all the little successes I'd totted up so happily at college fizzled to

1

nothing outside the slick marble and plate-glass fronts along Madison Avenue.

I was supposed to be having the time of my life.

I was supposed to be the envy of thousands of other college girls just like me all over America who wanted nothing more than to be tripping about in those same size-seven patent leather shoes I'd bought in Bloomingdale's one lunch hour with a black patent leather belt and black patent leather pocketbook to match. And when my picture came out in the magazine the twelve of us were working on—drinking martinis in a skimpy, imitation silver-lamé bodice stuck on to a big, fat cloud of white tulle, on some Starlight Roof, in the company of several anonymous young men with all-American bone structures hired or loaned for the occasion—everybody would think I must be having a real whirl.

Look what can happen in this country, they'd say. A girl lives in some out-of-the-way town for nineteen years, so poor she can't afford a magazine, and then she gets a scholarship to college and wins a prize here and a prize there and ends up steering New York like her own private car.

Only I wasn't steering anything, not even myself. I just bumped from my hotel to work and to parties and from parties to my hotel and back to work like a numb trolleybus. I guess I should have been excited the way most of the other girls were, but I couldn't get myself to react. I felt very still and very empty, the way the eye of a tornado must feel, moving dully along in the middle of the surrounding hullabaloo.

There were twelve of us at the hotel.

We had all won a fashion magazine contest, by writing essays and stories and poems and fashion blurbs, and as prizes they gave us jobs in New York for a month, expenses paid, and piles and piles of free bonuses, like ballet tickets and passes to fashion shows and hair stylings at a famous expensive salon and chances to meet successful people in the field of our desire and advice about what to do with our particular complexions.

I still have the make-up kit they gave me, fitted out for a

person with brown eyes and brown hair: an oblong of brown mascara with a tiny brush, and a round basin of blue eyeshadow just big enough to dab the tip of your finger in, and three lipsticks ranging from red to pink, all cased in the same little gilt box with a mirror on one side. I also have a white plastic sunglasses case with colored shells and sequins and a green plastic starfish sewed onto it.

I realized we kept piling up these presents because it was as good as free advertising for the firms involved, but I couldn't be cynical. I got such a kick out of all those free gifts showering on to us. For a long time afterward I hid them away, but later, when I was all right again, I brought them out, and I still have them around the house. I use the lipsticks now and then, and last week I cut the plastic starfish off the sunglasses case for the baby to play with.

So there were twelve of us at the hotel, in the same wing on the same floor in single rooms, one after the other, and it reminded me of my dormitory at college. It wasn't a proper hotel—I mean a hotel where there are both men and women mixed about here and there on the same floor.

This hotel—the Amazon—was for women only, and they were mostly girls my age with wealthy parents who wanted to be sure their daughters would be living where men couldn't get at them and deceive them; and they were all going to posh secretarial schools like Katy Gibbs, where they had to wear hats and stockings and gloves to class, or they had just graduated from places like Katy Gibbs and were secretaries to executives and simply hanging around in New York waiting to get married to some career man or other.

These girls looked awfully bored to me. I saw them on the sunroof, yawning and painting their nails and trying to keep up their Bermuda tans, and they seemed bored as hell. I talked with one of them, and she was bored with yachts and bored with flying around in airplanes and bored with skiing in Switzerland at Christmas and bored with the men in Brazil.

Girls like that make me sick. I'm so jealous I can't speak. Nineteen years, and I hadn't been out of New England except for this trip to New York. It was my first big chance, but here I was, sitting back and letting it run through my fingers like so much water.

I guess one of my troubles was Doreen.

I'd never known a girl like Doreen before. Doreen came from a society girls' college down South and had bright white hair standing out in a cotton candy fluff round her head and blue eyes like transparent agate marbles, hard and polished and just about indestructible, and a mouth set in a sort of perpetual sneer. I don't mean a nasty sneer, but an amused, mysterious sneer, as if all the people around her were pretty silly and she could tell some good jokes on them if she wanted to.

Doreen singled me out right away. She made me feel I was that much sharper than the others, and she really was wonderfully funny. She used to sit next to me at the conference table, and when the visiting celebrities were talking she'd whisper witty sarcastic remarks to me under her breath.

Her college was so fashion conscious, she said, that all the girls had pocketbook covers made out of the same material as their dresses, so each time they changed their clothes they had a matching pocketbook. This kind of detail impressed me. It suggested a whole life of marvelous, elaborate decadence that attracted me like a magnet.

The only thing Doreen ever bawled me out about was bothering to get my assignments in by a deadline.

"What are you sweating over that for?" Doreen lounged on my bed in a peach silk dressing gown, filing her long, nicotine-yellow nails with an emery board, while I typed up the draft of an interview with a best-selling novelist.

That was another thing—the rest of us had starched cotton summer nighties and quilted housecoats, or maybe terrycloth robes that doubled as beachcoats, but Doreen wore these full-length nylon and lace jobs you could half see through, and dressing gowns the color of skin, that stuck to her by some kind of electricity. She had an interesting, slightly sweaty smell that reminded me of those scallopy leaves of sweet fern you break off and crush between your fingers for the musk of them.

"You know old Jay Cee won't give a damn if that story's in tomorrow or Monday." Doreen lit a cigarette and let the smoke flare slowly from her nostrils so her eyes were veiled. "Jay Cee's ugly as sin," Doreen went on coolly. "I bet that old husband of hers turns out all the lights before he gets near her or he'd puke otherwise."

Jay Cee was my boss, and I liked her a lot, in spite of what Doreen said. She wasn't one of the fashion magazine gushers with fake eyelashes and giddy jewelry. Jay Cee had brains, so her plug-ugly looks didn't seem to matter. She read a couple of languages and knew all the quality writers in the business.

I tried to imagine Jay Cee out of her strict office suit and luncheon-duty hat and in bed with her fat husband, but I just couldn't do it. I always had a terribly hard time trying to imagine people in bed together.

Jay Cee wanted to teach me something, all the old ladies I ever knew wanted to teach me something, but I suddenly didn't think they had anything to teach me. I fitted the lid on my typewriter and clicked it shut.

Doreen grinned. "Smart girl."

Somebody tapped at the door.

"Who is it?" I didn't bother to get up.

"It's me, Betsy. Are you coming to the party?"

"I guess so." I still didn't go to the door.

They imported Betsy straight from Kansas with her bouncing blonde ponytail and Sweetheart-of-Sigma-Chi smile. I remember once the two of us were called over to the office of some blue-chinned TV producer in a pin-stripe suit to see if we had any angles he could build up for a program, and Betsy started to tell about the male and female corn in Kansas. She got so excited about that damn corn even the producer had tears in his eyes, only he couldn't use any of it, unfortunately, he said.

Later on, the Beauty Editor persuaded Betsy to cut her hair and made a cover girl out of her, and I still see her face now and then, smiling out of those "P.Q.'s wife wears B.H. Wragge" ads.

Betsy was always asking me to do things with her and the other girls as if she were trying to save me in some way. She never asked Doreen. In private, Doreen called her Pollyanna Cowgirl.

"Do you want to come in our cab?" Betsy said through the door.

Doreen shook her head.

"That's all right, Betsy," I said. "I'm going with Doreen."

"Okay." I could hear Betsy padding off down the hall.

"We'll just go till we get sick of it," Doreen told me, stubbing out her cigarette in the base of my bedside reading lamp, "then we'll go out on the town. Those parties they stage here remind me of the old dances in the school gym. Why do they always round up Yalies? They're so *stoo*-pit!"

Buddy Willard went to Yale, but now I thought of it, what was wrong with him was that he was stupid. Oh, he'd managed to get good marks all right, and to have an affair with some awful waitress on the Cape by the name of Gladys, but he didn't have one speck of intuition. Doreen had intuition. Everything she said was like a secret voice speaking straight out of my own bones.

We were stuck in the theater-hour rush. Our cab sat wedged in back of Betsy's cab and in front of a cab with four of the other girls, and nothing moved.

Doreen looked terrific. She was wearing a strapless white lace dress zipped up over a snug corset affair that curved her in at the middle and bulged her out again spectacularly above and below, and her skin had a bronzy polish under the pale dusting powder. She smelled strong as a whole perfume store.

I wore a black shantung sheath that cost me forty dollars. It was part of a buying spree I had with some of my scholarship money when I heard I was one of the lucky ones going to New York. This dress was cut so queerly I couldn't wear any sort of a bra under it, but that didn't matter much as I was skinny as a boy and barely rippled, and I liked feeling almost naked on the hot summer nights.

The city had faded my tan, though. I looked yellow as a Chinaman. Ordinarily, I would have been nervous about my dress and my odd color, but being with Doreen made me forget my worries. I felt wise and cynical as all hell.

When the man in the blue lumber shirt and black chinos and tooled leather cowboy boots started to stroll over to us from under the striped awning of the bar where he'd been eyeing our cab, I couldn't have any illusions. I knew perfectly well he'd come for Doreen. He threaded his way out between the stopped cars and leaned engagingly on the sill of our open window.

"And what, may I ask, are two nice girls like you doing all alone in a cab on a nice night like this?"

He had a big, wide, white toothpaste-ad smile.

"We're on our way to a party," I blurted, since Doreen had gone suddenly dumb as a post and was fiddling in a blasé way with her white lace pocketbook cover.

"That sounds boring," the man said. "Whyn't you both join me for a couple of drinks in that bar over there? I've some friends waiting as well."

He nodded in the direction of several informally dressed men slouching around under the awning. They had been following him with their eyes, and when he glanced back at them, they burst out laughing.

The laughter should have warned me. It was a kind of low, know-it-all snicker, but the traffic showed signs of moving again, and I knew that if I sat tight, in two seconds I'd be wishing I'd taken this gift of a chance to see something of New York besides what the people on the magazine had planned out for us so carefully.

"How about it, Doreen?" I said.

"How about it, Doreen?" the man said, smiling his big smile. To this day I can't remember what he looked like when he wasn't smiling. I think he must have been smiling the whole time. It must have been natural for him, smiling like that.

"Well, all right," Doreen said to me. I opened the door, and we stepped out of the cab just as it was edging ahead again and started to walk over to the bar.

There was a terrible shriek of brakes followed by a dull thump-thump.

"Hey you!" Our cabby was craning out of his window with a furious, purple expression. "Waddaya think you're doin'?"

He had stopped the cab so abruptly that the cab behind bumped smack into him, and we could see the four girls inside waving and struggling and scrambling up off the floor.

The man laughed and left us on the curb and went back and handed a bill to the driver in the middle of a great honking and some yelling, and then we saw the girls from the magazine moving off in a row, one cab after another, like a wedding party with nothing but bridesmaids.

"Come on, Frankie," the man said to one of his friends in the group, and a short, scrunty fellow detached himself and came into the bar with us.

He was the type of fellow I can't stand. I'm five feet ten in my stocking feet, and when I am with little men I stoop over a bit and slouch my hips, one up and one down, so I'll look shorter, and I feel gawky and morbid as somebody in a sideshow.

For a minute I had a wild hope we might pair off according to size, which would line me up with the man who had spoken to us in the first place, and he cleared a good six feet, but he went ahead with Doreen and didn't give me a second look. I tried to pretend I didn't see Frankie dogging along at my elbow and sat close by Doreen at the table.

It was so dark in the bar I could hardly make out anything except Doreen. With her white hair and white dress she was so white she looked silver. I think she must have reflected the neons over the bar. I felt myself melting into the shadows like the negative of a person I'd never seen before in my life.

"Well, what'll we have?" the man asked with a large smile.

"I think I'll have an old-fashioned," Doreen said to me.

Ordering drinks always floored me. I didn't know whisky from gin and never managed to get anything I really liked the taste of. Buddy Willard and the other college boys I knew were usually too poor to buy hard liquor or they scorned drinking altogether. It's amazing how many college boys don't drink or smoke. I seemed to know them all. The farthest Buddy Willard ever went was buying us a bottle of Dubonnet, which he only did because he was trying to prove he could be aesthetic in spite of being a medical student.

"I'll have a vodka," I said.

The man looked at me more closely. "With anything?"

"Just plain," I said. "I always have it plain."

I thought I might make a fool of myself by saying I'd have it with ice or gin or anything. I'd seen a vodka ad once, just a glass full of vodka standing in the middle of a snowdrift in a blue light, and the vodka looked clear and pure as water, so I thought having vodka plain must be all right. My dream was someday ordering a drink and finding out it tasted wonderful.

The waiter came up then, and the man ordered drinks for the four of us. He looked so at home in that citified bar in his ranch outfit I thought he might well be somebody famous.

Doreen wasn't saying a word, she only toyed with her cork placemat and eventually lit a cigarette, but the man didn't seem to mind. He kept staring at her the way people stare at the great white macaw in the zoo, waiting for it to say something human.

The drinks arrived, and mine looked clear and pure, just like the vodka ad.

"What do you do?" I asked the man, to break the silence shooting up around me on all sides, thick as jungle grass. "I mean what do you do here in New York?"

Slowly and with what seemed a great effort, the man dragged his eyes away from Doreen's shoulder. "I'm a disc jockey," he said. "You prob'ly must have heard of me. The name's Lenny Shepherd."

"I know you," Doreen said suddenly.

"I'm glad about that, honey," the man said, and burst out laughing. "That'll come in handy. I'm famous as hell."

Then Lenny Shepherd gave Frankie a long look.

"Say, where do you come from?" Frankie asked, sitting up with a jerk. "What's your name?"

"This here's Doreen." Lenny slid his hand around Doreen's bare arm and gave her a squeeze.

What surprised me was that Doreen didn't let on she noticed what he was doing. She just sat there, dusky as a bleached-blonde Negress in her white dress, and sipped daintily at her drink.

"My name's Elly Higginbottom," I said. "I come from Chicago." After that I felt safer. I didn't want anything I said or did that night to be associated with me and my real name and coming from Boston.

"Well, Elly, what do you say we dance some?"

The thought of dancing with that little runt in his orange suede elevator shoes and mingy T-shirt and droopy blue sports coat made me laugh. If there's anything I look down on, it's a man in a blue outfit. Black or gray, or brown, even. Blue makes me laugh.

"I'm not in the mood," I said coldly, turning my back on him and hitching my chair over nearer to Doreen and Lenny.

Those two looked as if they'd known each other for years by now. Doreen was spooning up the hunks of fruit at the bottom of her glass with a spindly silver spoon, and Lenny was grunting each time she lifted the spoon to her mouth, and snapping and pretending to be a dog or something, and trying to get the fruit off the spoon. Doreen giggled and kept spooning up the fruit.

I began to think vodka was my drink at last. It didn't taste like anything, but it went straight down into my stomach like a sword swallower's sword and made me feel powerful and godlike.

"I better go now," Frankie said, standing up.

I couldn't see him very clearly, the place was so dim, but for the first time I heard what a high, silly voice he had. Nobody paid him any notice.

"Hey, Lenny, you owe me something. Remember, Lenny, you owe me something, don't you, Lenny?"

I thought it odd Frankie should be reminding Lenny he owed him something in front of us, and we being perfect strangers, but Frankie stood there saying the same thing over and over until Lenny dug into his pocket and pulled out a big roll of green bills and peeled one off and handed it to Frankie. I think it was ten dollars.

"Shut up and scram."

For a minute I thought Lenny was talking to me as well, but then I heard Doreen say, "I won't come unless Elly comes." I had to hand it to her the way she picked up my fake name.

"Oh, Elly'll come, won't you, Elly?" Lenny said, giving me a wink.

"Sure I'll come," I said. Frankie had wilted away into the night, so I thought I'd string along with Doreen. I wanted to see as much as I could.

I liked looking on at other people in crucial situations. If there was a road accident or a street fight or a baby pickled in a laboratory jar for me to look at, I'd stop and look so hard I never forgot it.

I certainly learned a lot of things I never would have learned otherwise this way, and even when they surprised me or made me sick I never let on, but pretended that's the way I knew things were all the time.

Two

I WOULDN'T HAVE MISSED Lenny's place for anything.

It was built exactly like the inside of a ranch, only in the middle of a New York apartment house. He'd had a few partitions knocked down to make the place broaden out, he said, and then had them pine-panel the walls and fit up a special pine-paneled bar in the shape of a horseshoe. I think the floor was pine-paneled, too.

Great white bearskins lay about underfoot, and the only furniture was a lot of low beds covered with Indian rugs. Instead of pictures hung up on the walls, he had antlers and buffalo horns and a stuffed rabbit head. Lenny jutted a thumb at the meek little gray muzzle and stiff jackrabbit ears.

"Ran over that in Las Vegas."

He walked away across the room, his cowboy boots echoing like pistol shots. "Acoustics," he said, and grew smaller and smaller until he vanished through a door in the distance.

All at once music started to come out of the air on every side. Then it stopped, and we heard Lenny's voice say "This is your twelve o'clock disc jock, Lenny Shepherd, with a round-up of the tops in pops. Number Ten in the wagon train this week is none other than that little yaller-haired gal you been hearin' so much about lately . . . the one an' only *Sunflower!*"

> *I was born in Kansas, I was bred in Kansas,*
> *And when I marry I'll be wed in Kansas . . .*

"What a card!" Doreen said. "Isn't he a card?"

"You bet," I said.

"Listen, Elly, do me a favor." She seemed to think Elly was who I really was by now.

"Sure," I said.

12

"Stick around, will you? I wouldn't have a chance if he tried anything funny. Did you see that muscle?" Doreen giggled.

Lenny popped out of the back room. "I got twenty grand's worth of recording equipment in there." He ambled over to the bar and set out three glasses and a silver ice bucket and a big pitcher and began to mix drinks from several different bottles.

... to a true-blue gal who promised she would wait—
She's the sunflower of the Sunflower State.

"Terrific, huh?" Lenny came over, balancing three glasses. Big drops stood out on them like sweat, and the ice cubes jingled as he passed them around. Then the music twanged to a stop, and we heard Lenny's voice announcing the next number.

"Nothing like listening to yourself talk. Say," Lenny's eye lingered on me, "Frankie vamoosed, you ought to have somebody, I'll call up one of the fellers."

"That's okay," I said. "You don't have to do that." I didn't want to come straight out and ask for somebody several sizes larger than Frankie.

Lenny looked relieved. "Just so's you don't mind. I wouldn't want to do wrong by a friend of Doreen's." He gave Doreen a big white smile. "Would I, honeybun?"

He held out a hand to Doreen, and without a word they both started to jitterbug, still hanging onto their glasses.

I sat cross-legged on one of the beds and tried to look devout and impassive like some businessmen I once saw watching an Algerian belly dancer, but as soon as I leaned back against the wall under the stuffed rabbit, the bed started to roll out into the room, so I sat down on a bearskin on the floor and leaned back against the bed instead.

My drink was wet and depressing. Each time I took another sip it tasted more and more like dead water. Around the middle of the glass there was painted a pink lasso with yellow polka dots. I drank to about an inch below the lasso and waited a bit, and when I went to take another sip, the drink was up to lasso-level again.

Out of the air Lenny's voice boomed, "Wye oh wye did I ever leave Wyoming?"

The two of them didn't even stop jitterbugging during the intervals. I felt myself shrinking to a small black dot against all those red and white rugs and that pine paneling. I felt like a hole in the ground.

There is something demoralizing about watching two people get more and more crazy about each other, especially when you are the only extra person in the room.

It's like watching Paris from an express caboose heading in the opposite direction—every second the city gets smaller and smaller, only you feel it's really you getting smaller and smaller and lonelier and lonelier, rushing away from all those lights and that excitement at about a million miles an hour.

Every so often Lenny and Doreen would bang into each other and kiss and then swing to take a long drink and close in on each other again. I thought I might just lie down on the bearskin and go to sleep until Doreen felt ready to go back to the hotel.

Then Lenny gave a terrible roar. I sat up. Doreen was hanging on to Lenny's left earlobe with her teeth.

"Leggo, you bitch!"

Lenny stooped, and Doreen went flying up on to his shoulder, and her glass sailed out of her hand in a long, wide arc and fetched up against the pine paneling with a silly tinkle. Lenny was still roaring and whirling round so fast I couldn't see Doreen's face.

I noted, in the routine way you notice the color of somebody's eyes, that Doreen's breasts had popped out of her dress and were swinging out slightly like full brown melons as she circled belly-down on Lenny's shoulder, thrashing her legs in the air and screeching, and then they both started to laugh and slow up, and Lenny was trying to bite Doreen's hip through her skirt when I let myself out the door before anything more could happen and managed to get downstairs by leaning with both hands on the banister and half sliding the whole way.

I didn't realize Lenny's place had been air-conditioned until I wavered out onto the pavement. The tropical, stale heat the sidewalks had been sucking up all day hit me in the face like a last insult. I didn't know where in the world I was.

For a minute I entertained the idea of taking a cab to the party after all, but decided against it because the dance might be over by now, and I didn't feel like ending up in an empty barn of a ballroom strewn with confetti and cigarette butts and crumpled cocktail napkins.

I walked carefully to the nearest street corner, brushing the wall of the buildings on my left with the tip of one finger to steady myself. I looked at the street sign. Then I took my New York street map out of my pocketbook. I was exactly forty-three blocks by five blocks away from my hotel.

Walking has never fazed me. I just set out in the right direction, counting the blocks under my breath, and when I walked into the lobby of the hotel I was perfectly sober and my feet only slightly swollen, but that was my own fault because I hadn't bothered to wear any stockings.

The lobby was empty except for a night clerk dozing in his lit booth among the key rings and the silent telephones.

I slid into the self-service elevator and pushed the button for my floor. The doors folded shut like a noiseless accordion. Then my ears went funny, and I noticed a big, smudgy-eyed Chinese woman staring idiotically into my face. It was only me, of course. I was appalled to see how wrinkled and used up I looked.

There wasn't a soul in the hall. I let myself into my room. It was full of smoke. At first I thought the smoke had materialized out of thin air as a sort of judgment, but then I remembered it was Doreen's smoke and pushed the button that opened the window vent. They had the windows fixed so you couldn't really open them and lean out, and for some reason this made me furious.

By standing at the left side of the window and laying my cheek to the woodwork, I could see downtown to where the UN balanced itself in the dark, like a weird green Martian honeycomb. I could see the moving red and white lights along the drive and the lights of the bridges whose names I didn't know.

The silence depressed me. It wasn't the silence of silence. It was my own silence.

I knew perfectly well the cars were making noise, and the people in them and behind the lit windows of the buildings were making a noise, and the river was making a noise, but I couldn't hear a thing. The city hung in my window, flat as a poster, glittering and blinking, but it might just as well not have been there at all, for all the good it did me.

The china-white bedside telephone could have connected me up with things, but there it sat, dumb as a death's head. I tried to think of people I'd given my phone number to, so I could make a list of all the possible calls I might be about to receive, but all I could think of was that I'd given my phone number to Buddy Willard's mother so she could give it to a simultaneous interpreter she knew at the UN.

I let out a small, dry laugh.

I could imagine the sort of simultaneous interpreter Mrs. Willard would introduce me to when all the time she wanted me to marry Buddy, who was taking the cure for TB somewhere in upper New York State. Buddy's mother had even arranged for me to be given a job as a waitress at the TB sanatorium that summer so Buddy wouldn't be lonely. She and Buddy couldn't understand why I chose to go to New York City instead.

The mirror over my bureau seemed slightly warped and much too silver. The face in it looked like the reflection in a ball of dentist's mercury. I thought of crawling in between the bed sheets and trying to sleep, but that appealed to me about as much as stuffing a dirty, scrawled-over letter into a fresh, clean envelope. I decided to take a hot bath.

There must be quite a few things a hot bath won't cure, but I don't know many of them. Whenever I'm sad I'm going to die, or so nervous I can't sleep, or in love with somebody I won't be seeing for a week, I slump down just so far and then I say: "I'll go take a hot bath."

I meditate in the bath. The water needs to be very hot, so hot you can barely stand putting your foot in it. Then you lower yourself, inch by inch, till the water's up to your neck.

I remember the ceiling over every bathtub I've stretched out in. I remember the texture of the ceilings and the cracks and the colors and the damp spots and the light fixtures. I remember the tubs, too: the antique griffin-legged tubs, and the modern coffin-shaped tubs, and the fancy pink marble tubs overlooking indoor lily ponds, and I remember the shapes and sizes of the water taps and the different sorts of soap holders.

I never feel so much myself as when I'm in a hot bath.

I lay in that tub on the seventeenth floor of this hotel for-women-only, high up over the jazz and push of New York, for near onto an hour, and I felt myself growing pure again. I don't believe in baptism or the waters of Jordan or anything like that, but I guess I feel about a hot bath the way those religious people feel about holy water.

I said to myself: "Doreen is dissolving, Lenny Shepherd is dissolving, Frankie is dissolving, New York is dissolving, they are all dissolving away and none of them matter any more. I don't know them, I have never known them and I am very pure. All that liquor and those sticky kisses I saw and the dirt that settled on my skin on the way back is turning into something pure."

The longer I lay there in the clear hot water the purer I felt, and when I stepped out at last and wrapped myself in one of the big, soft white hotel bath towels I felt pure and sweet as a new baby.

I don't know how long I had been asleep when I heard the knocking. I didn't pay any attention at first, because the person knocking kept saying, "Elly, Elly, Elly, let me in," and I didn't know any Elly. Then another kind of knock sounded over the first dull, bumping knock—a sharp tap-tap, and another, much crisper voice said, "Miss Greenwood, your friend wants you," and I knew it was Doreen.

I swung to my feet and balanced dizzily for a minute in the middle of the dark room. I felt angry with Doreen for waking me up. All I stood a chance of getting out of that sad night was a good sleep, and she had to wake me up and spoil it. I thought if I pretended to be asleep the knocking might go away and leave me in peace, but I waited, and it didn't.

"Elly, Elly, Elly," the first voice mumbled, while the other voice went on hissing, "Miss Greenwood, Miss Greenwood, Miss Greenwood," as if I had a split personality or something.

I opened the door and blinked out into the bright hall. I had the impression it wasn't night and it wasn't day, but some lurid third interval that had suddenly slipped between them and would never end.

Doreen was slumped against the doorjamb. When I came out, she toppled into my arms. I couldn't see her face because her head was hanging down on her chest and her stiff blonde hair fell down from its dark roots like a hula fringe.

I recognized the short, squat, mustached woman in the black uniform as the night maid who ironed day dresses and party frocks in a crowded cubicle on our floor. I couldn't understand how she came to know Doreen or why she should want to help Doreen wake me up instead of leading her quietly back to her own room.

Seeing Doreen supported in my arms and silent except for a few wet hiccups, the woman strode away down the hall to her cubicle with its ancient Singer sewing machine and white ironing board. I wanted to run after her and tell her I had nothing to do with Doreen, because she looked stern and hardworking and moral as an old-style European immigrant and reminded me of my Austrian grandmother.

"Lemme lie down, lemme lie down," Doreen was muttering. "Lemme lie down, lemme lie down."

I felt if I carried Doreen across the threshold into my room and helped her onto my bed I would never get rid of her again.

Her body was warm and soft as a pile of pillows against my arm where she leaned her weight, and her feet, in their high, spiked heels, dragged foolishly. She was much too heavy for me to budge down the long hall.

I decided the only thing to do was to dump her on the carpet and shut and lock my door and go back to bed. When Doreen woke up she wouldn't remember what had happened and would think she must have passed out in front of my door while I slept, and she would get up of her own accord and go sensibly back to her room.

I started to lower Doreen gently onto the green hall carpet, but she gave a low moan and pitched forward out of my arms. A jet of brown vomit flew from her mouth and spread in a large puddle at my feet.

Suddenly Doreen grew even heavier. Her head drooped forward into the puddle, the wisps of her blonde hair dabbling in it like tree roots in a bog, and I realized she was asleep. I drew back. I felt half-asleep myself.

I made a decision about Doreen that night. I decided I would watch her and listen to what she said, but deep down I would have nothing at all to do with her. Deep down, I would be loyal to Betsy and her innocent friends. It was Betsy I resembled at heart.

Quietly, I stepped back into my room and shut the door. On second thought, I didn't lock it. I couldn't quite bring myself to do that.

When I woke up in the dull, sunless heat the next morning, I dressed and splashed my face with cold water and put on some lipstick and opened the door slowly. I think I still expected to see Doreen's body lying there in the pool of vomit like an ugly, concrete testimony to my own dirty nature.

There was nobody in the hall. The carpet stretched from one end of the hall to the other, clean and eternally verdant except for a faint, irregular dark stain before my door as if somebody had by accident spilled a glass of water there, but dabbed it dry again.

Three

ARRAYED ON THE *Ladies' Day* banquet table were yellow-green avocado pear halves stuffed with crabmeat and mayonnaise, and platters of rare roast beef and cold chicken, and every so often a cut-glass bowl heaped with black caviar. I hadn't had time to eat any breakfast at the hotel cafeteria that morning, except for a cup of overstewed coffee so bitter it made my nose curl, and I was starving.

Before I came to New York I'd never eaten out in a proper restaurant. I don't count Howard Johnson's, where I only had french fries and cheeseburgers and vanilla frappes with people like Buddy Willard. I'm not sure why it is, but I love food more than just about anything else. No matter how much I eat, I never put on weight. With one exception I've been the same weight for ten years.

My favorite dishes are full of butter and cheese and sour cream. In New York we had so many free luncheons with people on the magazine and various visiting celebrities I developed the habit of running my eye down those huge handwritten menus, where a tiny side dish of peas cost fifty or sixty cents, until I'd picked the richest, most expensive dishes and ordered a string of them.

We were always taken out on expense accounts, so I never felt guilty. I made a point of eating so fast I never kept the other people waiting who generally ordered only chef's salad and grapefruit juice because they were trying to reduce. Almost everybody I met in New York was trying to reduce.

"I want to welcome the prettiest, smartest bunch of young ladies our staff has yet had the good luck to meet," the plump, bald master-of-ceremonies wheezed into his lapel microphone. "This banquet is just a small sample of the hospitality our

Food Testing Kitchens here on *Ladies' Day* would like to offer in appreciation for your visit."

A delicate, ladylike spatter of applause, and we all sat at the enormous linen-draped table.

There were eleven of us girls from the magazine, together with most of our supervising editors, and the whole staff of the *Ladies' Day* Food Testing Kitchens in hygienic white smocks, neat hairnets and flawless makeup of a uniform peach-pie color.

There were only eleven of us, because Doreen was missing. They had set her place next to mine for some reason, and the chair stayed empty. I saved her placecard for her—a pocket mirror with "Doreen" painted along the top of it in lacy script and a wreath of frosted daisies around the edge, framing the silver hole where her face would show.

Doreen was spending the day with Lenny Shepherd. She spent most of her free time with Lenny Shepherd now.

In the hour before our luncheon at *Ladies' Day*—the big women's magazine that features lush double-page spreads of Technicolor meals, with a different theme and locale each month—we had been shown around the endless glossy kitchens and seen how difficult it is to photograph apple pie à la mode under bright lights because the ice cream keeps melting and has to be propped up from behind with toothpicks and changed every time it starts looking too soppy.

The sight of all the food stacked in those kitchens made me dizzy. It's not that we hadn't enough to eat at home, it's just that my grandmother always cooked economy joints and economy meat loafs and had the habit of saying, the minute you lifted the first forkful to your mouth, "I hope you enjoy that, it cost forty-one cents a pound," which always made me feel I was somehow eating pennies instead of Sunday roast.

While we were standing up behind our chairs listening to the welcome speech, I had bowed my head and secretly eyed the position of the bowls of caviar. One bowl was set strategically between me and Doreen's empty chair.

I figured the girl across from me couldn't reach it because of the mountainous centerpiece of marzipan fruit, and Betsy, on my right, would be too nice to ask me to share it with her if I just kept it out of the way at my elbow by my bread-and-butter plate. Besides, another bowl of caviar sat a little way to the right of the girl next to Betsy, and she could eat that.

My grandfather and I had a standing joke. He was the head waiter at a country club near my home town, and every Sunday my grandmother drove in to bring him home for his Monday off. My brother and I alternated going with her, and my grandfather always served Sunday supper to my grandmother and whichever of us was along as if we were regular club guests. He loved introducing me to special tidbits, and by the age of nine I had developed a passionate taste for cold vichyssoise and caviar and anchovy paste.

The joke was that at my wedding my grandfather would see I had all the caviar I could eat. It was a joke because I never intended to get married, and even if I did, my grandfather couldn't have afforded enough caviar unless he robbed the country club kitchen and carried it off in a suitcase.

Under cover of the clinking of water goblets and silverware and bone china, I paved my plate with chicken slices. Then I covered the chicken slices with caviar thickly as if I were spreading peanut butter on a piece of bread. Then I picked up the chicken slices in my fingers one by one, rolled them so the caviar wouldn't ooze off and ate them.

I'd discovered, after a lot of extreme apprehension about what spoons to use, that if you do something incorrect at table with a certain arrogance, as if you knew perfectly well you were doing it properly, you can get away with it and nobody will think you are bad-mannered or poorly brought up. They will think you are original and very witty.

I learned this trick the day Jay Cee took me to lunch with a famous poet. He wore a horrible, lumpy, speckled brown tweed jacket and gray pants and a red-and-blue checked open-throated jersey in a very formal restaurant full of fountains and chandeliers, where all the other men were dressed in dark suits and immaculate white shirts.

This poet ate his salad with his fingers, leaf by leaf, while talking to me about the antithesis of nature and art. I couldn't take my eyes off the pale, stubby white fingers traveling back and forth from the poet's salad bowl to the poet's mouth with one dripping lettuce leaf after another. Nobody giggled or whispered rude remarks. The poet made eating salad with your fingers seem to be the only natural and sensible thing to do.

None of our magazine editors or the *Ladies' Day* staff members sat anywhere near me, and Betsy seemed sweet and friendly, she didn't even seem to like caviar, so I grew more and more confident. When I finished my first plate of cold chicken and caviar, I laid out another. Then I tackled the avocado and crabmeat salad.

Avocados are my favorite fruit. Every Sunday my grandfather used to bring me an avocado pear hidden at the bottom of his briefcase under six soiled shirts and the Sunday comics. He taught me how to eat avocados by melting grape jelly and french dressing together in a saucepan and filling the cup of the pear with the garnet sauce. I felt homesick for that sauce. The crabmeat tasted bland in comparison.

"How was the fur show?" I asked Betsy, when I was no longer worried about competition over my caviar. I scraped the last few salty black eggs from the dish with my soup spoon and licked it clean.

"It was wonderful," Betsy smiled. "They showed us how to make an all-purpose neckerchief out of mink tails and a gold chain, the sort of chain you can get an exact copy of at Woolworth's for a dollar ninety-eight, and Hilda nipped down to the wholesale fur warehouses right afterward and bought a bunch of mink tails at a big discount and dropped in at Woolworth's and then stitched the whole thing together coming up on the bus."

I peered over at Hilda, who sat on the other side of Betsy. Sure enough, she was wearing an expensive-looking scarf of furry tails fastened on one side by a dangling gilt chain.

I never really understood Hilda. She was six feet tall, with huge, slanted green eyes and thick red lips and a vacant, Slavic expression. She made hats. She was apprenticed to the Fashion Editor, which set her apart from the more literary ones among us like Doreen and Betsy and I myself, who all wrote columns, even if some of them were only about health and beauty. I don't know if Hilda could read, but she made startling hats. She went to a special school for making hats in New York and every day she wore a new hat to work, constructed by her own hands out of bits of straw or fur or ribbon or veiling in subtle shades.

"That's amazing," I said. "Amazing." I missed Doreen. She would have murmured some fine, scalding remark about Hilda's miraculous furpiece to cheer me up.

I felt very low. I had been unmasked only that morning by Jay Cee herself, and I felt now that all the uncomfortable suspicions I had about myself were coming true, and I couldn't hide the truth much longer. After nineteen years of running after good marks and prizes and grants of one sort and another, I was letting up, slowing down, dropping clean out of the race.

"Why didn't you come along to the fur show with us?" Betsy asked. I had the impression she was repeating herself, and that she'd asked me the same question a minute ago, only I couldn't have been listening. "Did you go off with Doreen?"

"No," I said, "I wanted to go to the fur show, but Jay Cee called up and made me come into the office." That wasn't quite true about wanting to go to the show, but I tried to convince myself now that it was true, so I could be really wounded about what Jay Cee had done.

I told Betsy how I had been lying in bed that morning planning to go to the fur show. What I didn't tell her was that Doreen had come into my room earlier and said, "What do you want to go to that assy show for, Lenny and I are going to Coney Island, so why don't you come along? Lenny can get you a nice fellow, the day's shot to hell anyhow with that luncheon and then the film première in the afternoon, so nobody'll miss us."

For a minute I was tempted. The show certainly did seem stupid. I have never cared for furs. What I decided to do in the end was lie in bed as long as I wanted to and then go to Central Park and spend the day lying in the grass, the longest grass I could find in that bald, duck-ponded wilderness.

I told Doreen I would not go to the show or the luncheon or the film première, but that I would not go to Coney Island either, I would stay in bed. After Doreen left, I wondered why I couldn't go the whole way doing what I should any more. This made me sad and tired. Then I wondered why I couldn't go the whole way doing what I shouldn't, the way Doreen did, and this made me even sadder and more tired.

I didn't know what time it was, but I'd heard the girls bustling and calling in the hall and getting ready for the fur show, and then I'd heard the hall go still, and as I lay on my back in bed staring up at the blank, white ceiling the stillness seemed to grow bigger and bigger until I felt my eardrums would burst with it. Then the phone rang.

I stared at the phone for a minute. The receiver shook a bit in its bone-colored cradle, so I could tell it was really ringing. I thought I might have given my phone number to somebody at a dance or a party and then forgotten about it. I lifted the receiver and spoke in a husky, receptive voice.

"Hello?"

"Jay Cee here," Jay Cee rapped out with brutal promptitude. "I wondered if you happened to be planning to come into the office today?"

I sank down into the sheets. I couldn't understand why Jay Cee thought I'd be coming into the office. We had these mimeographed schedule cards so we could keep track of all our activities, and we spent a lot of mornings and afternoons away from the office going to affairs in town. Of course, some of the affairs were optional.

There was quite a pause. Then I said meekly, "I thought I was going to the fur show." Of course I hadn't thought any such thing, but I couldn't figure out what else to say.

"I told her I thought I was going to the fur show," I said to Betsy. "But she told me to come into the office, she wanted to have a little talk with me, and there was some work to do."

"Oh-oh!" Betsy said sympathetically. She must have seen the tears that plopped down into my dessert dish of meringue and brandy ice cream, because she pushed over her own untouched dessert and I started absently on that when I'd finished my own. I felt a bit awkward about the tears, but they were real enough. Jay Cee had said some terrible things to me.

When I made my wan entrance into the office at about ten o'clock, Jay Cee stood up and came round her desk to shut the door, and I sat in the swivel chair in front of my typewriter table facing her, and she sat in the swivel chair behind her desk facing me, with the window full of potted plants, shelf after shelf of them, springing up at her back like a tropical garden.

"Doesn't your work interest you, Esther?"

"Oh, it does, it does," I said. "It interests me very much." I felt like yelling the words, as if that might make them more convincing, but I controlled myself.

All my life I'd told myself studying and reading and writing and working like mad was what I wanted to do, and it actually seemed to be true, I did everything well enough and got all A's, and by the time I made it to college nobody could stop me.

I was college correspondent for the town *Gazette* and editor of the literary magazine and secretary of Honor Board, which deals with academic and social offenses and punishments —a popular office—and I had a well-known woman poet and professor on the faculty championing me for graduate school at the biggest universities in the east, and promises of full scholarships all the way, and now I was apprenticed to the best editor on an intellectual fashion magazine, and what did I do but balk and balk like a dull cart horse?

"I'm very interested in everything." The words fell with a hollow flatness on to Jay Cee's desk, like so many wooden nickels.

"I'm glad of that," Jay Cee said a bit waspishly. "You can learn a lot in this month on the magazine, you know, if you just roll up your shirtsleeves. The girl who was here before you didn't bother with any of the fashion-show stuff. She went straight from this office on to *Time.*"

"My!" I said, in the same sepulchral tone. "That was quick!"

"Of course, you have another year at college yet," Jay Cee went on a little more mildly. "What do you have in mind after you graduate?"

What I always thought I had in mind was getting some big scholarship to graduate school or a grant to study all over Europe, and then I thought I'd be a professor and write books of poems or write books of poems and be an editor of some sort. Usually I had these plans on the tip of my tongue.

"I don't really know," I heard myself say. I felt a deep shock, hearing myself say that, because the minute I said it, I knew it was true.

It sounded true, and I recognized it, the way you recognize some nondescript person that's been hanging around your door for ages and then suddenly comes up and introduces himself as your real father and looks exactly like you, so you know he really is your father, and the person you thought all your life was your father is a sham.

"I don't really know."

"You'll never get anywhere like that." Jay Cee paused. "What languages do you have?"

"Oh, I can read a bit of French, I guess, and I've always wanted to learn German." I'd been telling people I'd always wanted to learn German for about five years.

My mother spoke German during her childhood in America and was stoned for it during the First World War by the children at school. My German-speaking father, dead since I was nine, came from some manic-depressive hamlet in the black heart of Prussia. My youngest brother was at that moment on the Experiment in International Living in Berlin and speaking German like a native.

What I didn't say was that each time I picked up a German dictionary or a German book, the very sight of those dense, black, barbed-wire letters made my mind shut like a clam.

"I've always thought I'd like to go into publishing." I tried to recover a thread that might lead me back to my old, bright salesmanship. "I guess what I'll do is apply at some publishing house."

"You ought to read French and German," Jay Cee said mercilessly, "and probably several other languages as well, Spanish and Italian—better still, Russian. Hundreds of girls flood into New York every June thinking they'll be editors. You need to offer something more than the run-of-the-mill person. You better learn some languages."

I hadn't the heart to tell Jay Cee there wasn't one scrap of space on my senior year schedule to learn languages in. I was taking one of those honors programs that teach you to think

independently, and except for a course in Tolstoy and Dosto-
evsky and a seminar in advanced poetry composition, I would
spend my whole time writing on some obscure theme in the
works of James Joyce. I hadn't picked out my theme yet,
because I hadn't got round to reading *Finnegans Wake*, but
my professor was very excited about my thesis and had
promised to give me some leads on images about twins.

"I'll see what I can do," I told Jay Cee. "I probably might
just fit in one of those double-barreled accelerated courses in
elementary German they've rigged up." I thought at the time
I might actually do this. I had a way of persuading my Class
Dean to let me do irregular things. She regarded me as a sort
of interesting experiment.

At college I had to take a required course in physics and
chemistry. I had already taken a course in botany and done
very well. I never answered one test question wrong the
whole year, and for a while I toyed with the idea of being a
botanist and studying the wild grasses in Africa or the South
American rain forests, because you can win big grants to study
offbeat things like that in queer areas much more easily than
winning grants to study art in Italy or English in England;
there's not so much competition.

Botany was fine, because I loved cutting up leaves and
putting them under the microscope and drawing diagrams of
bread mold and the odd, heart-shaped leaf in the sex cycle of
the fern, it seemed so real to me.

The day I went into physics class it was death.

A short dark man with a high lisping voice, named Mr.
Manzi, stood in front of the class in a tight blue suit holding a
little wooden ball. He put the ball on a steep grooved slide
and let it run down to the bottom. Then he started talking
about let a equal acceleration and let t equal time and suddenly he was scribbling letters and numbers and equals signs all
over the blackboard and my mind went dead.

I took the physics book back to my dormitory. It was a
huge book on porous mimeographed paper—four hundred
pages long with no drawings or photographs, only diagrams
and formulas—between brick-red cardboard covers. This book
was written by Mr. Manzi to explain physics to college girls,
and if it worked on us he would try to have it published.

Well, I studied those formulas, I went to class and watched balls roll down slides and listened to bells ring and by the end of the semester most of the other girls had failed and I had a straight A. I heard Mr. Manzi saying to a bunch of the girls who were complaining that the course was too hard, "No, it can't be too hard, because one girl got a straight A." "Who is it? Tell us," they said, but he shook his head and didn't say anything and gave me a sweet little conspiring smile.

That's what gave me the idea of escaping the next semester of chemistry. I may have made a straight A in physics, but I was panic-struck. Physics made me sick the whole time I learned it. What I couldn't stand was this shrinking everything into letters and numbers. Instead of leaf shapes and enlarged diagrams of the holes the leaves breathe through and fascinating words like carotene and xanthophyll on the blackboard, there were these hideous, cramped, scorpion-lettered formulas in Mr. Manzi's special red chalk.

I knew chemistry would be worse, because I'd seen a big chart of the ninety-odd elements hung up in the chemistry lab, and all the perfectly good words like gold and silver and cobalt and aluminum were shortened to ugly abbreviations with different decimal numbers after them. If I had to strain my brain with any more of that stuff I would go mad. I would fail outright. It was only by a horrible effort of will that I had dragged myself through the first half of the year.

So I went to my Class Dean with a clever plan.

My plan was that I needed the time to take a course in Shakespeare, since I was, after all, an English major. She knew and I knew perfectly well I would get a straight A again in the chemistry course, so what was the point of my taking the exams; why couldn't I just go to the classes and look on and take it all in and forget about marks or credits? It was a case of honor among honorable people, and the content meant more than the form, and marks were really a bit silly anyway, weren't they, when you knew you'd always get an A? My plan was strengthened by the fact that the college had just dropped the second year of required science for the classes after me anyway, so my class was the last to suffer under the old ruling.

Mr. Manzi was in perfect agreement with my plan. I think

it flattered him that I enjoyed his classes so much I would take them for no materialistic reason like credit and an A, but for the sheer beauty of chemistry itself. I thought it was quite ingenious of me to suggest sitting in on the chemistry course even after I'd changed over to Shakespeare. It was quite an unnecessary gesture and made it seem I simply couldn't bear to give chemistry up.

Of course, I would never have succeeded with this scheme if I hadn't made that A in the first place. And if my Class Dean had known how scared and depressed I was, and how I seriously contemplated desperate remedies such as getting a doctor's certificate that I was unfit to study chemistry, the formulas made me dizzy and so on, I'm sure she wouldn't have listened to me for a minute, but would have made me take the course regardless.

As it happened, the Faculty Board passed my petition, and my Class Dean told me later that several of the professors were touched by it. They took it as a real step in intellectual maturity.

I had to laugh when I thought about the rest of that year. I went to the chemistry class five times a week and didn't miss a single one. Mr. Manzi stood at the bottom of the big, rickety old amphitheater, making blue flames and red flares and clouds of yellow stuff by pouring the contents of one test tube into another, and I shut his voice out of my ears by pretending it was only a mosquito in the distance and sat back enjoying the bright lights and the colored fires and wrote page after page of villanelles and sonnets.

Mr. Manzi would glance at me now and then and see me writing, and send up a sweet little appreciative smile. I guess he thought I was writing down all those formulas not for exam time, like the other girls, but because his presentation fascinated me so much I couldn't help it.

Four

I DON'T KNOW just why my successful evasion of chemistry should have floated into my mind there in Jay Cee's office.

All the time she talked to me, I saw Mr. Manzi standing on thin air in back of Jay Cee's head, like something conjured up out of a hat, holding his little wooden ball and the test tube that billowed a great cloud of yellow smoke the day before Easter vacation and smelt of rotten eggs and made all the girls and Mr. Manzi laugh.

I felt sorry for Mr. Manzi. I felt like going down to him on my hands and knees and apologizing for being such an awful liar.

Jay Cee handed me a pile of story manuscripts and spoke to me much more kindly. I spent the rest of the morning reading the stories and typing out what I thought of them on the pink Interoffice Memo sheets and sending them into the office of Betsy's editor to be read by Betsy the next day. Jay Cee interrupted me now and then to tell me something practical or a bit of gossip.

Jay Cee was going to lunch that noon with two famous writers, a man and a lady. The man had just sold six short stories to the *New Yorker* and six to Jay Cee. This surprised me, as I didn't know magazines bought stories in lots of six, and I was staggered by the thought of the amount of money six stories would probably bring in. Jay Cee said she had to be very careful at this lunch, because the lady writer wrote stories too, but she had never had any in the *New Yorker* and Jay Cee had only taken one from her in five years. Jay Cee had to flatter the more famous man at the same time as she was careful not to hurt the less famous lady.

When the cherubs in Jay Cee's French wall clock waved their wings up and down and put their little gilt trumpets to their lips and pinged out twelve notes one after the other, Jay Cee told me I'd done enough work for the day, and to go off to the *Ladies' Day* tour and banquet and to the film première, and she would see me bright and early tomorrow.

Then she slipped a suit jacket over her lilac blouse, pinned a hat of imitation lilacs on the top of her head, powdered her nose briefly and adjusted her thick spectacles. She looked terrible, but very wise. As she left the office, she patted my shoulder with one lilac-gloved hand.

"Don't let the wicked city get you down."

I sat quietly in my swivel chair for a few minutes and thought about Jay Cee. I tried to imagine what it would be like if I were Ee Gee, the famous editor, in an office full of potted rubber plants and African violets my secretary had to water each morning. I wished I had a mother like Jay Cee. Then I'd know what to do.

My own mother wasn't much help. My mother had taught shorthand and typing to support us ever since my father died, and secretly she hated it and hated him for dying and leaving no money because he didn't trust life insurance salesmen. She was always on to me to learn shorthand after college, so I'd have a practical skill as well as a college degree. "Even the apostles were tentmakers," she'd say. "They had to live, just the way we do."

I dabbled my fingers in the bowl of warm water a *Ladies' Day* waitress set down in place of my two empty ice cream dishes. Then I wiped each finger carefully with my linen napkin which was still quite clean. Then I folded the linen napkin and laid it between my lips and brought my lips down on it precisely. When I put the napkin back on the table a fuzzy pink lip shape bloomed right in the middle of it like a tiny heart.

I thought what a long way I had come.

The first time I saw a fingerbowl was at the home of my benefactress. It was the custom at my college, the little freckled lady in the Scholarships Office told me, to write to the person whose scholarship you had, if they were still alive, and thank them for it.

I had the scholarship of Philomena Guinea, a wealthy novelist who went to my college in the early nineteen hundreds and had her first novel made into a silent film with Bette Davis as well as a radio serial that was still running, and it turned out she was alive and lived in a large mansion not far from my grandfather's country club.

So I wrote Philomena Guinea a long letter in coal-black ink on gray paper with the name of the college embossed on it in red. I wrote what the leaves looked like in autumn when I bicycled out into the hills, and how wonderful it was to live on a campus instead of commuting by bus to a city college and having to live at home, and how all knowledge was opening up before me and perhaps one day I would be able to write great books the way she did.

I had read one of Mrs. Guinea's books in the town library— the college library didn't stock them for some reason—and it was crammed from beginning to end with long, suspenseful questions: "Would Evelyn discern that Gladys knew Roger in her past? wondered Hector feverishly" and "How could Donald marry her when he learned of the child Elsie, hidden away with Mrs. Rollmop on the secluded country farm? Griselda demanded of her bleak, moonlit pillow." These books earned Philomena Guinea, who later told me she had been very stupid at college, millions and millions of dollars.

Mrs. Guinea answered my letter and invited me to lunch at her home. That was where I saw my first fingerbowl.

The water had a few cherry blossoms floating in it, and I thought it must be some clear sort of Japanese after-dinner soup and ate every bit of it, including the crisp little blossoms. Mrs. Guinea never said anything, and it was only much later, when I told a debutante I knew at college about the dinner, that I learned what I had done.

When we came out of the sunnily lit interior of the *Ladies' Day* offices, the streets were gray and fuming with rain. It wasn't the nice kind of rain that rinses you clean, but the sort of rain I imagine they must have in Brazil. It flew straight down from the sky in drops the size of coffee saucers and hit

the hot sidewalks with a hiss that sent clouds of steam
writhing up from the gleaming, dark concrete.

My secret hope of spending the afternoon alone in Central
Park died in the glass eggbeater of *Ladies' Day's* revolving
doors. I found myself spewed out through the warm rain and
into the dim, throbbing cave of a cab, together with Betsy and
Hilda and Emily Ann Offenbach, a prim little girl with a bun
of red hair and a husband and three children in Teaneck, New
Jersey.

The movie was very poor. It starred a nice blonde girl who
looked like June Allyson but was really somebody else, and a
sexy black-haired girl who looked like Elizabeth Taylor but
was also somebody else, and two big, broad-shouldered bone-
heads with names like Rick and Gil.

It was a football romance and it was in Technicolor.

I hate Technicolor. Everybody in a Technicolor movie
seems to feel obliged to wear a lurid costume in each new
scene and to stand around like a clotheshorse with a lot of
very green trees or very yellow wheat or very blue ocean
rolling away for miles and miles in every direction.

Most of the action in this picture took place in the football
stands, with the two girls waving and cheering in smart suits
with orange chrysanthemums the size of cabbages on their
lapels, or in a ballroom, where the girls swooped across the
floor with their dates, in dresses like something out of *Gone
With the Wind,* and then sneaked off into the powder room
to say nasty intense things to each other.

Finally I could see the nice girl was going to end up with
the nice football hero and the sexy girl was going to end up
with nobody, because the man named Gil had only wanted a
mistress and not a wife all along and was now packing off to
Europe on a single ticket.

At about this point I began to feel peculiar. I looked round
me at all the rows of rapt little heads with the same silver
glow on them at the front and the same black shadow on
them at the back, and they looked like nothing more or less
than a lot of stupid moonbrains.

I felt in terrible danger of puking. I didn't know whether it
was the awful movie giving me a stomachache or all that
caviar I had eaten.

"I'm going back to the hotel," I whispered to Betsy through the half-dark.

Betsy was staring at the screen with deadly concentration. "Don't you feel good?" she whispered, barely moving her lips.

"No," I said. "I feel like hell."

"So do I, I'll come back with you."

We slipped out of our seats and said Excuse me Excuse me Excuse me down the length of our row, while the people grumbled and hissed and shifted their rain boots and umbrellas to let us pass, and I stepped on as many feet as I could because it took my mind off this enormous desire to puke that was ballooning up in front of me so fast I couldn't see round it.

The remains of a tepid rain were still sifting down when we stepped out into the street.

Betsy looked a fright. The bloom was gone from her cheeks and her drained face floated in front of me, green and sweating. We fell into one of those yellow checkered cabs that are always waiting at the curb when you are trying to decide whether or not you want a taxi, and by the time we reached the hotel I had puked once and Betsy had puked twice.

The cab driver took the corners with such momentum that we were thrown together first on one side of the back seat and then on the other. Each time one of us felt sick, she would lean over quietly as if she had dropped something and was picking it up off the floor, and the other one would hum a little and pretend to be looking out the window.

The cab driver seemed to know what we were doing, even so.

"Hey," he protested, driving through a light that had just turned red, "you can't do that in my cab, you better get out and do it in the street."

But we didn't say anything, and I guess he figured we were almost at the hotel so he didn't make us get out until we pulled up in front of the main entrance.

We didn't dare wait to add up the fare. We stuffed a pile of silver into the cabby's hand and dropped a couple of Kleenexes to cover the mess on the floor, and ran in through the lobby and on to the empty elevator. Luckily for us, it was a quiet time of day. Betsy was sick again in the elevator and I held her head, and then I was sick and she held mine.

Usually after a good puke you feel better right away. We hugged each other and then said good-bye and went off to opposite ends of the hall to lie down in our own rooms. There is nothing like puking with somebody to make you into old friends.

But the minute I'd shut the door behind me and undressed and dragged myself on to the bed, I felt worse than ever. I felt I just had to go to the toilet. I struggled into my white bathrobe with the blue cornflowers on it and staggered down to the bathroom.

Betsy was already there. I could hear her groaning behind the door, so I hurried on around the corner to the bathroom in the next wing. I thought I would die, it was so far.

I sat on the toilet and leaned my head over the edge of the washbowl and I thought I was losing my guts and my dinner both. The sickness rolled through me in great waves. After each wave it would fade away and leave me limp as a wet leaf and shivering all over and then I would feel it rising up in me again, and the glittering white torture chamber tiles under my feet and over my head and on all four sides closed in and squeezed me to pieces.

I don't know how long I kept at it. I let the cold water in the bowl go on running loudly with the stopper out, so anybody who came by would think I was washing my clothes, and then when I felt reasonably safe I stretched out on the floor and lay quite still.

It didn't seem to be summer any more. I could feel the winter shaking my bones and banging my teeth together, and the big white hotel towel I had dragged down with me lay under my head numb as a snowdrift.

I thought it very bad manners for anyone to pound on a bathroom door the way some person was pounding. They could just go around the corner and find another bathroom the way I had done and leave me in peace. But the person kept banging and pleading with me to let them in and I thought I dimly recognized the voice. It sounded a bit like Emily Ann Offenbach.

"Just a minute," I said then. My words bungled out thick as molasses.

I pulled myself together and slowly rose and flushed the toilet for the tenth time and sopped the bowl clean and rolled up the towel so the vomit stains didn't show very clearly and unlocked the door and stepped out into the hall.

I knew it would be fatal if I looked at Emily Ann or anybody else so I fixed my eyes glassily on a window that swam at the end of the hall and put one foot in front of the other.

The next thing I had a view of was somebody's shoe.

It was a stout shoe of cracked black leather and quite old, with tiny air holes in a scalloped pattern over the toe and a dull polish, and it was pointed at me. It seemed to be placed on a hard green surface that was hurting my right cheekbone.

I kept very still, waiting for a clue that would give me some notion of what to do. A little to the left of the shoe I saw a vague heap of blue cornflowers on a white ground and this made me want to cry. It was the sleeve of my own bathrobe I was looking at, and my left hand lay pale as a cod at the end of it.

"She's all right now."

The voice came from a cool, rational region far above my head. For a minute I didn't think there was anything strange about it, and then I thought it was strange. It was a man's voice, and no men were allowed to be in our hotel at any time of the night or day.

"How many others are there?" the voice went on.

I listened with interest. The floor seemed wonderfully solid. It was comforting to know I had fallen and could fall no farther.

"Eleven, I think," a woman's voice answered. I figured she must belong to the black shoe. "I think there's eleven more of 'um, but one's missin' so there's oney ten."

"Well, you get this one to bed and I'll take care of the rest."

I heard a hollow boomp boomp in my right ear that grew fainter and fainter. Then a door opened in the distance, and there were voices and groans, and the door shut again.

Two hands slid under my armpits and the woman's voice said, "Come, come, lovey, we'll make it yet," and I felt myself being half lifted, and slowly the doors began to move by, one by one, until we came to an open door and went in.

The sheet on my bed was folded back, and the woman helped me lie down and covered me up to the chin and rested for a minute in the bedside armchair, fanning herself with one plump, pink hand. She wore gilt-rimmed spectacles and a white nurse's cap.

"Who are you?" I asked in a faint voice.

"I'm the hotel nurse."

"What's the matter with me?"

"Poisoned," she said briefly. "Poisoned, the whole lot of you. I never seen anythin' like it. Sick here, sick there, whatever have you young ladies been stuffin' yourselves with?"

"Is everybody else sick too?" I asked with some hope.

"The whole of your lot," she affirmed with relish. "Sick as dogs and cryin' for ma."

The room hovered around me with great gentleness, as if the chairs and the tables and the walls were withholding their weight out of sympathy for my sudden frailty.

"The doctor's given you an injection," the nurse said from the doorway. "You'll sleep now."

And the door took her place like a sheet of blank paper, and then a larger sheet of paper took the place of the door, and I drifted toward it and smiled myself to sleep.

Somebody was standing by my pillow with a white cup.

"Drink this," they said.

I shook my head. The pillow crackled like a wad of straw.

"Drink this and you'll feel better."

A thick white china cup was lowered under my nose. In the wan light that might have been evening and might have been dawn I contemplated the clean amber liquid. Pads of butter floated on the surface and a faint chickeny aroma fumed up to my nostrils.

My eyes moved tentatively to the skirt behind the cup. "Betsy," I said.

"Betsy nothing, it's me."

I raised my eyes then, and saw Doreen's head silhouetted against the paling window, her blonde hair lit at the tips from behind like a halo of gold. Her face was in shadow, so I couldn't make out her expression, but I felt a sort of expert tenderness flowing from the ends of her fingers. She might have been Betsy or my mother or a fern-scented nurse.

I bent my head and took a sip of the broth. I thought my mouth must be made of sand. I took another sip and then another and another until the cup was empty.

I felt purged and holy and ready for a new life.

Doreen set the cup on the windowsill and lowered herself into the armchair. I noticed that she made no move to take out a cigarette, and as she was a chain smoker this surprised me.

"Well, you almost died," she said finally.

"I guess it was all that caviar."

"Caviar nothing! It was the crabmeat. They did tests on it and it was chock-full of ptomaine."

I had a vision of the celestially white kitchens of *Ladies' Day* stretching into infinity. I saw avocado pear after avocado pear being stuffed with crabmeat and mayonnaise and photographed under brilliant lights. I saw the delicate, pink-mottled claw meat poking seductively through its blanket of mayonnaise and the bland yellow pear cup with its rim of alligator-green cradling the whole mess.

Poison.

"Who did tests?" I thought the doctor might have pumped somebody's stomach and then analyzed what he found in his hotel laboratory.

"Those dodos on *Ladies' Day*. As soon as you all started keeling over like ninepins somebody called into the office and the office called across to *Ladies' Day* and they did tests on everything left over from the big lunch. Ha!"

"Ha!" I echoed hollowly. It was good to have Doreen back.

"They sent presents," she added. "They're in a big carton out in the hall."

"How did they get here so fast?"

"Special express delivery, what do you think? They can't afford to have the lot of you running around saying you got poisoned at *Ladies' Day*. You could sue them for every penny they own if you just knew some smart law man."

"What are the presents?" I began to feel if it was a good enough present I wouldn't mind about what happened, because I felt so pure as a result.

"Nobody's opened the box yet, they'll all out flat. I'm supposed to be carting soup in to everybody, seeing as I'm the only one on my feet, but I brought you yours first."

"See what the present is," I begged. Then I remembered and said, "I've a present for you as well."

Doreen went out into the hall. I could hear her rustling around for a minute and then the sound of paper tearing. Finally she came back carrying a thick book with a glossy cover and people's names printed all over it.

"The Thirty Best Short Stories of the Year." She dropped the book in my lap. "There's eleven more of them out there in that box. I suppose they thought it'd give you something to read while you were sick." She paused. "Where's mine?"

I fished in my pocketbook and handed Doreen the mirror with her name and the daisies on it. Doreen looked at me and I looked at her and we both burst out laughing.

"You can have my soup if you want," she said. "They put twelve soups on the tray by mistake and Lenny and I stuffed down so many hotdogs while we were waiting for the rain to stop I couldn't eat another mouthful."

"Bring it in," I said. "I'm starving."

Five

AT SEVEN THE NEXT MORNING the telephone rang.

Slowly I swam up from the bottom of a black sleep. I already had a telegram from Jay Cee stuck in my mirror, telling me not to bother to come in to work but to rest for a day and get completely well, and how sorry she was about the bad crabmeat, so I couldn't imagine who would be calling.

I reached out and hitched the receiver onto my pillow so the mouthpiece rested on my collarbone and the earpiece lay on my shoulder.

"Hello?"

A man's voice said, "Is that Miss Esther Greenwood?" I thought I detected a slight foreign accent.

"It certainly is," I said.

"This is Constantin Something-or-Other."

I couldn't make out the last name, but it was full of S's and K's. I didn't know any Constantin, but I hadn't the heart to say so.

Then I remembered Mrs. Willard and her simultaneous interpreter.

"Of course, of course!" I cried, sitting up and clutching the phone to me with both hands.

I'd never have given Mrs. Willard credit for introducing me to a man named Constantin.

I collected men with interesting names. I already knew a Socrates. He was tall and ugly and intellectual and the son of some big Greek movie producer in Hollywood, but also a Catholic, which ruined it for both of us. In addition to Socrates, I knew a White Russian named Attila at the Boston School of Business Administration.

Gradually I realized that Constantin was trying to arrange a meeting for us later in the day.

41

"Would you like to see the UN this afternoon?"

"I can already see the UN," I told him, with a little hysterical giggle.

He seemed nonplussed.

"I can see it from my window." I thought perhaps my English was a touch too fast for him.

There was a silence.

Then he said, "Maybe you would like a bite to eat afterward."

I detected the vocabulary of Mrs. Willard and my heart sank. Mrs. Willard always invited you for a bite to eat. I remembered that this man had been a guest at Mrs. Willard's house when he first came to America—Mrs. Willard had one of these arrangements where you open your house to foreigners and then when you go abroad they open their houses to you.

I now saw quite clearly that Mrs. Willard had simply traded her open house in Russia for my bite to eat in New York.

"Yes, I would like a bite to eat," I said stiffly. "What time will you come?"

"I'll call for you in my car about two. It's the Amazon, isn't it?"

"Yes."

"Ah, I know where that is."

For a moment I thought his tone was laden with special meaning, and then I figured that probably some of the girls at the Amazon were secretaries at the UN and maybe he had taken one of them out at one time. I let him hang up first, and then I hung up and lay back in the pillows, feeling grim.

There I went again, building up a glamorous picture of a man who would love me passionately the minute he met me, and all out of a few prosy nothings. A duty tour of the UN and a post-UN sandwich!

I tried to jack up my morale.

Probably Mrs. Willard's simultaneous interpreter would be short and ugly and I would come to look down on him in the end the way I looked down on Buddy Willard. This thought gave me a certain satisfaction. Because I did look down on Buddy Willard, and although everybody still thought I would marry him when he came out of the TB place, I knew I would never marry him if he were the last man on earth.

Buddy Willard was a hypocrite.

Of course, I didn't know he was a hypocrite at first. I thought he was the most wonderful boy I'd ever seen. I'd adored him from a distance for five years before he even looked at me, and then there was a beautiful time when I still adored him and he started looking at me, and then just as he was looking at me more and more I discovered quite by accident what an awful hypocrite he was, and now he wanted me to marry him and I hated his guts.

The worst part of it was I couldn't come straight out and tell him what I thought of him, because he caught TB before I could do that, and now I had to humor him along till he got well again and could take the unvarnished truth.

I decided not to go down to the cafeteria for breakfast. It would only mean getting dressed, and what was the point of getting dressed if you were staying in bed for the morning? I could have called down and asked for a breakfast tray in my room, I guess, but then I would have to tip the person who brought it up and I never knew how much to tip. I'd had some very upsetting experiences trying to tip people in New York.

When I first arrived at the Amazon a dwarfish, bald man in a bellhop's uniform carried my suitcase up in the elevator and unlocked my room for me. Of course I rushed immediately to the window and looked out to see what the view was. After a while I was aware of this bellhop turning on the hot and cold taps in the washbowl and saying "This is the hot and this is the cold" and switching on the radio and telling me all the names of all the New York stations and I began to get uneasy, so I kept my back to him and said firmly, "Thank you for bringing up my suitcase."

"Thank you thank you thank you. Ha!" he said in a very nasty insinuating tone, and before I could wheel round to see what had come over him he was gone, shutting the door behind him with a rude slam.

Later, when I told Doreen about his curious behavior, she said, "You ninny, he wanted his tip."

I asked how much I should have given and she said a

quarter at least and thirty-five cents if the suitcase was too heavy. Now I could have carried that suitcase to my room perfectly well by myself, only the bellhop seemed so eager to do it that I let him. I thought that sort of service came along with what you paid for your hotel room.

I hate handing over money to people for doing what I could just as easily do myself, it makes me nervous.

Doreen said ten per cent was what you should tip a person, but I somehow never had the right change and I'd have felt awfully silly giving somebody half a dollar and saying, "Fifteen cents of this is a tip for you, please give me thirty-five cents back."

The first time I took a taxi in New York I tipped the driver ten cents. The fare was a dollar, so I thought ten cents was exactly right and gave the driver my dime with a little flourish and a smile. But he only held it in the palm of his hand and stared and stared at it, and when I stepped out of the cab, hoping I had not handed him a Canadian dime by mistake, he started yelling, "Lady, I gotta live like you and everybody else," in a loud voice which scared me so much I broke into a run. Luckily he was stopped at a traffic light or I think he would have driven along beside me yelling in that embarrassing way.

When I asked Doreen about this she said the tipping percentage might well have risen from ten to fifteen per cent since she was last in New York. Either that, or that particular cabdriver was an out-and-out louse.

I reached for the book the people from *Ladies' Day* had sent.

When I opened it a card fell out. The front of the card showed a poodle in a flowered bedjacket sitting in a poodle basket with a sad face, and the inside of the card showed the poodle lying down in the basket with a smile, sound asleep under an embroidered sampler that said, "You'll get well best with lots and lots of rest." At the bottom of the card somebody had written, "Get well quick! from all of your good friends at *Ladies' Day,*" in lavender ink.

I flipped through one story after another until finally I came to a story about a fig tree.

This fig grew on a green lawn between the house of a Jewish man and a convent, and the Jewish man and a beautiful dark nun kept meeting at the tree to pick the ripe figs, until one day they saw an egg hatching in a bird's nest on a branch of the tree, and as they watched the little bird peck its way out of the egg, they touched the backs of their hands together, and then the nun didn't come out to pick figs with the Jewish man any more but a mean-faced Catholic kitchen maid came to pick them instead and counted up the figs the man picked after they were both through to be sure he hadn't picked any more than she had, and the man was furious.

I thought it was a lovely story, especially the part about the fig tree in winter under the snow and then the fig tree in spring with all the green fruit. I felt sorry when I came to the last page. I wanted to crawl in between those black lines of print the way you crawl through a fence, and go to sleep under that beautiful big green fig tree.

It seemed to me Buddy Willard and I were like that Jewish man and that nun, although of course we weren't Jewish or Catholic but Unitarian. We had met together under our own imaginary fig tree, and what we had seen wasn't a bird coming out of an egg but a baby coming out of a woman, and then something awful happened and we went our separate ways.

As I lay there in my white hotel bed feeling lonely and weak, I thought I was up in that sanatorium in the Adirondacks, and I felt like a heel of the worst sort. In his letters Buddy kept telling me how he was reading poems by a poet who was also a doctor and how he'd found out about some famous dead Russian short-story writer who had been a doctor too, so maybe doctors and writers could get along fine after all.

Now this was a very different tune from what Buddy Willard had been singing all the two years we were getting to know each other. I remember the day he smiled at me and said, "Do you know what a poem is, Esther?"

"No, what?" I said.

"A piece of dust." And he looked so proud of having thought of this that I just stared at his blond hair and his blue eyes and his white teeth—he had very long, strong white teeth—and said, "I guess so."

It was only in the middle of New York a whole year later that I finally thought of an answer to that remark.

I spent a lot of time having imaginary conversations with Buddy Willard. He was a couple of years older than I was and very scientific, so he could always prove things. When I was with him I had to work to keep my head above water.

These conversations I had in my mind usually repeated the beginnings of conversations I'd really had with Buddy, only they finished with me answering him back quite sharply, instead of just sitting around and saying, "I guess so."

Now, lying on my back in bed, I imagined Buddy saying, "Do you know what a poem is, Esther?"

"No, what?" I would say.

"A piece of dust."

Then just as he was smiling and starting to look proud, I would say, "So are the cadavers you cut up. So are the people you think you're curing. They're dust as dust as dust. I reckon a good poem lasts a whole lot longer than a hundred of those people put together."

And of course Buddy wouldn't have any answer to that, because what I said was true. People were made of nothing so much as dust, and I couldn't see that doctoring all that dust was a bit better than writing poems people would remember and repeat to themselves when they were unhappy or sick and couldn't sleep.

My trouble was I took everything Buddy Willard told me as the honest-to-God truth. I remember the first night he kissed me. It was after the Yale Junior Prom.

It was strange, the way Buddy had invited me to that prom.

He popped into my house out of the blue one Christmas vacation, wearing a thick white turtleneck sweater and looking so handsome I could hardly stop staring, and said, "I might drop over to see you at college some day, all right?"

I was flabbergasted. I only saw Buddy at church on Sundays when we were both home from college, and then at a distance, and I couldn't figure what had put it into his head to run over and see me—he had run the two miles between our houses for cross-country practice, he said.

Of course, our mothers were good friends. They had gone to school together and then both married their professors and settled down in the same town, but Buddy was always off on a scholarship at prep school in the fall or earning money by fighting blister rust in Montana in the summer, so our mothers being old school chums really didn't matter a bit.

After this sudden visit I didn't hear a word from Buddy until one fine Saturday morning in early March. I was up in my room at college, studying about Peter the Hermit and Walter the Penniless for my history exam on the crusades the coming Monday, when the hall phone rang.

Usually people are supposed to take turns answering the hall phone, but as I was the only freshman on a floor with all seniors they made me answer it most of the time. I waited a minute to see if anybody would beat me to it. Then I figured everybody was probably out playing squash or away on weekends, so I answered it myself.

"Is that you, Esther?" the girl on watch downstairs said, and when I said yes, she said, "There's a man to see you."

I was surprised to hear this, because of all the blind dates I'd had that year not one called me up again for a second date. I just didn't have any luck. I hated coming downstairs sweaty-handed and curious every Saturday night and having some senior introduce me to her aunt's best friend's son and finding some pale, mushroomy fellow with protruding ears or buck teeth or a bad leg. I didn't think I deserved it. After all, I wasn't crippled in any way, I just studied too hard, I didn't know when to stop.

Well, I combed my hair and put on some more lipstick and took my history book—so I could say I was on my way to the library if it turned out to be somebody awful—and went down, and there was Buddy Willard leaning against the mail table in a khaki zipper jacket and blue dungarees and frayed gray sneakers and grinning up at me.

"I just came over to say hello," he said.

I thought it odd he should come all the way up from Yale even hitchhiking, as he did, to save money, just to say hello.

"Hello," I said. "Let's go out and sit on the porch."

I wanted to go out on the porch because the girl on watch

was a nosy senior and eyeing me curiously. She obviously thought Buddy had made a big mistake.

We sat side by side in two wicker rocking chairs. The sunlight was clean and windless and almost hot.

"I can't stay for more than a few minutes," Buddy said.

"Oh, come on, stay for lunch," I said.

"Oh, I can't do that. I'm up here for the Sophomore Prom with Joan."

I felt like a prize idiot.

"How *is* Joan?" I asked coldly.

Joan Gilling come from our home town and went to our church and was a year ahead of me at college. She was a big wheel—president of her class and a physics major and the college hockey champion. She always made me feel squirmy with her starey pebble-colored eyes and her gleaming tombstone teeth and her breathy voice. She was big as a horse, too. I began to think Buddy had pretty poor taste.

"Oh, Joan," he said. "She asked me up to this dance two months ahead of time and her mother asked my mother if I would take her, so what could I do?"

"Well, why did you say you'd take her if you didn't want to?" I asked meanly.

"Oh, I like Joan. She never cares whether you spend any money on her or not and she enjoys doing things out-of-doors. The last time she came down to Yale for house weekend we went on a bicycle trip to East Rock and she's the only girl I haven't had to push up hills. Joan's all right."

I went cold with envy. I had never been to Yale, and Yale was the place all the seniors in my house liked to go best on weekends. I decided to expect nothing from Buddy Willard. If you expect nothing from somebody you are never disappointed.

"You better go and find Joan then," I said in a matter-of-fact voice. "I've a date coming any minute and he won't like seeing me sitting around with you."

"A date?" Buddy looked surprised. "Who is it?"

"It's two," I said, "Peter the Hermit and Walter the Penniless."

Buddy didn't say anything, so I said, "Those are their nicknames."

Then I added, "They're from Dartmouth."

I guess Buddy never read much history, because his mouth stiffened. He swung up from the wicker rocking chair and gave it a sharp little unnecessary push. Then he dropped a pale blue envelope with a Yale crest into my lap.

"Here's a letter I meant to leave for you if you weren't in. There's a question in it you can answer by mail. I don't feel like asking you about it right now."

After Buddy had gone I opened the letter. It was a letter inviting me to the Yale Junior Prom.

I was so surprised I let out a couple of yips and ran into the house shouting, "I'm going I'm going I'm going." After the bright white sun on the porch it looked pitch dark in there, and I couldn't make out a thing. I found myself hugging the senior on watch. When she heard I was going to the Yale Junior Prom she treated me with amazement and respect.

Oddly enough, things changed in the house after that. The seniors on my floor started speaking to me and every now and then one of them would answer the phone quite spontaneously and nobody made any more nasty loud remarks outside my door about people wasting their golden college days with their noses stuck in a book.

Well, all during the Junior Prom Buddy treated me like a friend or a cousin.

We danced about a mile apart the whole time, until during "Auld Lang Syne" he suddenly rested his chin on the tip of my head as if he were very tired. Then in the cold, black, three-o'clock wind we walked very slowly the five miles back to the house where I was sleeping in the living room on a couch that was too short because it only cost fifty cents a night instead of two dollars like most of the other places with proper beds.

I felt dull and flat and full of shattered visions.

I had imagined Buddy would fall in love with me that weekend and that I wouldn't have to worry about what I was doing on any more Saturday nights the rest of the year. Just as we approached the house where I was staying Buddy said, "Let's go up to the chemistry lab."

I was aghast. "The *chemistry* lab?"

"Yes." Buddy reached for my hand. "There's a beautiful view up there behind the chemistry lab."

And sure enough, there was a sort of hilly place behind the chemistry lab from which you could see the lights of a couple of houses in New Haven.

I stood pretending to admire them while Buddy got a good footing on the rough soil. While he kissed me I kept my eyes open and tried to memorize the spacing of the house lights so I would never forget them.

Finally Buddy stepped back. "Wow!" he said.

"Wow what?" I said, surprised. It had been a dry, uninspiring little kiss, and I remember thinking it was too bad both our mouths were so chapped from walking five miles in that cold wind.

"Wow, it makes me feel terrific to kiss you."

I modestly didn't say anything.

"I guess you go out with a lot of boys," Buddy said then.

"Well, I guess I do." I thought I must have gone out with a different boy for every week in the year.

"Well, I have to study a lot."

"So do I," I put in hastily. "I have to keep my scholarship after all."

"Still, I think I could manage to see you every third weekend."

"That's nice." I was almost fainting and dying to get back to college and tell everybody.

Buddy kissed me again in front of the house steps, and the next fall, when his scholarship to medical school came through, I went there to see him instead of to Yale and it was there I found out how he had fooled me all those years and what a hypocrite he was.

I found out on the day we saw the baby born.

Six

I HAD KEPT BEGGING Buddy to show me some really interesting hospital sights, so one Friday I cut all my classes and came down for a long weekend and he gave me the works.

I started out by dressing in a white coat and sitting on a tall stool in a room with four cadavers, while Buddy and his friends cut them up. These cadavers were so unhuman-looking they didn't bother me a bit. They had stiff, leathery, purple-black skin and they smelt like old pickle jars.

After that, Buddy took me out into the hall where they had some big glass bottles full of babies that had died before they were born. The baby in the first bottle had a large white head bent over a tiny curled-up body the size of a frog. The baby in the next bottle was bigger and the baby next to that one was bigger still and the baby in the last bottle was the size of a normal baby and he seemed to be looking at me and smiling a little piggy smile.

I was quite proud of the calm way I stared at all these gruesome things. The only time I jumped was when I leaned my elbow on Buddy's cadaver's stomach to watch him dissect a lung. After a minute or two I felt this burning sensation in my elbow and it occurred to me the cadaver might just be half alive since it was still warm, so I leapt off my stool with a small exclamation. Then Buddy explained the burning was only from the pickling fluid, and I sat back in my old position.

In the hour before lunch Buddy took me to a lecture on sickle-cell anemia and some other depressing diseases, where they wheeled sick people out onto the platform and asked them questions and then wheeled them off and showed colored slides.

One slide I remember showed a beautiful laughing girl with a black mole on her cheek. "Twenty days after that mole

appeared the girl was dead," the doctor said, and everybody
went very quiet for a minute and then the bell rang, so I
never really found out what the mole was or why the girl
died.

In the afternoon we went to see a baby born.

First we found a linen closet in the hospital corridor where
Buddy took out a white mask for me to wear and some gauze.

A tall fat medical student, big as Sydney Greenstreet,
lounged nearby, watching Buddy wind the gauze round and
round my head until my hair was completely covered and only
my eyes peered out over the white mask.

The medical student gave an unpleasant little snicker. "At
least your mother loves you," he said.

I was so busy thinking how very fat he was and how
unfortunate it must be for a man and especially a young man
to be fat, because what woman could stand leaning over that
big stomach to kiss him, that I didn't immediately realize what
this student had said to me was an insult. By the time I
figured he must consider himself quite a fine fellow and had
thought up a cutting remark about how only a mother loves a
fat man, he was gone.

Buddy was examining a queer wooden plaque on the wall
with a row of holes in it, starting from a hole about the size
of a silver dollar and ending with one the size of a dinner
plate.

"Fine, fine," he said to me. "There's somebody about to
have a baby this minute."

At the door of the delivery room stood a thin, stoop-
shouldered medical student Buddy knew.

"Hello, Will," Buddy said. "Who's on the job?"

"I am," Will said gloomily, and I noticed little drops of
sweat beading his high pale forehead. "I am, and it's my first."

Buddy told me Will was a third-year man and had to
deliver eight babies before he could graduate.

Then he noticed a bustle at the far end of the hall and some
men in lime-green coats and skull caps and a few nurses came
moving toward us in a ragged procession wheeling a trolley
with a big white lump on it.

"You oughtn't to see this," Will muttered in my ear.

"You'll never want to have a baby if you do. They oughtn't to let women watch. It'll be the end of the human race."

Buddy and I laughed, and then Buddy shook Will's hand and we all went into the room.

I was so struck by the sight of the table where they were lifting the woman I didn't say a word. It looked like some awful torture table, with these metal stirrups sticking up in mid-air at one end and all sorts of instruments and wires and tubes I couldn't make out properly at the other.

Buddy and I stood together by the window, a few feet away from the woman, where we had a perfect view.

The woman's stomach stuck up so high I couldn't see her face or the upper part of her body at all. She seemed to have nothing but an enormous spider-fat stomach and two little ugly spindly legs propped in the high stirrups, and all the time the baby was being born she never stopped making this unhuman whooing noise.

Later Buddy told me the woman was on a drug that would make her forget she'd had any pain and that when she swore and groaned she really didn't know what she was doing because she was in a kind of twilight sleep.

I thought it sounded just like the sort of drug a man would invent. Here was a woman in terrible pain, obviously feeling every bit of it or she wouldn't groan like that, and she would go straight home and start another baby, because the drug would make her forget how bad the pain had been, when all the time, in some secret part of her, that long, blind, doorless and windowless corridor of pain was waiting to open up and shut her in again.

The head doctor, who was supervising Will, kept saying to the woman, "Push down, Mrs. Tomolillo, push down, that's a good girl, push down," and finally through the split, shaven place between her legs, lurid with disinfectant, I saw a dark fuzzy thing appear.

"The baby's head," Buddy whispered under cover of the woman's groans.

But the baby's head stuck for some reason, and the doctor told Will he'd have to make a cut. I heard the scissors close on the woman's skin like cloth and the blood began to run down—a fierce, bright red. Then all at once the baby seemed to pop out into Will's hands, the color of a blue plum and floured with white stuff and streaked with blood, and Will kept saying, "I'm going to drop it, I'm going to drop it, I'm going to drop it," in a terrified voice.

"No, you're not," the doctor said, and took the baby out of Will's hands and started massaging it, and the blue color went away and the baby started to cry in a lorn, croaky voice and I could see it was a boy.

The first thing that baby did was pee in the doctor's face. I told Buddy later I didn't see how that was possible, but he said it was quite possible, though unusual, to see something like that happen.

As soon as the baby was born the people in the room divided up into two groups, the nurses tying a metal dog tag on the baby's wrist and swabbing its eyes with cotton on the end of a stick and wrapping it up and putting it in a canvas-sided cot, while the doctor and Will started sewing up the woman's cut with a needle and a long thread.

I think somebody said, "It's a boy, Mrs. Tomolillo," but the woman didn't answer or raise her head.

"Well, how was it?" Buddy asked with a satisfied expression as we walked across the green quadrangle to his room.

"Wonderful," I said. "I could see something like that every day."

I didn't feel up to asking him if there were any other ways to have babies. For some reason the most important thing to me was actually seeing the baby come out of you yourself and making sure it was yours. I thought if you had to have all that pain anyway you might just as well stay awake.

I had always imagined myself hitching up on to my elbows on the delivery table after it was all over—dead white, of course, with no makeup and from the awful ordeal, but smiling and radiant, with my hair down to my waist, and reaching out for my first little squirmy child and saying its name, whatever it was.

"Why was it all covered with flour?" I asked then, to keep the conversation going, and Buddy told me about the waxy stuff that guarded the baby's skin.

When we were back in Buddy's room, which reminded me of nothing so much as a monk's cell, with its bare walls and bare bed and bare floor and the desk loaded with Gray's *Anatomy* and other thick gruesome books, Buddy lit a candle and uncorked a bottle of Dubonnet. Then we lay down side by side on the bed and Buddy sipped his wine while I read aloud "somewhere I have never travelled" and other poems from a book I'd brought.

Buddy said he figured there must be something in poetry if a girl like me spent all her days over it, so each time we met I read him some poetry and explained to him what I found in it. It was Buddy's idea. He always arranged our weekends so we'd never regret wasting our time in any way. Buddy's father was a teacher, and I think Buddy could have been a teacher as well, he was always trying to explain things to me and introduce me to new knowledge.

Suddenly, after I finished a poem, he said, "Esther, have you ever seen a man?"

The way he said it I knew he didn't mean a regular man or a man in general, I knew he meant a man naked.

"No," I said. "Only statues."

"Well, don't you think you would like to see me?"

I didn't know what to say. My mother and my grandmother had started hinting around to me a lot lately about what a fine, clean boy Buddy Willard was, coming from such a fine, clean family, and how everybody at church thought he was a model person, so kind to his parents and to older people, as well as so athletic and so handsome and so intelligent.

All I'd heard about, really, was how fine and clean Buddy was and how he was the kind of a person a girl should stay fine and clean for. So I didn't really see the harm in anything Buddy would think up to do.

"Well, all right, I guess so," I said.

I stared at Buddy while he unzipped his chino pants and took them off and laid them on a chair and then took off his underpants that were made of something like nylon fishnet.

"They're cool," he explained, "and my mother says they wash easily."

Then he just stood there in front of me and I kept staring at him. The only thing I could think of was turkey neck and turkey gizzards and I felt very depressed.

Buddy seemed hurt I didn't say anything. "I think you

ought to get used to me like this," he said. "Now let me see you."

But undressing in front of Buddy suddenly appealed to me about as much as having my Posture Picture taken at college, where you have to stand naked in front of a camera, knowing all the time that a picture of you stark naked, both full view and side view, is going into the college gym files to be marked A B C or D depending on how straight you are.

"Oh, some other time," I said.

"All right." Buddy got dressed again.

Then we kissed and hugged a while and I felt a little better. I drank the rest of the Dubonnet and sat cross-legged at the end of Buddy's bed and asked for a comb. I began to comb my hair down over my face so Buddy couldn't see it. Suddenly I said, "Have you ever had an affair with anyone, Buddy?"

I don't know what made me say it, the words just popped out of my mouth. I never thought for one minute that Buddy Willard would have an affair with anyone. I expected him to say, "No, I have been saving myself for when I get married to somebody pure and a virgin like you."

But Buddy didn't say anything, he just turned pink.

"Well, have you?"

"What do you mean, an affair?" Buddy asked then in a hollow voice.

"You know, have you ever gone to bed with anyone?" I kept rhythmically combing the hair down over the side of my face nearest to Buddy, and I could feel the little electric filaments clinging to my hot cheeks and I wanted to shout, "Stop, stop, don't tell me, don't say anything." But I didn't, I just kept still.

"Well, yes, I have," Buddy said finally.

I almost fell over. From the first night Buddy Willard kissed me and said I must go out with a lot of boys, he made me feel I was much more sexy and experienced than he was and that everything he did like hugging and kissing and petting was simply what I made him feel like doing out of the blue, he couldn't help it and didn't know how it came about.

Now I saw he had only been pretending all this time to be so innocent.

"Tell me about it." I combed my hair slowly over and over,

feeling the teeth of the comb dig into my cheek at every stroke. "Who was it?"

Buddy seemed relieved I wasn't angry. He even seemed relieved to have somebody to tell about how he was seduced.

Of course, somebody had seduced Buddy, Buddy hadn't started it and it wasn't really his fault. It was this waitress at the hotel he worked at as a busboy the last summer at Cape Cod. Buddy had noticed her staring at him queerly and shoving her breasts up against him in the confusion of the kitchen, so finally one day he asked her what the trouble was and she looked him straight in the eye and said, "I want you."

"Served up with parsley?" Buddy had laughed innocently.

"No," she had said. "Some night."

And that's how Buddy had lost his pureness and his virginity.

At first I thought he must have slept with the waitress only the once, but when I asked how many times, just to make sure, he said he couldn't remember but a couple of times a week for the rest of the summer. I multiplied three by ten and got thirty, which seemed beyond all reason.

After that something in me just froze up.

Back at college I started asking a senior here and a senior there what they would do if a boy they knew suddenly told them he'd slept thirty times with some slutty waitress one summer, smack in the middle of knowing them. But these seniors said most boys were like that and you couldn't honestly accuse them of anything until you were at least pinned or engaged to be married.

Actually, it wasn't the idea of Buddy sleeping with somebody that bothered me. I mean I'd read about all sorts of people sleeping with each other, and if it had been any other boy I would merely have asked him the most interesting details, and maybe gone out and slept with somebody myself just to even things up, and then thought no more about it.

What I couldn't stand was Buddy's pretending I was so sexy and he was so pure, when all the time he'd been having an affair with that tarty waitress and must have felt like laughing in my face.

"What does your mother think about this waitress?" I asked Buddy that weekend.

Buddy was amazingly close to his mother. He was always quoting what she said about the relationship between a man and a woman, and I knew Mrs. Willard was a real fanatic about virginity for men and women both. When I first went to her house for supper she gave me a queer, shrewd, searching look, and I knew she was trying to tell whether I was a virgin or not.

Just as I thought, Buddy was embarrassed. "Mother asked me about Gladys," he admitted.

"Well, what did you say?"

"I said Gladys was free, white and twenty-one."

Now I knew Buddy would never talk to his mother as rudely as that for my sake. He was always saying how his mother said, "What a man wants is a mate and what a woman wants is infinite security," and, "What a man is is an arrow into the future and what a woman is is the place the arrow shoots off from," until it made me tired.

Every time I tried to argue, Buddy would say his mother still got pleasure out of his father and wasn't that wonderful for people their age, it must mean she really knew what was what.

Well, I had just decided to ditch Buddy Willard for once and for all, not because he'd slept with that waitress but because he didn't have the honest guts to admit it straight off to everybody and face up to it as part of his character, when the phone in the hall rang and somebody said in a little knowing singsong, "It's for you, Esther, it's from Boston."

I could tell right away something must be wrong, because Buddy was the only person I knew in Boston, and he never called me long distance because it was so much more expensive than letters. Once, when he had a message he wanted me to get almost immediately, he went all round his entry at medical school asking if anybody was driving up to my college that weekend, and sure enough, somebody was, so he gave them a note for me and I got it the same day. He didn't even have to pay for a stamp.

It was Buddy all right. He told me that the annual fall chest X-ray showed he had caught TB and he was going off on a scholarship for medical students who caught TB to a TB place in the Adirondacks. Then he said I hadn't written since that last weekend and he hoped nothing was the matter between us, and would I please try to write him at least once a week and come to visit him at this TB place in my Christmas vacation?

I had never heard Buddy so upset. He was very proud of his perfect health and was always telling me it was psychosomatic when my sinuses blocked up and I couldn't breathe. I thought this an odd attitude for a doctor to have and perhaps he should study to be a psychiatrist instead, but of course I never came right out and said so.

I told Buddy how sorry I was about the TB and promised to write, but when I hung up I didn't feel one bit sorry. I only felt a wonderful relief.

I thought the TB might just be a punishment for living the kind of double life Buddy lived and feeling so superior to people. And I thought how convenient it would be now I didn't have to announce to everybody at college I had broken off with Buddy and start the boring business of blind dates all over again.

I simply told everyone that Buddy had TB and we were practically engaged, and when I stayed in to study on Saturday nights they were extremely kind to me because they thought I was so brave, working the way I did just to hide a broken heart.

Seven

OF COURSE, Constantin was much too short, but in his own way he was handsome, with light brown hair and dark blue eyes and a lively, challenging expression. He could almost have been an American, he was so tan and had such good teeth, but I could tell straight away that he wasn't. He had what no American man I've ever met has had, and that's intuition.

From the start Constantin guessed I wasn't any protégé of Mrs. Willard's. I raised an eyebrow here and dropped a dry little laugh there, and pretty soon we were both openly raking Mrs. Willard over the coals and I thought, "This Constantin won't mind if I'm too tall and don't know enough languages and haven't been to Europe, he'll see through all that stuff to what I really am."

Constantin drove me to the UN in his old green convertible with cracked, comfortable brown leather seats and the top down. He told me his tan came from playing tennis, and when we were sitting there side by side flying down the streets in the open sun he took my hand and squeezed it, and I felt happier than I had been since I was about nine and running along the hot white beaches with my father the summer before he died.

And while Constantin and I sat in one of those hushed plush auditoriums in the UN, next to a stern muscular Russian girl with no makeup who was a simultaneous interpreter like Constantin, I thought how strange it had never occurred to me before that I was only purely happy until I was nine years old.

After that—in spite of the Girl Scouts and the piano lessons and the water-color lessons and the dancing lessons and the sailing camp, all of which my mother scrimped to give me,

60

and college, with crewing in the mist before breakfast and blackbottom pies and the little new firecrackers of ideas going off every day—I had never been really happy again.

I stared through the Russian girl in her double-breasted gray suit, rattling off idiom after idiom in her own unknowable tongue—which Constantin said was the most difficult part because the Russians didn't have the same idioms as our idioms—and I wished with all my heart I could crawl into her and spend the rest of my life barking out one idiom after another. It mightn't make me any happier, but it would be one more little pebble of efficiency among all the other pebbles.

Then Constantin and the Russian girl interpreter and the whole bunch of black and white and yellow men arguing down there behind their labeled microphones seemed to move off at a distance. I saw their mouths going up and down without a sound, as if they were sitting on the deck of a departing ship, stranding me in the middle of a huge silence.

I started adding up all the things I couldn't do.

I began with cooking.

My grandmother and my mother were such good cooks that I left everything to them. They were always trying to teach me one dish or another, but I would just look on and say, "Yes, yes, I see," while the instructions slid through my head like water, and then I'd always spoil what I did so nobody would ask me to do it again.

I remember Jody, my best and only girlfriend at college in my freshman year, making me scrambled eggs at her house one morning. They tasted unusual, and when I asked her if she had put in anything extra, she said cheese and garlic salt. I asked who told her to do that, and she said nobody, she just thought it up. But then, she was practical and a sociology major.

I didn't know shorthand either.

This meant I couldn't get a good job after college. My mother kept telling me nobody wanted a plain English major. But an English major who knew shorthand was something else again. Everybody would want her. She would be in demand among all the up-and-coming young men and she would transcribe letter after thrilling letter.

The trouble was, I hated the idea of serving men in any way. I wanted to dictate my own thrilling letters. Besides, those little shorthand symbols in the book my mother showed me seemed just as bad as let t equal time and let s equal the total distance.

My list grew longer.

I was a terrible dancer. I couldn't carry a tune. I had no sense of balance, and when we had to walk down a narrow board with our hands out and a book on our heads in gym class I always fell over. I couldn't ride a horse or ski, the two things I wanted to do most, because they cost too much money. I couldn't speak German or read Hebrew or write Chinese. I didn't even know where most of the old out-of-the-way countries the UN men in front of me represented fitted in on the map.

For the first time in my life, sitting there in the soundproof heart of the UN building between Constantin who could play tennis as well as simultaneouly interpret and the Russian girl who knew so many idioms, I felt dreadfully inadequate. The trouble was, I had been inadequate all along, I simply hadn't thought about it.

The one thing I was good at was winning scholarships and prizes, and that era was coming to an end.

I felt like a racehorse in a world without racetracks or a champion college footballer suddenly confronted by Wall Street and a business suit, his days of glory shrunk to a little gold cup on his mantel with a date engraved on it like the date on a tombstone.

I saw my life branching out before me like the green fig tree in the story.

From the tip of every branch, like a fat purple fig, a wonderful future beckoned and winked. One fig was a husband and a happy home and children, and another fig was a famous poet and another fig was a brilliant professor, and another fig was Ee Gee, the amazing editor, and another fig was Europe and Africa and South America, and another fig was Constantin and Socrates and Attila and a pack of other lovers with queer names and offbeat professions, and another fig was an Olympic lady crew champion, and beyond and above these figs were many more figs I couldn't quite make out.

I saw myself sitting in the crotch of this fig tree, starving to death, just because I couldn't make up my mind which of the figs I would choose. I wanted each and every one of them, but choosing one meant losing all the rest, and, as I sat there, unable to decide, the figs began to wrinkle and go black, and, one by one, they plopped to the ground at my feet.

Constantin's restaurant smelt of herbs and spices and sour cream. All the time I had been in New York I had never found such a restaurant. I only found those Heavenly Hamburger places, where they serve giant hamburgers and soup-of-the-day and four kinds of fancy cake at a very clean counter facing a long glarey mirror.

To reach this restaurant we had to climb down seven dimly lit steps into a sort of cellar.

Travel posters plastered the smoke-dark walls, like so many picture windows overlooking Swiss lakes and Japanese mountains and African velds, and thick, dusty bottle-candles, that seemed for centuries to have wept their colored waxes red over blue over green in a fine, three-dimensional lace, cast a circle of light round each table where the faces floated, flushed and flamelike themselves.

I don't know what I ate, but I felt immensely better after the first mouthful. It occurred to me that my vision of the fig tree and all the fat figs that withered and fell to earth might well have arisen from the profound void of an empty stomach.

Constantin kept refilling our glasses with a sweet Greek wine that tasted of pine bark, and I found myself telling him how I was going to learn German and go to Europe and be a war correspondent like Maggie Higgins.

I felt so fine by the time we came to the yogurt and strawberry jam that I decided I would let Constantin seduce me.

Ever since Buddy Willard had told me about that waitress I had been thinking I ought to go out and sleep with somebody myself. Sleeping with Buddy wouldn't count, though, because he would still be one person ahead of me, it would have to be with somebody else.

The only boy I ever actually discussed going to bed with was a bitter, hawk-nosed Southerner from Yale, who came to college one weekend only to find his date had eloped with a taxi driver the day before. As the girl had lived in my house and I was the only one home that particular night, it was my job to cheer him up.

At the local coffee shop, hunched in one of the secretive, high-backed booths with hundreds of people's names gouged into the wood, we drank cup after cup of black coffee and talked frankly about sex.

This boy—his name was Eric—said he thought it disgusting the way all the girls at my college stood around on the porches under the lights and in the bushes in plain view, necking madly before the one o'clock curfew, so everybody passing by could see them. A million years of evolution, Eric said bitterly, and what are we? Animals.

Then Eric told me how he had slept with his first woman.

He went to a Southern prep school that specialized in building all-round gentlemen, and by the time you graduated it was an unwritten rule that you had to have known a woman. Known in the Biblical sense, Eric said.

So one Saturday Eric and a few of his classmates took a bus into the nearest city and visited a notorious whorehouse. Eric's whore hadn't even taken off her dress. She was a fat, middle-aged woman with dyed red hair and suspiciously thick lips and rat-colored skin and she wouldn't turn off the light, so he had had her under a fly-spotted twenty-five-watt bulb, and it was nothing like it was cracked up to be. It was boring as going to the toilet.

I said maybe if you loved a woman it wouldn't seem so boring, but Eric said it would be spoiled by thinking this woman too was just an animal like the rest, so if he loved anybody he would never go to bed with her. He'd go to a whore if he had to and keep the woman he loved free of all that dirty business.

It had crossed my mind at the time that Eric might be a good person to go to bed with, since he had already done it and, unlike the usual run of boys, didn't seem dirty-minded or silly when he talked about it. But then Eric wrote me a letter saying he thought he might really be able to love me, I was so

intelligent and cynical and yet had such a kind face, surprisingly like his older sister's; so I knew it was no use, I was the
type he would never go to bed with, and wrote him I was
unfortunately about to marry a childhood sweetheart.

The more I thought about it the better I liked the idea of
being seduced by a simultaneous interpreter in New York
City. Constantin seemed mature and considerate in every way.
There were no people I knew he would want to brag to about
it, the way college boys bragged about sleeping with girls in
the backs of cars to their roommates or their friends on the
basketball team. And there would be a pleasant irony in
sleeping with a man Mrs. Willard had introduced me to, as if
she were, in a roundabout way, to blame for it.

When Constantin asked if I would like to come up to his
apartment to hear some balalaika records I smiled to myself.
My mother had always told me never under any circumstances
to go with a man to a man's rooms after an evening out, it
could mean only one thing.

"I am very fond of balalaika music," I said.

Constantin's room had a balcony, and the balcony overlooked the river, and we could hear the hooing of the tugs
down in the darkness. I felt moved and tender and perfectly
certain about what I was going to do.

I knew I might have a baby, but that thought hung far and
dim in the distance and didn't trouble me at all. There was no
one hundred per cent sure way not to have a baby, it said in
an article my mother cut out of the *Reader's Digest* and
mailed to me at college. This article was written by a married
woman lawyer with children and called "In Defense of
Chastity."

It gave all the reasons a girl shouldn't sleep with anybody
but her husband and then only after they were married.

The main point of the article was that a man's world is
different from a woman's world and a man's emotions are
different from a woman's emotions and only marriage can
bring the two worlds and the two different sets of emotions
together properly. My mother said this was something a girl
didn't know about till it was too late, so she had to take the

advice of people who were already experts, like a married
woman.

This woman lawyer said the best men wanted to be pure
for their wives, and even if they weren't pure, they wanted to
be the ones to teach their wives about sex. Of course they
would try to persuade a girl to have sex and say they would
marry her later, but as soon as she gave in, they would lose all
respect for her and start saying that if she did that with them
she would do that with other men and they would end up by
making her life miserable.

The woman finished her article by saying better be safe
than sorry and besides, there was no sure way of not getting
stuck with a baby and then you'd really be in a pickle.

Now the one thing this article didn't seem to me to consider was how a girl felt.

It might be nice to be pure and then to marry a pure man,
but what if he suddenly confessed he wasn't pure after we
were married, the way Buddy Willard had? I couldn't stand
the idea of a woman having to have a single pure life and a
man being able to have a double life, one pure and one not.

Finally I decided that if it was so difficult to find a red-
blooded intelligent man who was still pure by the time he was
twenty-one I might as well forget about staying pure myself
and marry somebody who wasn't pure either. Then when he
started to make my life miserable I could make his miserable
as well.

When I was nineteen, pureness was the great issue.

Instead of the world being divided up into Catholics and
Protestants or Republicans and Democrats or white men and
black men or even men and women, I saw the world divided
into people who had slept with somebody and people who
hadn't, and this seemed the only really significant difference
between one person and another.

I thought a spectacular change would come over me the day
I crossed the boundary line.

I thought it would be the way I'd feel if I ever visited
Europe. I'd come home, and if I looked closely into the
mirror I'd be able to make out a little white Alp at the back
of my eye. Now I thought that if I looked into the mirror

tomorrow I'd see a doll-size Constantin sitting in my eye and smiling out at me.

Well, for about an hour we lounged on Constantin's balcony in two separate slingback chairs with the victrola playing and the balalaika records stacked between us. A faint milky light diffused from the street lights or the half moon or the cars or the stars, I couldn't tell what, but apart from holding my hand Constantin showed no desire to seduce me whatsoever.

I asked if he was engaged or had any special girlfriend, thinking maybe that's what was the matter, but he said no, he made a point of keeping clear of such attachments.

At last I felt a powerful drowsiness drifting through my veins from all the pine-bark wine I had drunk.

"I think I'll go in and lie down," I said.

I strolled casually into the bedroom and stooped over to nudge off my shoes. The clean bed bobbed before me like a safe boat. I stretched full length and shut my eyes. Then I heard Constantin sigh and come in from the balcony. One by one his shoes clonked on to the floor, and he lay down by my side.

I looked at him secretly from under a fall of hair.

He was lying on his back, his hands under his head, staring at the ceiling. The starched white sleeves of his shirt, rolled up to the elbows, glimmered eerily in the half dark and his tan skin seemed almost black. I thought he must be the most beautiful man I'd ever seen.

I thought if only I had a keen, shapely bone structure to my face or could discuss politics shrewdly or was a famous writer Constantin might find me interesting enough to sleep with.

And then I wondered if as soon as he came to like me he would sink into ordinariness, and if as soon as he came to love me I would find fault after fault, the way I did with Buddy Willard and the boys before him.

The same thing happened over and over:

I would catch sight of some flawless man off in the distance, but as soon as he moved closer I immediately saw he wouldn't do at all.

That's one of the reasons I never wanted to get married.

The last thing I wanted was infinite security and to be the place an arrow shoots off from. I wanted change and excitement and to shoot off in all directions myself, like the colored arrows from a Fourth of July rocket.

I woke to the sound of rain.

It was pitch dark. After a while I deciphered the faint outlines of an unfamiliar window. Every so often a beam of light appeared out of thin air, traversed the wall like a ghostly, exploratory finger, and slid off into nothing again.

Then I heard the sound of somebody breathing.

At first I thought it was only myself, and that I was lying in the dark in my hotel room after being poisoned. I held my breath, but the breathing kept on.

A green eye glowed on the bed beside me. It was divided into quarters like a compass. I reached out slowly and closed my hand on it. I lifted it up. With it came an arm, heavy as a dead man's, but warm with sleep.

Constantin's watch said three o'clock.

He was lying in his shirt and trousers and stocking feet just as I had left him when I dropped asleep, and as my eyes grew used to the darkness I made out his pale eyelids and his straight nose and his tolerant, shapely mouth, but they seemed insubstantial, as if drawn on fog. For a few minutes I leaned over, studying him. I had never fallen asleep beside a man before.

I tried to imagine what it would be like if Constantin were my husband.

It would mean getting up at seven and cooking him eggs and bacon and toast and coffee and dawdling about in my nightgown and curlers after he'd left for work to wash up the dirty plates and make the bed, and then when he came home after a lively, fascinating day he'd expect a big dinner, and I'd spend the evening washing up even more dirty plates till I fell into bed, utterly exhausted.

This seemed a dreary and wasted life for a girl with fifteen years of straight A's, but I knew that's what marriage was like, because cook and clean and wash was just what Buddy Willard's mother did from morning till night, and she was the wife of a university professor and had been a private school teacher herself.

Once when I visited Buddy I found Mrs. Willard braiding a rug out of strips of wool from Mr. Willard's old suits. She'd spent weeks on that rug, and I had admired the tweedy browns and greens and blues patterning the braid, but after Mrs. Willard was through, instead of hanging the rug on the wall the way I would have done, she put it down in place of her kitchen mat, and in a few days it was soiled and dull and indistinguishable from any mat you could buy for under a dollar in the five and ten.

And I knew that in spite of all the roses and kisses and restaurant dinners a man showered on a woman before he married her, what he secretly wanted when the wedding service ended was for her to flatten out underneath his feet like Mrs. Willard's kitchen mat.

Hadn't my own mother told me that as soon as she and my father left Reno on their honeymoon—my father had been married before, so he needed a divorce—my father said to her, "Whew, that's a relief, now we can stop pretending and be ourselves"?—and from that day on my mother never had a minute's peace.

I also remembered Buddy Willard saying in a sinister, knowing way that after I had children I would feel differently, I wouldn't want to write poems any more. So I began to think maybe it was true that when you were married and had children it was like being brainwashed, and afterward you went about numb as a slave in some private, totalitarian state.

As I stared down at Constantin the way you stare down at a bright, unattainable pebble at the bottom of a deep well, his eyelids lifted and he looked through me, and his eyes were full of love. I watched dumbly as a shutter of recognition clicked across the blur of tenderness and the wide pupils went glossy and depthless as patent leather.

Constantin sat up, yawning. "What time is it?"

"Three," I said in a flat voice. "I better go home. I have to be at work first thing in the morning."

"I'll drive you."

As we sat back to back on our separate sides of the bed fumbling with our shoes in the horrid cheerful white light of the bed lamp, I sensed Constantin turn round. "Is your hair always like that?"

"Like what?"

He didn't answer but reached over and put his hand at the root of my hair and ran his fingers out slowly to the tip ends like a comb. A little electric shock flared through me and I sat quite still. Ever since I was small I loved feeling somebody comb my hair. It made me go all sleepy and peaceful.

"Ah, I know what it is," Constantin said. "You've just washed it."

And he bent to lace up his tennis shoes.

An hour later I lay in my hotel bed, listening to the rain. It didn't even sound like rain, it sounded like a tap running. The ache in the middle of my left shin bone came to life, and I abandoned any hope of sleep before seven, when my radio-alarm clock would rouse me with its hearty renderings of Sousa.

Every time it rained the old leg-break seemed to remember itself, and what it remembered was a dull hurt.

Then I thought, "Buddy Willard made me break that leg."

Then I thought, "No, I broke it myself. I broke it on purpose to pay myself back for being such a heel."

Eight

MR. WILLARD drove me up to the Adirondacks.

It was the day after Christmas and a gray sky bellied over us, fat with snow. I felt overstuffed and dull and disappointed, the way I always do the day after Christmas, as if whatever it was the pine boughs and the candles and the silver and gilt-ribboned presents and the birch-log fires and the Christmas turkey and the carols and the piano promised never came to pass.

At Christmas I almost wished I was a Catholic.

First Mr. Willard drove and then I drove. I don't know what we talked about, but as the countryside, already deep under old falls of snow, turned us a bleaker shoulder, and as the fir trees crowded down from the gray hills to the road edge, so darkly green they looked black, I grew gloomier and gloomier.

I was tempted to tell Mr. Willard to go ahead alone, I would hitchhike home.

But one glance at Mr. Willard's face—the silver hair in its boyish crewcut, the clear blue eyes, the pink cheeks, all frosted like a sweet wedding cake with the innocent, trusting expression—and I knew I couldn't do it. I'd have to see the visit through to the end.

At midday the grayness paled a bit, and we parked in an icy turnoff and shared out the tunafish sandwiches and the oatmeal cookies and the apples and the thermos of black coffee Mrs. Willard had packed for our lunch.

Mr. Willard eyed me kindly. Then he cleared his throat and brushed a few last crumbs from his lap. I could tell he was going to say something serious, because he was very shy, and I'd heard him clear his throat in that same way before giving an important economics lecture.

71

"Nelly and I have always wanted a daughter."

For one crazy minute I thought, Mr. Willard was going to announce that Mrs. Willard was pregnant and expecting a baby girl. Then he said, "But I don't see how any daughter could be nicer than you."

Mr. Willard must have thought I was crying because I was so glad he wanted to be a father to me. "There, there," he patted my shoulder and cleared his throat once or twice. "I think we understand each other."

Then he opened the car door on his side and strolled round to my side, his breath shaping tortuous smoke signals in the gray air. I moved over to the seat he had left and he started the car and we drove on.

I'm not sure what I expected of Buddy's sanatorium.

I think I expected a kind of wooden chalet perched up on top of a small mountain, with rosy-cheeked young men and women, all very attractive but with hectic glittering eyes, lying covered with thick blankets on outdoor balconies.

"TB is like living with a bomb in your lung," Buddy had written to me at college. "You just lie around very quietly hoping it won't go off."

I found it hard to imagine Buddy lying quietly. His whole philosophy of life was to be up and doing every second. Even when we went to the beach in the summer he never lay down to drowse in the sun the way I did. He ran back and forth or played ball or did a little series of rapid pushups to use the time.

Mr. Willard and I waited in the reception room for the end of the afternoon rest cure.

The color scheme of the whole sanatorium seemed to be based on liver. Dark, glowering woodwork, burnt-brown leather chairs, walls that might once have been white but had succumbed under a spreading malady of mold or damp. A mottled brown linoleum sealed off the floor.

On a low coffee table, with circular and semicircular stains bitten into the dark veneer, lay a few wilted numbers of *Time* and *Life*. I flipped to the middle of the nearest magazine. The face of Eisenhower beamed up at me, bald and blank as the face of a fetus in a bottle.

After a while I became aware of a sly, leaking noise. For a

minute I thought the walls had begun to discharge the moisture that must saturate them, but then I saw the noise came from a small fountain in one corner of the room.

The fountain spurted a few inches into the air from a rough length of pipe, threw up its hands, collapsed and drowned its ragged dribble in a stone basin of yellowing water. The basin was paved with the white hexagonal tiles one finds in public lavatories.

A buzzer sounded. Doors opened and shut in the distance. Then Buddy came in.

"Hello, Dad."

Buddy hugged his father, and promptly, with a dreadful brightness, came over to me and held out his hand. I shook it. It felt moist and fat.

Mr. Willard and I sat together on a leather couch. Buddy perched opposite us on the edge of a slippery armchair. He kept smiling, as if the corners of his mouth were strung up on invisible wire.

The last thing I expected was for Buddy to be fat. All the time I thought of him at the sanatorium I saw shadows carving themselves under his cheekbones and his eyes burning out of almost fleshless sockets.

But everything concave about Buddy had suddenly turned convex. A pot belly swelled under the tight white nylon shirt and his cheeks were round and ruddy as marzipan fruit. Even his laugh sounded plump.

Buddy's eyes met mine. "It's the eating," he said. "They stuff us day after day and then just make us lie around. But I'm allowed out on walk hours now, so don't worry, I'll thin down in a couple of weeks." He jumped up, smiling like a glad host. "Would you like to see my room?"

I followed Buddy, and Mr. Willard followed me, through a pair of swinging doors set with panes of frosted glass down a dim, liver-colored corridor smelling of floor wax and Lysol and another vaguer odor, like bruised gardenias.

Buddy threw open a brown door, and we filed into the narrow room.

A lumpy bed, shrouded by a thin white spread, pencil-striped with blue, took up most of the space. Next to it stood a bed table with a pitcher and a water glass and the silver twig of a thermometer poking up from a jar of pink disinfectant. A second table, covered with books and papers and off-kilter clay pots—baked and painted, but not glazed—squeezed itself between the bed foot and the closet door.

"Well," Mr. Willard breathed, "it looks comfortable enough."

Buddy laughed.

"What are these?" I picked up a clay ashtray in the shape of a lilypad, with the veinings carefully drawn in yellow on a murky green ground. Buddy didn't smoke.

"That's an ashtray," Buddy said. "It's for you."

I put the tray down. "I don't smoke."

"I know," Buddy said. "I thought you might like it, though."

"Well," Mr. Willard rubbed one papery lip against another. "I guess I'll be getting on. I guess I'll be leaving you two young people . . ."

"Fine, Dad. You be getting on."

I was surprised. I had thought Mr. Willard was going to stay the night before driving me back the next day.

"Shall I come too?"

"No, no." Mr. Willard peeled a few bills from his wallet and handed them to Buddy. "See that Esther gets a comfortable seat on the train. She'll stay a day or so, maybe."

Buddy escorted his father to the door.

I felt Mr. Willard had deserted me. I thought he must have planned it all along, but Buddy said no, his father simply couldn't stand the sight of sickness and especially his own son's sickness, because he thought all sickness was sickness of the will. Mr. Willard had never been sick a day in his life.

I sat down on Buddy's bed. There simply wasn't anywhere else to sit.

Buddy rummaged among his papers in a businesslike way. Then he handed me a thin, gray magazine. "Turn to page eleven."

The magazine was printed somewhere in Maine and full of stenciled poems and descriptive paragraphs separated from each other by asterisks. On page eleven I found a poem titled "Florida Dawn." I skipped down through image after image about watermelon lights and turtle-green palms and shells fluted like bits of Greek architecture.

"Not bad." I thought it was dreadful.

"Who wrote it?" Buddy asked with an odd, pigeony smile.

My eye dropped to the name on the lower right-hand corner of the page. B. S. Willard.

"I don't know." Then I said, "Of course I know, Buddy. You wrote it."

Buddy edged over to me.

I edged back. I have very little knowledge about TB, but it seemed to me an extremely sinister disease, the way it went on so invisibly. I thought Buddy might well be sitting in his own little murderous aura of TB germs.

"Don't worry," Buddy laughed. "I'm not positive."

"Positive?"

"You can't catch anything."

Buddy stopped for a breath, the way you do in the middle of climbing something very steep.

"I want to ask you a question." He had a disquieting new habit of boring into my eyes with his look as if actually bent on piercing my head, the better to analyze what went on inside it.

"I'd thought of asking it by letter."

I had a fleeting vision of a pale blue envelope with a Yale crest on the back flap.

"But then I decided it would be better if I waited until you came up, so I could ask you in person." He paused. "Well, don't you want to know what it is?"

"What?" I said in a small, unpromising voice.

Buddy sat down beside me. He put his arm around my waist and brushed the hair from my ear. I didn't move. Then I heard him whisper, "How would you like to be Mrs. Buddy Willard?"

I had an awful impulse to laugh.

I thought how that question would have bowled me over at any time in my five- or six-year period of adoring Buddy Willard from a distance.

Buddy saw me hesitate.

"Oh, I'm in no shape now, I know," he said quickly. "I'm still on P.A.S. and I may yet lose a rib or two, but I'll be back at med school by next fall. A year from this spring at the latest . . ."

"I think I should tell you something, Buddy."

"I know," Buddy said stiffly. "You've met someone."

"No, it's not that."

"What is it, then?"

"I'm never going to get married."

"You're crazy." Buddy brightened. "You'll change your mind."

"No. My mind's made up."

But Buddy just went on looking cheerful.

"Remember," I said, "that time you hitchhiked back to college with me after Skit Night?"

"I remember."

"Remember how you asked me where would I like to live best, the country or the city?"

"And you said . . ."

"And I said I wanted to live in the country and in the city both?"

Buddy nodded.

"And you," I continued with sudden force, "laughed and said I had the perfect setup of a true neurotic and that that question came from some questionnaire you'd had in psychology class that week?"

Buddy's smile dimmed.

"Well, you were right. I *am* neurotic. I could never settle down in either the country *or* the city."

"You could live between them," Buddy suggested helpfully. "Then you could go to the city sometimes and to the country sometimes."

"Well, what's so neurotic about that?"

Buddy didn't answer.

"Well?" I rapped out, thinking, You can't coddle these sick people, it's the worst thing for them, it'll spoil them to bits.

"Nothing," Buddy said in a pale, still voice.

"Neurotic, ha!" I let out a scornful laugh. "If neurotic is wanting two mutually exclusive things at one and the same time, then I'm neurotic as hell. I'll be flying back and forth between one mutually exclusive thing and another for the rest of my days."

Buddy put his hand on mine.

"Let me fly with you."

I stood at the top of the ski slope on Mount Pisgah, looking down. I had no business to be up there. I had never skied before in my life. Still, I thought I would enjoy the view while I had the chance.

At my left, the rope tow deposited skier after skier on the snowy summit which, packed by much crossing and recrossing and slightly melted in the noon sun, had hardened to the consistency and polish of glass. The cold air punished my lungs and sinuses to a visionary clearness.

On every side of me the red and blue and white jacketed skiers tore away down the blinding slope like fugitive bits of an American flag. From the foot of the ski run, the imitation log cabin lodge piped its popular songs into the overhang of silence.

> *Gazing down on the Jungfrau*
> *From our chalet for two ...*

The lilt and boom threaded by me like an invisible rivulet in a desert of snow. One careless, superb gesture, and I would be hurled into motion down the slope toward the small khaki spot in the sidelines, among the spectators, which was Buddy Willard.

All morning Buddy had been teaching me how to ski.

First, Buddy borrowed skis and ski poles from a friend of his in the village, and ski boots from a doctor's wife whose feet were only one size larger than my own, and a red ski jacket from a student nurse. His persistence in the face of mulishness was astounding.

Then I remembered that at medical school Buddy had won a prize for persuading the most relatives of dead people to have their dead ones cut up whether they needed it or not, in the interests of science. I forget what the prize was, but I could just see Buddy in his white coat with his stethoscope sticking out of a side pocket like part of his anatomy, smiling and bowing and talking those numb, dumb relatives into signing the postmortem papers.

Next, Buddy borrowed a car from his own doctor, who'd had TB himself and was very understanding, and we drove off as the buzzer for walk hour rasped along the sunless sanatorium corridors.

Buddy had never skied before either, but he said that the elementary principles were quite simple, and as he'd often watched the ski instructors and their pupils he could teach me all I'd need to know.

For the first half hour I obediently herringboned up a small slope, pushed off with my poles and coasted straight down. Buddy seemed pleased with my progress.

"That's fine, Esther," he observed, as I negotiated my slope for the twentieth time. "Now let's try you on the rope tow."

I stopped in my tracks, flushed and panting.

"But Buddy, I don't know how to zigzag yet. All those people coming down from the top know how to zigzag."

"Oh, you need only go halfway. Then you won't gain very much momentum."

And Buddy accompanied me to the rope tow and showed me how to let the rope run through my hands, and then told me to close my fingers round it and go up.

It never occurred to me to say no.

I wrapped my fingers around the rough, bruising snake of a rope that slithered through them, and went up.

But the rope dragged me, wobbling and balancing, so rapidly I couldn't hope to dissociate myself from it halfway. There was a skier in front of me and a skier behind me, and I'd have been knocked over and stuck full of skis and poles the minute I let go, and I didn't want to make trouble, so I hung quietly on.

At the top, though, I had second thoughts.

Buddy singled me out, hesitating there in the red jacket. His arms chopped the air like khaki windmills. Then I saw he was signaling me to come down a path that had opened in the middle of the weaving skiers. But as I poised, uneasy, with a dry throat, the smooth white path from my feet to his feet blurred.

A skier crossed it from the left, another crossed it from the right, and Buddy's arms went on waving feebly as antennae from the other side of a field swarming with tiny moving animalcules like germs, or bent, bright exclamation marks.

I looked up from that churning amphitheater to the view beyond it.

The great, gray eye of the sky looked back at me, its mist-shrouded sun focusing all the white and silent distances that poured from every point of the compass, hill after pale hill, to stall at my feet.

The interior voice nagging me not to be a fool—to save my skin and take off my skis and walk down, camouflaged by the scrub pines bordering the slope—fled like a disconsolate mosquito. The thought that I might kill myself formed in my mind coolly as a tree or a flower.

I measured the distance to Buddy with my eye.

His arms were folded, now, and he seemed of a piece with the split-rail fence behind him—numb, brown and inconsequential.

Edging to the rim of the hilltop, I dug the spikes of my poles into the snow and pushed myself into a flight I knew I couldn't stop by skill or any belated access of will.

I aimed straight down.

A keen wind that had been hiding itself struck me full in the mouth and raked the hair back horizontal on my head. I was descending, but the white sun rose no higher. It hung over the suspended waves of the hills, an insentient pivot without which the world would not exist.

A small, answering point in my own body flew toward it. I felt my lungs inflate with the inrush of scenery—air, mountains, trees, people. I thought, "This is what it is to be happy."

I plummeted down past the zigzaggers, the students, the experts, through year after year of doubleness and smiles and compromise, into my own past.

People and trees receded on either hand like the dark sides of a tunnel as I hurtled on to the still, bright point at the end of it, the pebble at the bottom of the well, the white sweet baby cradled in its mother's belly.

My teeth crunched a gravelly mouthful. Ice water seeped down my throat.

Buddy's face hung over me, near and huge, like a distracted

planet. Other faces showed themselves up in back of his. Behind him, black dots swarmed on a plane of whiteness. Piece by piece, as at the strokes of a dull godmother's wand, the old world sprang back into position.

"You were doing fine," a familiar voice informed my ear, "until that man stepped into your path."

People were unfastening my bindings and collecting my ski poles from where they poked skyward, askew, in their separate snowbanks. The lodge fence propped itself at my back.

Buddy bent to pull off my boots and the several pairs of white wool socks that padded them. His plump hand shut on my left foot, then inched up my ankle, closing and probing, as if feeling for a concealed weapon.

A dispassionate white sun shone at the summit of the sky. I wanted to hone myself on it till I grew saintly and thin and essential as the blade of a knife.

"I'm going up," I said. "I'm going to do it again."

"No, you're not."

A queer, satisfied expression came over Buddy's face.

"No, you're not," he repeated with a final smile. "Your leg's broken in two places. You'll be stuck in a cast for months."

Nine

"I'M SO GLAD THEY'RE GOING TO DIE."

Hilda arched her cat-limbs in a yawn, buried her head in her arms on the conference table and went back to sleep. A wisp of bilious green straw perched on her brow like a tropical bird.

Bile green. They were promoting it for fall, only Hilda, as usual, was half a year ahead of time. Bile green with black, bile green with white, bile green with nile green, its kissing cousin.

Fashion blurbs, silver and full of nothing, sent up their fishy bubbles in my brain. They surfaced with a hollow pop.

I'm so glad they're going to die.

I cursed the luck that had timed my arrival in the hotel cafeteria to coincide with Hilda's. After a late night I felt too dull to think up the excuse that would take me back to my room for the glove, the handkerchief, the umbrella, the notebook I forgot. My penalty was the long, dead walk from the frosted glass doors of the Amazon to the strawberry-marble slab of our entry on Madison Avenue.

Hilda moved like a mannequin the whole way.

"That's a lovely hat, did you make it?"

I half expected Hilda to turn on me and say, "You sound sick," but she only extended and then retracted her swanny neck.

"Yes."

The night before I'd seen a play where the heroine was possessed by a dybbuk, and when the dybbuk spoke from her mouth its voice sounded so cavernous and deep you couldn't tell whether it was a man or a woman. Well, Hilda's voice sounded just like the voice of that dybbuk.

She stared at her reflection in the glossed shop windows as

81

if to make sure, moment by moment, that she continued to exist. The silence between us was so profound I thought part of it must be my fault.

So I said, "Isn't it awful about the Rosenbergs?"

The Rosenbergs were to be electrocuted late that night.

"Yes!" Hilda said, and at last I felt I had touched a human string in the cat's cradle of her heart. It was only as the two of us waited for the others in the tomblike morning gloom of the conference room that Hilda amplified that Yes of hers.

"It's awful such people should be alive."

She yawned then, and her pale orange mouth opened on a large darkness. Fascinated, I stared at the blind cave behind her face until the two lips met and moved and the dybbuk spoke out of its hiding place, "I'm so glad they're going to die."

"Come on, give us a smile."

I sat on the pink velvet loveseat in Jay Cee's office, holding a paper rose and facing the magazine photographer. I was the last of the twelve to have my picture taken. I had tried concealing myself in the powder room, but it didn't work. Betsy had spied my feet under the doors.

I didn't want my picture taken because I was going to cry. I didn't know why I was going to cry, but I knew that if anybody spoke to me or looked at me too closely the tears would fly out of my eyes and the sobs would fly out of my throat and I'd cry for a week. I could feel the tears brimming and sloshing in me like water in a glass that is unsteady and too full.

This was the last round of photographs before the magazine went to press and we returned to Tulsa or Biloxi or Teaneck or Coos Bay or wherever we'd come from, and we were supposed to be photographed with props to show what we wanted to be.

Betsy held an ear of corn to show she wanted to be a farmer's wife, and Hilda held the bald, faceless head of a hatmaker's dummy to show she wanted to design hats, and Doreen held a gold embroidered sari to show she wanted to be a social worker in India (she didn't really, she told me, she only wanted to get her hands on a sari).

When they asked me what I wanted to be I said I didn't know.

"Oh, sure you know," the photographer said.

"She wants," said Jay Cee wittily, "to be everything."

I said I wanted to be a poet.

Then they scouted about for something for me to hold.

Jay Cee suggested a book of poems, but the photographer said no, that was too obvious. It should be something that showed what inspired the poems. Finally Jay Cee unclipped the single, long-stemmed paper rose from her latest hat.

The photographer fiddled with his hot white lights. "Show us how happy it makes you to write a poem."

I stared through the frieze of rubber-plant leaves in Jay Cee's window to the blue sky beyond. A few stagey cloud puffs were traveling from right to left. I fixed my eyes on the largest cloud, as if, when it passed out of sight, I might have the good luck to pass with it.

I felt it was very important to keep the line of my mouth level.

"Give us a smile."

At last, obediently, like the mouth of a ventriloquist's dummy, my own mouth started to quirk up.

"Hey," the photographer protested, with sudden foreboding, "you look like you're going to cry."

I couldn't stop.

I buried my face in the pink velvet façade of Jay Cee's loveseat and with immense relief the salt tears and miserable noises that had been prowling around in me all morning burst out into the room.

When I lifted my head, the photographer had vanished. Jay Cee had vanished as well. I felt limp and betrayed, like the skin shed by a terrible animal. It was a relief to be free of the animal, but it seemed to have taken my spirit with it, and everything else it could lay its paws on.

I fumbled in my pocketbook for the gilt compact with the mascara and the mascara brush and the eyeshadow and the three lipsticks and the side mirror. The face that peered back at me seemed to be peering from the grating of a prison cell after a prolonged beating. It looked bruised and puffy and all the wrong colors. It was a face that needed soap and water and Christian tolerance.

I started to paint it with small heart.

Jay Cee breezed back after a decent interval with an armful of manuscripts.

"These'll amuse you," she said. "Have a good read."

Every morning a snowy avalanche of manuscripts swelled the dust-gray piles in the office of the Fiction Editor. Secretly, in studies and attics and schoolrooms all over America, people must be writing. Say someone or other finished a manuscript every minute; in five minutes that would be five manuscripts stacked on the Fiction Editor's desk. Within the hour there would be sixty, crowding each other onto the floor. And in a year ...

I smiled, seeing a pristine, imaginary manuscript floating in mid-air, with Esther Greenwood typed in the upper-right-hand corner. After my month on the magazine I'd applied for a summer school course with a famous writer where you sent in the manuscript of a story and he read it and said whether you were good enough to be admitted into his class.

Of course, it was a very small class, and I had sent in my story a long time ago and hadn't heard from the writer yet, but I was sure I'd find the letter of acceptance waiting on the mail table at home.

I decided I'd surprise Jay Cee and send in a couple of the stories I wrote in this class under a pseudonym. Then one day the Fiction Editor would come in to Jay Cee personally and plop the stories down on her desk and say, "Here's something a cut above the usual," and Jay Cee would agree and accept them and ask the author to lunch and it would be me.

"Honestly," Doreen said, "this one'll be different."

"Tell me about him," I said stonily.

"He's from Peru."

"They're squat," I said. "They're ugly as Aztecs."

"No, no, no, sweetie, I've already met him."

We were sitting on my bed in a mess of dirty cotton dresses and laddered nylons and gray underwear, and for ten

minutes Doreen had been trying to persuade me to go to a
country club dance with a friend of somebody Lenny knew
which, she insisted, was a very different thing from a friend of
Lenny's, but as I was catching the eight o'clock train home the
next morning I felt I should make some attempt to pack.

I also had a dim idea that if I walked the streets of New
York by myself all night something of the city's mystery and
magnificence might rub off on to me at last.

But I gave it up.

It was becoming more and more difficult for me to decide
to do anything in those last days. And when I eventually *did*
decide to do something, such as packing a suitcase, I only
dragged all my grubby, expensive clothes out of the bureau
and the closet and spread them on the chairs and the bed and
the floor and then sat and stared at them, utterly perplexed.
They seemed to have a separate, mulish identity of their own
that refused to be washed and folded and stowed.

"It's these clothes," I told Doreen. "I just can't face these
clothes when I come back."

"That's easy."

And in her beautiful, one-track way, Doreen started to
snatch up slips and stockings and the elaborate strapless bra,
full of steel springs—a free gift from the Primrose Corset
Company, which I'd never had the courage to wear—and
finally, one by one, the sad array of queerly cut forty-dollar
dresses. . . .

"Hey, leave that one out. I'm wearing it."

Doreen extricated a black scrap from her bundle and
dropped it in my lap. Then, snowballing the rest of the clothes
into one soft, conglomerate mass, she stuffed them out of
sight under the bed.

Doreen knocked on the green door with the gold knob.

Scuffling and a man's laugh, cut short, sounded from inside.
Then a tall boy in shirtsleeves and a blond crewcut inched the
door open and peered out.

"Baby!" he roared.

Doreen disappeared in his arms. I thought it must be the
person Lenny knew.

I stood quietly in the doorway in my black sheath and my black stole with the fringe, yellower than ever, but expecting less. "I am an observer," I told myself, as I watched Doreen being handed into the room by the blond boy to another man, who was also tall, but dark, with slightly longer hair. This man was wearing an immaculate white suit, a pale blue shirt and a yellow satin tie with a bright stickpin.

I couldn't take my eyes off that stickpin.

A great white light seemed to shoot out of it, illuminating the room. Then the light withdrew into itself, leaving a dewdrop on a field of gold.

I put one foot in front of the other.

"That's a diamond," somebody said, and a lot of people burst out laughing.

My nail tapped a glassy facet.

"Her first diamond."

"Give it to her, Marco."

Marco bowed and deposited the stickpin in my palm.

It dazzled and danced with light like a heavenly ice cube. I slipped it quickly into my imitation jet bead evening bag and looked around. The faces were empty as plates, and nobody seemed to be breathing.

"Fortunately," a dry, hard hand encircled my upper arm, "I am escorting the lady for the rest of the evening. Perhaps," the spark in Marco's eyes extinguished, and they went black, "I shall perform some small service . . ."

Somebody laughed.

". . . worthy of a diamond."

The hand round my arm tightened.

"Ouch!"

Marco removed his hand. I looked down at my arm. A thumbprint purpled into view. Marco watched me. Then he pointed to the underside of my arm. "Look there."

I looked, and saw four, faint matching prints.

"You see, I am quite serious."

Marco's small, flickering smile reminded me of a snake I'd teased in the Bronx Zoo. When I tapped my finger on the stout cage glass the snake had opened its clockwork jaws and seemed to smile. Then it struck and struck and struck at the invisible pane till I moved off.

I had never met a woman-hater before.

I could tell Marco was a woman-hater, because in spite of all the models and TV starlets in the room that night he paid attention to nobody but me. Not out of kindness or even curiosity, but because I'd happened to be dealt to him, like a playing card in a pack of identical cards.

A man in the country club band stepped up to the mike and started shaking those seedpod rattles that mean South American music.

Marco reached for my hand, but I hung on to my fourth daiquiri and stayed put. I'd never had a daiquiri before. The reason I had a daiquiri was because Marco ordered it for me, and I felt so grateful he hadn't asked what sort of drink I wanted that I didn't say a word, I just drank one daiquiri after another.

Marco looked at me.

"No," I said.

"What do you mean, no?"

"I can't dance to that kind of music."

"Don't be stupid."

"I want to sit here and finish my drink."

Marco bent toward me with a tight smile, and in one swoop my drink took wing and landed in a potted palm. Then Marco gripped my hand in such a way I had to choose between following him on to the floor or having my arm torn off.

"It's a tango." Marco maneuvered me out among the dancers. "I love tangos."

"I can't dance."

"You don't have to dance. I'll do the dancing."

Marco hooked an arm around my waist and jerked me up against his dazzling white suit. Then he said, "Pretend you are drowning."

I shut my eyes, and the music broke over me like a rainstorm. Marco's leg slid forward against mine and my leg slid back and I seemed to be riveted to him, limb for limb, moving as he moved, without any will or knowledge of my own, and after a while I thought, "It doesn't take two to dance, it only takes one," and I let myself blow and bend like a tree in the wind.

"What did I tell you?" Marco's breath scorched my ear. "You're a perfectly respectable dancer."

I began to see why woman-haters could make such fools of women. Woman-haters were like gods: invulnerable and chock-full of power. They descended, and then they disappeared. You could never catch one.

After the South American music there was an interval.

Marco led me through the French doors into the garden. Lights and voices spilled from the ballroom window, but a few yards beyond the darkness drew up its barricade and sealed them off. In the infinitesimal glow of the stars, the trees and flowers were strewing their cool odors. There was no moon.

The box hedges shut behind us. A deserted golf course stretched away toward a few hilly clumps of trees, and I felt the whole desolate familiarity of the scene—the country club and the dance and the lawn with its single cricket.

I didn't know where I was, but it was somewhere in the wealthy suburbs of New York.

Marco produced a slim cigar and a silver lighter in the shape of a bullet. He set the cigar between his lips and bent over the small flare. His face, with its exaggerated shadows and planes of light, looked alien and pained, like a refugee's.

I watched him.

"Who are you in love with?" I said then.

For a minute Marco didn't say anything, he simply opened his mouth and breathed out a blue, vaporous ring.

"Perfect!" he laughed.

The ring widened and blurred, ghost-pale on the dark air.

Then he said, "I am in love with my cousin."

I felt no surprise.

"Why don't you marry her?"

"Impossible."

"Why?"

Marco shrugged. "She's my first cousin. She's going to be a nun."

"Is she beautiful?"

"'There's no one to touch her."

"Does she know you love her?"

"Of course."

I paused. The obstacle seemed unreal to me.

"If you love her," I said, "you'll love somebody else some-day."

Marco dashed his cigar underfoot.

The ground soared and struck me with a soft shock. Mud squirmed through my fingers. Marco waited until I half rose. Then he put both hands on my shoulders and flung me back.

"My dress . . ."

"Your dress!" The mud oozed and adjusted itself to my shoulder blades. "Your dress!" Marco's face lowered cloudily over mine. A few drops of spit struck my lips. "Your dress is black and the dirt is black as well."

Then he threw himself face down as if he would grind his body through me and into the mud.

"It's happening," I thought. "It's happening. If I just lie here and do nothing it will happen."

Marco set his teeth to the strap at my shoulder and tore my sheath to the waist. I saw the glimmer of bare skin, like a pale veil separating two bloody-minded adversaries.

"Slut!"

The words hissed by my ear.

"Slut!"

The dust cleared, and I had a full view of the battle.

I began to writhe and bite.

Marco weighed me to the earth.

"Slut!"

I gouged at his leg with the sharp heel of my shoe. He turned, fumbling for the hurt.

Then I fisted my fingers together and smashed them at his nose. It was like hitting the steel plate of a battleship. Marco sat up. I began to cry.

Marco pulled out a white handkerchief and dabbed his nose. Blackness, like ink, spread over the pale cloth.

I sucked at my salty knuckles.

"I want Doreen."

Marco stared off across the golf links.

"I want Doreen. I want to go home."

"Sluts, all sluts." Marco seemed to be talking to himself. "Yes or no, it is all the same."

I poked Marco's shoulder.

"Where's Doreen?"

Marco snorted. "Go to the parking lot. Look in the backs of all the cars."

Then he spun around.

"My diamond."

I got up and retrieved my stole from the darkness. I started to walk off. Marco sprang to his feet and blocked my path. Then, deliberately, he wiped his finger under his bloody nose and with two strokes stained my cheeks. "I have earned my diamond with this blood. Give it to me."

"I don't know where it is."

Now I knew perfectly well that the diamond was in my evening bag and that when Marco knocked me down my evening bag had soared, like a night bird, into the enveloping darkness. I began to think I would lead him away and then return on my own and hunt for it.

I had no idea what a diamond that size would buy, but whatever it was, I knew it would be a lot.

Marco took my shoulders in both hands.

"Tell me," he said, giving each word equal emphasis. "Tell me, or I'll break your neck."

Suddenly I didn't care.

"It's in my imitation jet bead evening bag," I said. "Somewhere in the muck."

I left Marco on his hands and knees, scrabbling in the darkness for another, smaller darkness that hid the light of his diamond from his furious eyes.

Doreen was not in the ballroom nor in the parking lot.

I kept to the fringe of the shadows so nobody would notice the grass plastered to my dress and shoes, and with my black stole I covered my shoulders and bare breasts.

Luckily for me, the dance was nearly over, and groups of people were leaving and coming out to the parked cars. I asked at one car after another until finally I found a car that had room and would drop me in the middle of Manhattan.

At that vague hour between dark and dawn, the sunroof of the Amazon was deserted.

Quiet as a burglar in my cornflower-sprigged bathrobe, I crept to the edge of the parapet. The parapet reached almost to my shoulders, so I dragged a folding chair from the stack against the wall, opened it, and climbed onto the precarious seat.

A stiff breeze lifted the hair from my head. At my feet, the city doused its lights in sleep, its buildings blackened, as if for a funeral.

It was my last night.

I grasped the bundle I carried and pulled at a pale tail. A strapless elasticized slip which, in the course of wear, had lost its elasticity, slumped into my hand. I waved it, like a flag of truce, once, twice. . . . The breeze caught it, and I let go.

A white flake floated out into the night, and began its slow descent. I wondered on what street or rooftop it would come to rest.

I tugged at the bundle again.

The wind made an effort, but failed, and a batlike shadow sank toward the roof garden of the penthouse opposite.

Piece by piece, I fed my wardrobe to the night wind, and flutteringly, like a loved one's ashes, the gray scraps were ferried off, to settle here, there, exactly where I would never know, in the dark heart of New York.

Ten

THE FACE IN THE MIRROR looked like a sick Indian.

I dropped the compact into my pocketbook and stared out of the train window. Like a colossal junkyard, the swamps and back lots of Connecticut flashed past, one broken-down fragment bearing no relation to another.

What a hotchpotch the world was!

I glanced down at my unfamiliar skirt and blouse.

The skirt was a green dirndl with tiny black, white and electric-blue shapes swarming across it, and it stuck out like a lampshade. Instead of sleeves, the white eyelet blouse had frills at the shoulder, floppy as the wings of a new angel.

I'd forgotten to save any day clothes from the ones I let fly over New York, so Betsy had traded me a blouse and skirt for my bathrobe with the cornflowers on it.

A wan reflection of myself, white wings, brown ponytail and all, ghosted over the landscape.

"Pollyanna Cowgirl," I said out loud.

A woman in the seat opposite looked up from her magazine.

I hadn't, at the last moment, felt like washing off the two diagonal lines of dried blood that marked my cheeks. They seemed touching, and rather spectacular, and I thought I would carry them around with me, like the relic of a dead lover, till they wore off of their own accord.

Of course, if I smiled or moved my face much, the blood would flake away in no time, so I kept my face immobile, and when I had to speak I spoke through my teeth, without disturbing my lips.

I didn't really see why people should look at me.

Plenty of people looked queerer than I did.

My gray suitcase rode on the rack over my head, empty

except for *The Thirty Best Short Stories of the Year*, a white plastic sunglasses case and two dozen avocado pears, a parting present from Doreen.

The pears were unripe, so they would keep well, and whenever I lifted my suitcase up or down or simply carried it along, they cannoned from one end to the other with a special little thunder of their own.

"Root Wan Twenny Ate!" the conductor bawled.

The domesticated wilderness of pine, maple and oak rolled to a halt and stuck in the frame of the train window like a bad picture. My suitcase grumbled and bumped as I negotiated the long aisle.

I stepped from the air-conditioned compartment onto the station platform, and the motherly breath of the suburbs enfolded me. It smelt of lawn sprinklers and station wagons and tennis rackets and dogs and babies.

A summer calm laid its soothing hand over everything, like death.

My mother was waiting by the glove-gray Chevrolet.

"Why lovey, what's happened to your face?"

"Cut myself," I said briefly, and crawled into the back seat after my suitcase. I didn't want her staring at me the whole way home.

The upholstery felt slippery and clean.

My mother climbed behind the wheel and tossed a few letters into my lap, then turned her back.

The car purred into life.

"I think I should tell you right away," she said, and I could see bad news in the set of her neck, "you didn't make that writing course."

The air punched out of my stomach.

All through June the writing course stretched before me like a bright, safe bridge over the dull gulf of the summer. Now I saw it totter and dissolve, and a body in a white blouse and green skirt plummet into the gap.

Then my mouth shaped itself sourly.

I had expected it.

I slunk down on the middle of my spine, my nose level with the rim of the window, and watched the houses of outer

Boston glide by. As the houses grew more familiar, I slunk still lower.

I felt it was very important not to be recognized.

The gray, padded car roof closed over my head like the roof of a prison van, and the white, shining, identical clapboard houses with their interstices of well-groomed green proceeded past, one bar after another in a large but escape-proof cage.

I had never spent a summer in the suburbs before.

The soprano screak of carriage wheels punished my ear. Sun, seeping through the blinds, filled the bedroom with a sulphurous light. I didn't know how long I had slept, but I felt one big twitch of exhaustion.

The twin bed next to mine was empty and unmade.

At seven I had heard my mother get up, slip into her clothes and tiptoe out of the room. Then the buzz of the orange squeezer sounded from downstairs, and the smell of coffee and bacon filtered under my door. Then the sink water ran from the tap and dishes clinked as my mother dried them and put them back in the cupboard.

Then the front door opened and shut. Then the car door opened and shut, and the motor went broom-broom and, edging off with a crunch of gravel, faded into the distance.

My mother was teaching shorthand and typing to a lot of city college girls and wouldn't be home till the middle of the afternoon.

The carriage wheels screaked past again. Somebody seemed to be wheeling a baby back and forth under my window.

I slipped out of bed and onto the rug, and quietly, on my hands and knees, crawled over to see who it was.

Ours was a small, white clapboard house set in the middle of a small green lawn on the corner of two peaceful suburban streets, but in spite of the little maple trees planted at intervals around our property, anybody passing along the sidewalk could glance up at the second story windows and see just what was going on.

This was brought home to me by our next-door neighbor, a spiteful woman named Mrs. Ockenden.

Mrs. Ockenden was a retired nurse who had just married her third husband—the other two died in curious circumstances—and she spent an inordinate amount of time peering from behind the starched white curtains of her windows.

She had called my mother up twice about me—once to report that I had been sitting in front of the house for an hour under the streetlight and kissing somebody in a blue Plymouth, and once to say that I had better pull the blinds down in my room, because she had seen me half-naked getting ready for bed one night when she happened to be out walking her Scotch terrier.

With great care, I raised my eyes to the level of the windowsill.

A woman not five feet tall, with a grotesque, protruding stomach, was wheeling an old black baby carriage down the street. Two or three small children of various sizes, all pale, with smudgy faces and bare smudgy knees, wobbled along in the shadow of her skirts.

A serene, almost religious smile lit up the woman's face. Her head tilted happily back, like a sparrow egg perched on a duck egg, she smiled into the sun.

I knew the woman well.

It was Dodo Conway.

Dodo Conway was a Catholic who had gone to Barnard and then married an architect who had gone to Columbia and was also a Catholic. They had a big, rambling house up the street from us, set behind a morbid façade of pine trees, and surrounded by scooters, tricycles, doll carriages, toy fire trucks, baseball bats, badminton nets, croquet wickets, hamster cages and cocker spaniel puppies—the whole sprawling paraphernalia of suburban childhood.

Dodo interested me in spite of myself.

Her house was unlike all the others in our neighborhood in its size (it was much bigger) and its color (the second story was constructed of dark brown clapboard and the first of gray stucco, studded with gray and purple golfball-shaped stones), and the pine trees completely screened it from view, which was considered unsociable in our community of adjoining lawns and friendly, waist-high hedges.

Dodo raised her six children—and would no doubt raise her

seventh—on Rice Krispies, peanut-butter-and-marshmallow sandwiches, vanilla ice cream and gallon upon gallon of Hoods milk. She got a special discount from the local milkman.

Everybody loved Dodo, although the swelling size of her family was the talk of the neighborhood. The older people around, like my mother, had two children, and the younger, more prosperous ones had four, but nobody but Dodo was on the verge of a seventh. Even six was considered excessive, but then, everybody said, of course Dodo was a Catholic.

I watched Dodo wheel the youngest Conway up and down. She seemed to be doing it for my benefit.

Children made me sick.

A floorboard creaked, and I ducked down again, just as Dodo Conway's face, by instinct, or some gift of supernatural hearing, turned on the little pivot of its neck.

I felt her gaze pierce through the white clapboard and the pink wallpaper roses and uncover me, crouching there behind the silver pickets of the radiator.

I crawled back into bed and pulled the sheet over my head. But even that didn't shut out the light, so I buried my head under the darkness of the pillow and pretended it was night. I couldn't see the point of getting up.

I had nothing to look forward to.

After a while I heard the telephone ringing in the downstairs hall. I stuffed the pillow into my ears and gave myself five minutes. Then I lifted my head from its bolt hole. The ringing had stopped.

Almost at once it started up again.

Cursing whatever friend, relative or stranger had sniffed out my homecoming, I padded barefoot downstairs. The black instrument on the hall table trilled its hysterical note over and over, like a nervous bird.

I picked up the receiver.

"Hullo," I said, in a low, disguised voice.

"Hullo, Esther, what's the matter, have you got laryngitis?"

It was my old friend Jody, calling from Cambridge.

Jody was working at the Coop that summer and taking a lunchtime course in sociology. She and two other girls from my college had rented a big apartment from four Harvard law students, and I'd been planning to move in with them when my writing course began.

Jody wanted to know when they could expect me.

"I'm not coming," I said. "I didn't make the course."

There was a small pause.

"He's an ass," Jody said then. "He doesn't know a good thing when he sees it."

"My sentiments exactly." My voice sounded strange and hollow in my ears.

"Come anyway. Take some other course."

The notion of studying German or abnormal psychology flitted through my head. After all, I'd saved nearly the whole of my New York salary, so I could just about afford it.

But the hollow voice said, "You better count me out."

"Well," Jody began, "there's this other girl who wanted to come in with us if anybody dropped out. ..."

"Fine. Ask her."

The minute I hung up I knew I should have said I would come. One morning listening to Dodo Conway's baby carriage would drive me crazy. And I made a point of never living in the same house with my mother for more than a week.

I reached for the receiver.

My hand advanced a few inches, then retreated and fell limp. I forced it toward the receiver again, but again it stopped short, as if it had collided with a pane of glass.

I wandered into the dining room.

Propped on the table I found a long, businesslike letter from the summer school and a thin blue letter on leftover Yale stationery, addressed to me in Buddy Willard's lucid hand.

I slit open the summer school letter with a knife.

Since I wasn't accepted for the writing course, it said, I could choose some other course instead, but I should call in to the Admissions Office that same morning, or it would be too late to register, the courses were almost full.

I dialed the Admissions Office and listened to the zombie voice leave a message that Miss Esther Greenwood was canceling all arrangements to come to summer school.

Then I opened Buddy Willard's letter.

Buddy wrote that he was probably falling in love with a

nurse who also had TB, but his mother had rented a cottage in the Adirondacks for the month of July, and if I came along with her, he might well find his feeling for the nurse was mere infatuation.

I snatched up a pencil and crossed out Buddy's message. Then I turned the letter paper over and on the opposite side wrote that I was engaged to a simultaneous interpreter and never wanted to see Buddy again as I did not want to give my children a hypocrite for a father.

I stuck the letter back in the envelope, Scotch-taped it together, and readdressed it to Buddy, without putting on a new stamp. I thought the message was worth a good three cents.

Then I decided I would spend the summer writing a novel.

That would fix a lot of people.

I strolled into the kitchen, dropped a raw egg into a teacup of raw hamburger, mixed it up and ate it. Then I set up the card table on the screened breezeway between the house and the garage.

A great wallowing bush of mock orange shut off the view of the street in front, the house wall and the garage wall took care of either side, and a clump of birches and a box hedge protected me from Mrs. Ockenden at the back.

I counted out three hundred and fifty sheets of corrasable bond from my mother's stock in the hall closet, secreted away under a pile of old felt hats and clothes brushes and woolen scarves.

Back on the breezeway, I fed the first, virgin sheet into my old portable and rolled it up.

From another, distanced mind, I saw myself sitting on the breezeway, surrounded by two white clapboard walls, a mock orange bush and a clump of birches and a box hedge, small as a doll in a doll's house.

A feeling of tenderness filled my heart. My heroine would be myself, only in disguise. She would be called Elaine. Elaine. I counted the letters on my fingers. There were six letters in Esther, too. It seemed a lucky thing.

Elaine sat on the breezeway in an old yellow nightgown of her mother's waiting for something to happen. It was a sweltering morning in July, and drops of sweat crawled down her back one by one, like slow insects.

I leaned back and read what I had written.

It seemed lively enough, and I was quite proud of the bit about the drops of sweat like insects, only I had the dim impression I'd probably read it somewhere else a long time ago.

I sat like that for about an hour, trying to think what would come next, and in my mind, the barefoot doll in her mother's old yellow nightgown sat and stared into space as well.

"Why, honey, don't you want to get dressed?"

My mother took care never to tell me to do anything. She would only reason with me sweetly, like one intelligent mature person with another.

"It's almost three in the afternoon."

"I'm writing a novel," I said. "I haven't got time to change out of this and change into that."

I lay on the couch on the breezeway and shut my eyes. I could hear my mother clearing the typewriter and the papers from the card table and laying out the silver for supper, but I didn't move.

Inertia oozed like molasses through Elaine's limbs. That's what it must feel like to have malaria, she thought.

At any rate, I'd be lucky if I wrote a page a day.

Then I knew what the trouble was.

I needed experience.

How could I write about life when I'd never had a love affair or a baby or even seen anybody die? A girl I knew had just won a prize for a short story about her adventures among the pygmies in Africa. How could I compete with that sort of thing?

By the end of supper my mother had convinced me I should study shorthand in the evenings. Then I would be killing two birds with one stone, writing a novel and learning something practical as well. I would also be saving a whole lot of money.

That same evening, my mother unearthed an old blackboard

from the cellar and set it up on the breezeway. Then she stood at the blackboard and scribbled little curlicues in white chalk while I sat in a chair and watched.

At first I felt hopeful.

I thought I might learn shorthand in no time, and when the freckled lady in the Scholarships Office asked me why I hadn't worked to earn money in July and August, the way you were supposed to if you were a scholarship girl, I could tell her I had taken a free shorthand course instead, so I could support myself right after college.

The only thing was, when I tried to picture myself in some job, briskly jotting down line after line of shorthand, my mind went blank. There wasn't one job I felt like doing where you used shorthand. And, as I sat there and watched, the white chalk curlicues blurred into senselessness.

I told my mother I had a terrible headache, and went to bed.

An hour later the door inched open, and she crept into the room. I heard the whisper of her clothes as she undressed. She climbed into bed. Then her breathing grew slow and regular.

In the dim light of the streetlamp that filtered through the drawn blinds, I could see the pin curls on her head glittering like a row of little bayonets.

I decided I would put off the novel until I had gone to Europe and had a lover, and that I would never learn a word of shorthand. If I never learned shorthand I would never have to use it.

I thought I would spend the summer reading *Finnegans Wake* and writing my thesis.

Then I would be way ahead when college started at the end of September, and able to enjoy my last year instead of swotting away with no makeup and stringy hair, on a diet of coffee and Benzedrine, the way most of the seniors taking honors did, until they finished their thesis.

Then I thought I might put off college for a year and apprentice myself to a pottery maker.

Or work my way to Germany and be a waitress, until I was bilingual.

Then plan after plan started leaping through my head, like a family of scatty rabbits.

I saw the years of my life spaced along a road in the form of telephone poles, threaded together by wires. I counted one, two, three . . . nineteen telephone poles, and then the wires dangled into space, and try as I would, I couldn't see a single pole beyond the nineteenth.

The room blued into view, and I wondered where the night had gone. My mother turned from a foggy log into a slumbering, middle-aged woman, her mouth slightly open and a snore raveling from her throat. The piggish noise irritated me, and for a while it seemed to me that the only way to stop it would be to take the column of skin and sinew from which it rose and twist it to silence between my hands.

I feigned sleep until my mother left for school, but even my eyelids didn't shut out the light. They hung the raw, red screen of their tiny vessels in front of me like a wound. I crawled between the mattress and the padded bedstead and let the mattress fall across me like a tombstone. It felt dark and safe under there, but the mattress was not heavy enough.

It needed about a ton more weight to make me sleep.

riverrun, past Eve and Adam's, from swerve of shore to bend of bay, brings us by a commodius vicus of recirculation back to Howth Castle and Environs. . . .

The thick book made an unpleasant dent in my stomach.

riverrun, past Eve and Adam's . . .

I thought the small letter at the start might mean that nothing ever really began all new, with a capital, but that it just flowed on from what came before. Eve and Adam's was Adam and Eve, or course, but it probably signified something else as well.

Maybe it was a pub in Dublin.

My eyes sank through an alphabet soup of letters to the long word in the middle of the page.

bababadalgharaghtakamminarronnkonnbronntonnerronntuonn-thunntrovarrhounawnskawntoohoohoordenenthurnuk!

I counted the letters. There were exactly a hundred of them. I thought this must be important.

Why should there be a hundred letters?

Haltingly, I tried the word aloud.

It sounded like a heavy wooden object falling downstairs, boomp boomp boomp, step after step. Lifting the pages of the book, I let them fan slowly by my eyes. Words, dimly familiar but twisted all awry, like faces in a funhouse mirror, fled past, leaving no impression on the glassy surface of my brain.

I squinted at the page.

The letters grew barbs and rams' horns. I watched them separate, each from the other, and jiggle up and down in a silly way. Then they associated themselves in fantastic, untranslatable shapes, like Arabic or Chinese.

I decided to junk my thesis.

I decided to junk the whole honors program and become an ordinary English major. I went to look up the requirements of an ordinary English major at my college.

There were lots of requirements, and I didn't have half of them. One of the requirements was a course in the eighteenth century. I hated the very idea of the eighteenth century, with all those smug men writing tight little couplets and being so dead keen on reason. So I'd skipped it. They let you do that in honors, you were much freer. I had been so free I'd spent most of my time on Dylan Thomas.

A friend of mine, also in honors, had managed never to read a word of Shakespeare; but she was a real expert on the *Four Quartets*.

I saw how impossible and embarrassing it would be for me to try to switch from my free program into the stricter one. So I looked up the requirements for English majors at the city college where my mother taught.

They were even worse.

You had to know Old English and the History of the English Language and a representative selection of all that had been written from Beowulf to the present day.

This surprised me. I had always looked down on my mother's college, as it was coed, and filled with people who couldn't get scholarships to the big eastern colleges.

Now I saw that the stupidest person at my mother's college knew more than I did. I saw they wouldn't even let me in through the door, let alone give me a large scholarship like the one I had at my own college.

I thought I'd better go to work for a year and think things over. Maybe I could study the eighteenth century in secret.

But I didn't know shorthand, so what could I do?

I could be a waitress or a typist.

But I couldn't stand the idea of being either one.

"You say you want more sleeping pills?"

"Yes."

"But the ones I gave you last week are very strong."

"They don't work any more."

Teresa's large, dark eyes regarded me thoughtfully. I could hear the voices of her three children in the garden under the consulting-room window. My Aunt Libby had married an Italian, and Teresa was my aunt's sister-in-law and our family doctor.

I liked Teresa. She had a gentle, intuitive touch.

I thought it must be because she was Italian.

There was a little pause.

"What seems to be the matter?" Teresa said then.

"I can't sleep. I can't read." I tried to speak in a cool, calm way, but the zombie rose up in my throat and choked me off. I turned my hands palm up.

"I think," Teresa tore off a white slip from her prescription pad and wrote down a name and address, "you'd better see another doctor I know. He'll be able to help you more than I can."

I peered at the writing, but I couldn't read it.

"Doctor Gordon," Teresa said. "He's a psychiatrist."

Eleven

DOCTOR GORDON'S WAITING ROOM was hushed and beige.

The walls were beige, and the carpets were beige, and the upholstered chairs and sofas were beige. There were no mirrors or pictures, only certificates from different medical schools, with Doctor Gordon's name in Latin, hung about the walls. Pale green loopy ferns and spiked leaves of a much darker green filled the ceramic pots on the end table and the coffee table and the magazine table.

At first I wondered why the room felt so safe. Then I realized it was because there were no windows.

The air-conditioning made me shiver.

I was still wearing Betsy's white blouse and dirndl skirt. They drooped a bit now, as I hadn't washed them in my three weeks at home. The sweaty cotton gave off a sour but friendly smell.

I hadn't washed my hair for three weeks, either.

I hadn't slept for seven nights.

My mother told me I must have slept, it was impossible not to sleep in all that time, but if I slept, it was with my eyes wide open, for I had followed the green, luminous course of the second hand and the minute hand and the hour hand of the bedside clock through their circles and semi-circles, every night for seven nights, without missing a second, or a minute, or an hour.

The reason I hadn't washed my clothes or my hair was because it seemed so silly.

I saw the days of the year stretching ahead like a series of bright, white boxes, and separating one box from another was sleep, like a black shade. Only for me, the long perspective of shades that set off one box from the next had suddenly snapped up, and I could see day after day after day glaring ahead of me like a white, broad, infinitely desolate avenue.

It seemed silly to wash one day when I would only have to wash again the next.

It made me tired just to think of it.

I wanted to do everything once and for all and be through with it.

Doctor Gordon twiddled a silver pencil.

"Your mother tells me you are upset."

I curled in the cavernous leather chair and faced Doctor Gordon across an acre of highly polished desk.

Doctor Gordon waited. He tapped his pencil—tap, tap, tap—across the neat green field of his blotter.

His eyelashes were so long and thick they looked artificial. Black plastic reeds fringing two green, glacial pools.

Doctor Gordon's features were so perfect he was almost pretty.

I hated him the minute I walked in through the door.

I had imagined a kind, ugly, intuitive man looking up and saying "Ah!" in an encouraging way, as if he could see something I couldn't, and then I would find words to tell him how I was so scared, as if I were being stuffed farther and farther into a black, airless sack with no way out.

Then he would lean back in his chair and match the tips of his fingers together in a little steeple and tell me why I couldn't sleep and why I couldn't read and why I couldn't eat and why everything people did seemed so silly, because they only died in the end.

And then, I thought, he would help me, step by step, to be myself again.

But Doctor Gordon wasn't like that at all. He was young and good-looking, and I could see right away he was conceited.

Doctor Gordon had a photograph on his desk, in a silver frame, that half faced him and half faced my leather chair. It was a family photograph, and it showed a beautiful dark-haired woman, who could have been Doctor Gordon's sister, smiling out over the heads of two blond children.

I think one child was a boy and one was a girl, but it may have been that both children were boys or that both were girls, it is hard to tell when children are so small. I think there was also a dog in the picture, toward the bottom—a kind of airedale or a golden retriever—but it may have only been the pattern in the woman's skirt.

For some reason the photograph made me furious.

I didn't see why it should be turned half toward me unless Doctor Gordon was trying to show me right away that he was married to some glamorous woman and I'd better not get any funny ideas.

Then I thought, how could this Doctor Gordon help me anyway, with a beautiful wife and beautiful children and a beautiful dog haloing him like the angels on a Christmas card?

"Suppose you try and tell me what you think is wrong."

I turned the words over suspiciously, like round, sea-polished pebbles that might suddenly put out a claw and change into something else.

What did I *think* was wrong?

That made it sound as if nothing was *really* wrong, I only *thought* it was wrong.

In a dull, flat voice—to show I was not beguiled by his good looks or his family photograph—I told Doctor Gordon about not sleeping and not eating and not reading. I didn't tell him about the handwriting, which bothered me most of all.

That morning I had tried to write a letter to Doreen, down in West Virginia, asking whether I could come and live with her and maybe get a job at her college waiting on table or something.

But when I took up my pen, my hand made big, jerky letters like those of a child, and the lines sloped down the page from left to right almost diagonally, as if they were loops of string lying on the paper, and someone had come along and blown them askew.

I knew I couldn't send a letter like that, so I tore it up in little pieces and put them in my pocketbook, next to my all-purpose compact, in case the psychiatrist asked to see them.

But of course Doctor Gordon didn't ask to see them, as I hadn't mentioned them, and I began to feel pleased at my cleverness. I thought I only need tell him what I wanted to, and that I could control the picture he had of me by hiding this and revealing that, all the while he thought he was so smart.

The whole time I was talking, Doctor Gordon bent his head as if he were praying, and the only noise apart from the dull, flat voice was the tap, tap, tap of Doctor Gordon's pencil at the same point on the green blotter, like a stalled walking stick.

When I had finished, Doctor Gordon lifted his head.

"Where did you say you went to college?"

Baffled, I told him. I didn't see where college fitted in.

"Ah!" Doctor Gordon leaned back in his chair, staring into the air over my shoulder with a reminiscent smile.

I thought he was going to tell me his diagnosis, and that perhaps I had judged him too hastily and too unkindly. But he only said, "I remember your college well. I was up there, during the war. They had a WAC station, didn't they? Or was it WAVES?"

I said I didn't know.

"Yes, a WAC station, I remember now. I was doctor for the lot, before I was sent overseas. My, they were a pretty bunch of girls."

Doctor Gordon laughed.

Then, in one smooth move, he rose to his feet and strolled toward me round the corner of his desk. I wasn't sure what he meant to do, so I stood up as well.

Doctor Gordon reached for the hand that hung at my right side and shook it.

"See you next week, then."

The full, bosomy elms made a tunnel of shade over the yellow and red brick fronts along Commonwealth Avenue, and a trolley car was threading itself toward Boston down its slim, silver track. I waited for the trolley to pass, then crossed to the gray Chevrolet at the opposite curb.

I could see my mother's face, anxious and sallow as a slice of lemon, peering up at me through the windshield.

"Well, what did he say?"

I pulled the car door shut. It didn't catch. I pushed it out and drew it in again with a dull slam.

"He said he'll see me next week."

My mother sighed.

Doctor Gordon cost twenty-five dollars an hour.

"Hi there, what's your name?"

"Elly Higginbottom."

The sailor fell into step beside me, and I smiled.

I thought there must be as many sailors on the Common as there were pigeons. They seemed to come out of a dun-colored recruiting house on the far side, with blue and white "Join the Navy" posters stuck up on billboards round it and all over the inner walls.

"Where do you come from, Elly?"

"Chicago."

I had never been to Chicago, but I knew one or two boys who went to Chicago University, and it seemed the sort of place where unconventional, mixed-up people would come from.

"You sure are a long way from home."

The sailor put his arm around my waist, and for a long time we walked around the Common like that, the sailor stroking my hip through the green dirndl skirt, and me smiling myste-riously and trying not to say anything that would show I was from Boston and might at any moment meet Mrs. Willard, or one of my mother's other friends, crossing the Common after tea on Beacon Hill or shopping in Filene's Basement.

I thought if I ever did get to Chicago, I might change my name to Elly Higginbottom for good. Then nobody would know I had thrown up a scholarship at a big eastern women's college and mucked up a month in New York and refused a perfectly solid medical student for a husband who would one day be a member of the AMA and earn pots of money.

In Chicago, people would take me for what I was.

I would be simple Elly Higgenbottom, the orphan. People would love me for my sweet, quiet nature. They wouldn't be after me to read books and write long papers on the twins in James Joyce. And one day I might just marry a virile, but tender, garage mechanic and have a big cowy family, like Dodo Conway.

If I happened to feel like it.

"What do you want to do when you get out of the Navy?" I asked the sailor suddenly.

It was the longest sentence I had said, and he seemed taken aback. He pushed his white cupcake cap to one side and scratched his head.

"Well, I dunno, Elly," he said. "I might just go to college on the G.I. Bill."

I paused. Then I said suggestively, "You ever thought of opening a garage?"

"Nope," said the sailor. "Never have."

I peered at him from the corner of my eye. He didn't look a day over sixteen.

"Do you know how old I am?" I said accusingly.

The sailor grinned at me. "Nope, and I don't care either."

It occurred to me that this sailor was really remarkably handsome. He looked Nordic and virginal. Now I was simple-minded it seemed I attracted clean, handsome people.

"Well, I'm thirty," I said, and waited.

"Gee, Elly, you don't look it." The sailor squeezed my hip.

Then he glanced quickly from left to right. "Listen, Elly, if we go round to those steps over there, under the monument, I can kiss you."

At that moment I noticed a brown figure in sensible flat brown shoes striding across the Common in my direction. From the distance, I couldn't make out any features on the dime-sized face, but I knew it was Mrs. Willard.

"Could you please tell me the way to the subway?" I said to the sailor in a loud voice.

"Huh?"

"The subway that goes out to the Deer Island Prison?"

When Mrs. Willard came up I would have to pretend I was only asking the sailor directions, and didn't really know him at all.

"Take your hands off me," I said between my teeth.

"Say, Elly, what's up?"

The woman approached and passed by without a look or a nod, and of course it wasn't Mrs. Willard. Mrs. Willard was at her cottage in the Adirondacks.

I fixed the woman's receding back with a vengeful stare.

"Say, Elly ..."

"I thought it was somebody I knew," I said. "Some blasted lady from this orphan home in Chicago."

The sailor put his arm around me again.

"You mean you got no mom and dad, Elly?"

"No." I let out a tear that seemed ready. It made a little hot track down my cheek.

"Say, Elly, don't cry. This lady, was she mean to you?"

"She was ... she was *aw*ful!"

The tears came in a rush, then, and while the sailor was holding me and patting them dry with a big, clean, white linen handkerchief in the shelter of an American elm, I thought what an awful woman that lady in the brown suit had been, and how she, whether she knew it or not, was responsible for my taking the wrong turn here and the wrong path there and for everything bad that happened after that.

"Well, Esther, how do you feel this week?"

Doctor Gordon cradled his pencil like a slim, silver bullet.

"The same."

"The same?" He quirked an eyebrow, as if he didn't believe it.

So I told him again, in the same dull, flat voice, only it was angrier this time, because he seemed so slow to understand, how I hadn't slept for fourteen nights and how I couldn't read or write or swallow very well.

Doctor Gordon seemed unimpressed.

I dug into my pocketbook and found the scraps of my letter to Doreen. I took them out and let them flutter on to Doctor Gordon's immaculate green blotter. They lay there, dumb as daisy petals in a summer meadow.

"What," I said, "do you think of that?"

I thought Doctor Gordon must immediately see how bad the handwriting was, but he only said, "I think I would like to speak to your mother. Do you mind?"

"No." But I didn't like the idea of Doctor Gordon talking to my mother one bit. I thought he might tell her I should be locked up. I picked up every scrap of my letter to Doreen, so Doctor Gordon couldn't piece them together and see I was planning to run away, and walked out of his office without another word.

I watched my mother grow smaller and smaller until she disappeared into the door of Doctor Gordon's office building. Then I watched her grow larger and larger as she came back to the car.

"Well?" I could tell she had been crying.

My mother didn't look at me. She started the car.

Then she said, as we glided under the cool, deep-sea shade of the elms, "Doctor Gordon doesn't think you've improved at all. He thinks you should have some shock treatments at his private hospital in Walton."

I felt a sharp stab of curiosity, as if I had just read a terrible newspaper headline about somebody else.

"Does he mean *live* there?"

"No," my mother said, and her chin quivered.

I thought she must be lying.

"You tell me the truth," I said, "or I'll never speak to you again."

"Don't I *al*ways tell you the truth?" my mother said, and burst into tears.

SUICIDE SAVED FROM 7-STORY LEDGE!

After two hours on a narrow ledge seven stories above a concrete parking lot and gathered crowds, Mr. George Pollucci let himself be helped to safety through a nearby window by Sgt. Will Kilmartin of the Charles Street police force.

I cracked open a peanut from the ten-cent bag I had bought to feed the pigeons, and ate it. It tasted dead, like a bit of old tree bark.

I brought the newspaper close up to my eyes to get a better view of George Pollucci's face, spotlighted like a three-quarter moon against a vague background of brick and black sky. I felt he had something important to tell me, and whatever it was might just be written on his face.

But the smudgy crags of George Pollucci's features melted away as I peered at them, and resolved themselves into a regular pattern of dark and light and medium-gray dots.

The inky-black newspaper paragraph didn't tell why Mr. Pollucci was on the ledge, or what Sgt. Kilmartin did to him when he finally got him in through the window.

The trouble about jumping was that if you didn't pick the right number of stories, you might still be alive when you hit bottom. I thought seven stories must be a safe distance.

I folded the paper and wedged it between the slats of the park bench. It was what my mother called a scandal sheet, full of the local murders and suicides and beatings and robbings, and just about every page had a half-naked lady on it with her breasts surging over the edge of her dress and her legs arranged so you could see to her stocking tops.

I didn't know why I had never bought any of these papers before. They were the only things I could read. The little paragraphs between the pictures ended before the letters had a chance to get cocky and wiggle about. At home, all I ever saw was the *Christian Science Monitor,* which appeared on the doorstep at five o'clock every day but Sunday and treated suicides and sex crimes and airplane crashes as if they didn't happen.

A big white swan full of little children approached my bench, then turned around a bosky islet covered with ducks and paddled back under the dark arch of the bridge. Everything I looked at seemed bright and extremely tiny.

I saw, as if through the keyhole of a door I couldn't open, myself and my younger brother, knee-high and holding rabbit-eared balloons, climb aboard a swanboat and fight for a seat at the edge, over the peanut-shell-paved water. My mouth tasted of cleanness and peppermint. If we were good at the dentist's, my mother always bought us a swanboat ride.

I circled the Public Garden—over the bridge and under the blue-green monuments, past the American flag flowerbed and the entrance where you could have your picture taken in an orange-and-white striped canvas booth for twenty-five cents—reading the names of the trees.

My favorite tree was the Weeping Scholar Tree. I thought

it must come from Japan. They understood things of the spirit in Japan.

They disemboweled themselves when anything went wrong.

I tried to imagine how they would go about it. They must have an extremely sharp knife. No, probably two extremely sharp knives. Then they would sit down, cross-legged, a knife in either hand. Then they would cross their hands and point a knife at each side of their stomach. They would have to be naked, or the knife would get stuck in their clothes.

Then in one quick flash, before they had time to think twice, they would jab the knives in and zip them round, one on the upper crescent and one on the lower crescent, making a full circle. Then their stomach skin would come loose, like a plate, and their insides would fall out, and they would die.

It must take a lot of courage to die like that.

My trouble was I hated the sight of blood.

I thought I might stay in the park all night.

The next morning Dodo Conway was driving my mother and me to Walton, and if I was to run away before it was too late, now was the time. I looked in my pocketbook and counted out a dollar bill and seventy-nine cents in dimes and nickels and pennies.

I had no idea how much it would cost to get to Chicago, and I didn't dare go to the bank and draw out all my money, because I thought Doctor Gordon might well have warned the bank clerk to intercept me if I made an obvious move.

Hitchhiking occurred to me, but I had no idea which of all the routes out of Boston led to Chicago. It's easy enough to find directions on a map, but I had very little knowledge of directions when I was smack in the middle of somewhere. Every time I wanted to figure what was east or what was west it seemed to be noon, or cloudy, which was no help at all, or nighttime, and except for the Big Dipper and Cassiopeia's Chair, I was hopeless at stars, a failing which always disheartened Buddy Willard.

I decided to walk to the bus terminal and inquire about the fares to Chicago. Then I might go to the bank and withdraw precisely that amount, which would not cause so much suspicion.

I had just strolled in through the glass doors of the terminal and was browsing over the rack of colored tour leaflets and schedules, when I realized that the bank in my home town would be closed, as it was already mid-afternoon, and I couldn't get any money out till the next day.

My appointment at Walton was for ten o'clock.

At that moment, the loudspeaker crackled into life and started announcing the stops of a bus getting ready to leave in the parking lot outside. The voice on the loudspeaker went bockle bockle bockle, the way they do, so you can't understand a word, and then, in the middle of all the static, I heard a familiar name clear as A on the piano in the middle of all the tuning instruments of an orchestra.

It was a stop two blocks from my house.

I hurried out into the hot, dusty, end-of-July afternoon, sweating and sandy-mouthed, as if late for a difficult interview, and boarded the red bus, whose motor was already running.

I handed my fare to the driver, and silently, on gloved hinges, the door folded shut at my back.

Twelve

DOCTOR GORDON'S private hospital crowned a grassy rise at the end of a long, secluded drive that had been whitened with broken quahog shells. The yellow clapboard walls of the large house, with its encircling veranda, gleamed in the sun, but no people strolled on the green dome of the lawn.

As my mother and I approached the summer heat bore down on us, and a cicada started up, like an aerial lawnmower, in the heart of a copper beech tree at the back. The sound of the cicada only served to underline the enormous silence.

A nurse met us at the door.

"Will you wait in the living room, please. Doctor Gordon will be with you presently."

What bothered me was that everything about the house seemed normal, although I knew it must be chock-full of crazy people. There were no bars on the windows that I could see, and no wild or disquieting noises. Sunlight measured itself out in regular oblongs on the shabby, but soft red carpets, and a whiff of fresh-cut grass sweetened the air.

I paused in the doorway of the living room.

For a minute I thought it was the replica of a lounge in a guest house I visited once on an island off the coast of Maine. The French doors let in a dazzle of white light, a grand piano filled the far corner of the room, and people in summer clothes were sitting about at card tables and in the lopsided wicker armchairs one so often finds at down-at-heel seaside resorts.

Then I realized that none of the people were moving.

I focused more closely, trying to pry some clue from their stiff postures. I made out men and women, and boys and girls who must be as young as I, but there was a uniformity to

115

their faces, as if they had lain for a long time on a shelf, out of the sunlight, under siftings of pale, fine dust.

Then I saw that some of the people were indeed moving, but with such small, birdlike gestures I had not at first discerned them.

A gray-faced man was counting out a deck of cards, one, two, three, four. . . . I thought he must be seeing if it was a full pack, but when he had finished counting, he started over again. Next to him, a fat lady played with a string of wooden beads. She drew all the beads up to one end of the string. Then click, click, click, she let them fall back on each other.

At the piano, a young girl leafed through a few sheets of music, but when she saw me looking at her, she ducked her head crossly and tore the sheets in half.

My mother touched my arm, and I followed her into the room.

We sat, without speaking, on a lumpy sofa that creaked each time one stirred.

Then my gaze slid over the people to the blaze of green beyond the diaphanous curtains, and I felt as if I were sitting in the window of an enormous department store. The figures around me weren't people, but shop dummies, painted to resemble people and propped up in attitudes counterfeiting life.

I climbed after Doctor Gordon's dark-jacketed back.

Downstairs, in the hall, I had tried to ask him what the shock treatment would be like, but when I opened my mouth no words came out, my eyes only widened and stared at the smiling, familiar face that floated before me like a plate full of assurances.

At the top of the stairs, the garnet-colored carpet stopped. A plain, brown linoleum, tacked to the floor, took its place, and extended down a corridor lined with shut white doors. As I followed Doctor Gordon, a door opened somewhere in the distance, and I heard a woman shouting.

All at once a nurse popped around the corner of the corridor ahead of us leading a woman in a blue bathrobe with shaggy, waist-length hair. Doctor Gordon stepped back, and I flattened against the wall.

As the woman was dragged by, waving her arms and struggling in the grip of the nurse, she was saying, "I'm going to jump out of the window, I'm going to jump out of the window, I'm going to jump out of the window."

Dumpy and muscular in her smudge-fronted uniform, the wall-eyed nurse wore such thick spectacles that four eyes peered out at me from behind the round, twin panes of glass. I was trying to tell which eyes were the real eyes and which the false eyes, and which of the real eyes was the wall-eye and which the straight eye, when she brought her face up to mine with a large, conspiratorial grin and hissed, as if to reassure me, "She thinks she's going to jump out the window but she can't jump out the window because they're all barred!"

And as Doctor Gordon led me into a bare room at the back of the house, I saw that the windows in that part were indeed barred, and that the room door and the closet door and the drawers of the bureau and everything that opened and shut was fitted with a keyhole so it could be locked up.

I lay down on the bed.

The wall-eyed nurse came back. She unclasped my watch and dropped it in her pocket. Then she started tweaking the hairpins from my hair.

Doctor Gordon was unlocking the closet. He dragged out a table on wheels with a machine on it and rolled it behind the head of the bed. The nurse started swabbing my temples with a smelly grease.

As she leaned over to reach the side of my head nearest the wall, her fat breast muffled my face like a cloud or a pillow. A vague, medicinal stench emanated from her flesh.

"Don't worry," the nurse grinned down at me. "Their first time everybody's scared to death."

I tried to smile, but my skin had gone stiff, like parchment.

Doctor Gordon was fitting two metal plates on either side of my head. He buckled them into place with a strap that dented my forehead, and gave me a wire to bite.

I shut my eyes.

There was a brief silence, like an indrawn breath.

Then something bent down and took hold of me and shook me like the end of the world. Whee-ee-ee-ee-ee, it shrilled, through an air crackling with blue light, and with each flash a great jolt drubbed me till I thought my bones would break and the sap fly out of me like a split plant.

I wondered what terrible thing it was that I had done.

I was sitting in a wicker chair, holding a small cocktail glass of tomato juice. The watch had been replaced on my wrist, but it looked odd. Then I realized it had been fastened upside down. I sensed the unfamiliar positioning of the hairpins in my hair.

"How do you feel?"

An old metal floor lamp surfaced in my mind. One of the few relics of my father's study, it was surmounted by a copper bell which held the light bulb, and from which a frayed, tiger-colored cord ran down the length of the metal stand to a socket in the wall.

One day I decided to move this lamp from the side of my mother's bed to my desk at the other end of the room. The cord would be long enough, so I didn't unplug it. I closed both hands around the lamp and the fuzzy cord and gripped them tight.

Then something leapt out of the lamp in a blue flash and shook me till my teeth rattled, and I tried to pull my hands off, but they were stuck, and I screamed, or a scream was torn from my throat, for I didn't recognize it, but heard it soar and quaver in the air like a violently disembodied spirit.

Then my hands jerked free, and I fell back onto my mother's bed. A small hole, blackened as if with pencil lead, pitted the center of my right palm.

"How do you feel?"

"All right."

But I didn't. I felt terrible.

"Which college did you say you went to?"

I said what college it was.

"Ah!" Doctor Gordon's face lighted with a slow, almost tropical smile. "They had a WAC station up there, didn't they, during the war?"

My mother's knuckles were bone-white, as if the skin had worn off them in the hour of waiting. She looked past me to

Doctor Gordon, and he must have nodded, or smiled, because her face relaxed.

"A few more shock treatments, Mrs. Greenwood," I heard Doctor Gordon say, "and I think you'll notice a wonderful improvement."

The girl was still sitting on the piano stool, the torn sheet of music splayed at her feet like a dead bird. She stared at me, and I stared back. Her eyes narrowed. She stuck out her tongue.

My mother was following Doctor Gordon to the door. I lingered behind, and when their backs were turned, I rounded on the girl and thumbed both ears at her. She pulled her tongue in, and her face went stony.

I walked out into the sun.

Pantherlike in a dapple of tree shadow, Dodo Conway's black station wagon lay in wait.

The station wagon had been ordered originally by a wealthy society lady, black, without a speck of chrome, and with black leather upholstery, but when it came, it depressed her. It was the dead spit of a hearse, she said, and everybody else thought so too, and nobody would buy it, so the Conways drove it home, cut-price, and saved themselves a couple of hundred dollars.

Sitting in the front seat, between Dodo and my mother, I felt dumb and subdued. Every time I tried to concentrate, my mind glided off, like a skater, into a large empty space, and pirouetted there, absently.

"I'm through with that Doctor Gordon," I said, after we had left Dodo and her black station wagon behind the pines. "You can call him up and tell him I'm not coming next week."

My mother smiled. "I knew my baby wasn't like that."

I looked at her. "Like what?"

"Like those awful people. Those awful dead people at that hospital." She paused. "I knew you'd decide to be all right again."

STARLET SUCCUMBS AFTER 68-HOUR COMA.

I felt in my pocketbook among the paper scraps and the compact and the peanut shells and the dimes and nickels and the blue jiffy box containing nineteen Gillette blades, till I unearthed the snapshot I'd had taken that afternoon in the orange-and-white striped booth.

I brought it up next to the smudgy photograph of the dead girl. It matched, mouth for mouth, nose for nose. The only difference was the eyes. The eyes in the snapshot were open, and those in the newspaper photograph were closed. But I knew if the dead girl's eyes were to be thumbed wide, they would look at me with the same dead, black, vacant expression as the eyes in the snapshot.

I stuffed the snapshot back in my pocketbook.

"I will just sit here in the sun on this park bench five minutes more by the clock on that building over there," I told myself, "and then I will go somewhere and do it."

I summoned my little chorus of voices.

Doesn't your work interest you, Esther?

You know, Esther, you've got the perfect setup of a true neurotic.

You'll never get anywhere like that, you'll never get anywhere like that, you'll never get anywhere like that.

Once on a hot summer night, I had spent an hour kissing a hairy, ape-shaped law student from Yale because I felt sorry for him, he was so ugly. When I had finished, he said, "I have you typed, baby. You'll be a prude at forty."

"Factitious!" my creative writing professor at college scrawled on a story of mine called "The Big Weekend."

I hadn't known what factitious meant, so I looked it up in the dictionary.

Factitious, artificial, sham.

You'll never get anywhere like that.

I hadn't slept for twenty-one nights.

I thought the most beautiful thing in the world must be shadow, the million moving shapes and cul-de-sacs of shadow. There was shadow in bureau drawers and closets and suitcases, and shadow under houses and trees and stones, and shadow at the back of people's eyes and smiles, and shadow, miles and miles and miles of it, on the night side of the earth.

I looked down at the two flesh-colored Band-Aids forming a cross on the calf of my right leg.

That morning I had made a start.

I had locked myself in the bathroom, and run a tub full of warm water, and taken out a Gillette blade.

When they asked some old Roman philosopher or other how he wanted to die, he said he would open his veins in a warm bath. I thought it would be easy, lying in the tub and seeing the redness flower from my wrists, flush after flush through the clear water, till I sank to sleep under a surf gaudy as poppies.

But when it came right down to it, the skin of my wrist looked so white and defenseless that I couldn't do it. It was as if what I wanted to kill wasn't in that skin or the thin blue pulse that jumped under my thumb, but somewhere else, deeper, more secret, a whole lot harder to get at.

It would take two motions. One wrist, then the other wrist. Three motions, if you counted changing the razor from hand to hand. Then I would step into the tub and lie down.

I moved in front of the medicine cabinet. If I looked in the mirror while I did it, it would be like watching somebody else, in a book or a play.

But the person in the mirror was paralyzed and too stupid to do a thing.

Then I thought maybe I ought to spill a little blood for practice, so I sat on the edge of the tub and crossed my right ankle over my left knee. Then I lifted my right hand with the razor and let it drop of its own weight, like a guillotine, onto the calf of my leg.

I felt nothing. Then I felt a small, deep thrill, and a bright seam of red welled up at the lip of the slash. The blood gathered darkly, like fruit, and rolled down my ankle into the cup of my black patent leather shoe.

I thought of getting into the tub then, but I realized my dallying had used up the better part of the morning, and that my mother would probably come home and find me before I was done.

So I bandaged the cut, packed up my Gillette blades and caught the eleven-thirty bus to Boston.

"Sorry, baby, there's no subway to the Deer Island Prison, it's on a niland."

"No, it's not on an island, it used to be on an island, but they filled up the water with dirt and now it joins on to the mainland."

"There's no subway."

"I've got to get there."

"Hey," the fat man in the ticket booth peered at me through the grating, "don't cry. Who you got there, honey, some relative?"

People shoved and bumped by me in the artificially lit dark, hurrying after the trains that rumbled in and out of the intestinal tunnels under Scollay Square. I could feel the tears start to spurt from the screwed-up nozzles of my eyes.

"It's my *fa*ther."

The fat man consulted a diagram on the wall of his booth. "Here's how you do," he said, "you take a car from that track over there and get off at Orient Heights and then hop a bus with The Point on it." He beamed at me. "It'll run you straight to the prison gate."

"Hey you!" A young fellow in a blue uniform waved from the hut.

I waved back and kept on going.

"Hey you!"

I stopped and walked slowly over to the hut that perched like a circular living room on the waste of sands.

"Hey, you can't go any further. That's prison property, no trespassers allowed."

"I thought you could go anyplace along the beach," I said. "So long as you stayed under the tideline."

The fellow thought a minute.

Then he said, "Not this beach."

He had a pleasant, fresh face.

"You've a nice place here," I said. "It's like a little house."

He glanced back into the room, with its braided rug and chintz curtains. He smiled.

"We even got a coffee pot."

"I used to live near here."

"No kidding. I was born and brought up in this town myself."

I looked across the sands to the parking lot and the barred gate, and past the barred gate to the narrow road, lapped by the ocean on both sides, that led out to the one-time island.

The red brick buildings of the prison looked friendly, like the buildings of a seaside college. On a green hump of lawn to the left, I could see small white spots and slightly larger pink spots moving about. I asked the guard what they were, and he said, "Them's pigs 'n' chickens."

I was thinking that if I'd had the sense to go on living in that old town I might just have met this prison guard in school and married him and had a parcel of little kids by now. It would be nice, living by the sea with piles of little kids and pigs and chickens, wearing what my grandmother called wash dresses, and sitting about in some kitchen with bright linoleum and fat arms, drinking pots of coffee.

"How do you get into that prison?"

"You get a pass."

"No, how do you get *locked* in?"

"Oh," the guard laughed, "you steal a car, you rob a store."

"You got any murderers in there?"

"No. Murderers go to a big state place."

"Who else is in there?"

"Well, the first day of winter we get these old bums out of Boston. They heave a brick through a window, and then they get picked up and spend the winter out of the cold, with TV and plenty to eat, and basketball games on the weekend."

"That's nice."

"Nice if you like it," said the guard.

I said good-bye and started to move off, glancing back over my shoulder only once. The guard still stood in the doorway of his observation booth, and when I turned he lifted his arm in a salute.

The log I sat on was lead-heavy and smelled of tar. Under the stout, gray cylinder of the water tower on its commanding hill, the sandbar curved out into the sea. At high tide the bar completely submerged itself.

I remembered that sandbar well. It harbored, in the crook of its inner curve, a particular shell that could be found nowhere else on the beach.

The shell was thick, smooth, big as a thumb joint, and usually white, although sometimes pink or peach-colored. It resembled a sort of modest conch.

"Mummy, that girl's *still* sitting there."

I looked up, idly, and saw a small, sandy child being dragged up from the sea's edge by a skinny, bird-eyed woman in red shorts and a red-and-white polka-dot halter.

I hadn't counted on the beach being overrun with summer people. In the ten years of my absence, fancy blue and pink and pale green shanties had sprung up on the flat sands of the Point like a crop of tasteless mushrooms, and the silver airplanes and cigar-shaped blimps had given way to jets that scoured the rooftops in their loud offrush from the airport across the bay.

I was the only girl on the beach in a skirt and high heels, and it occurred to me I must stand out. I had removed my patent leather shoes after a while, for they foundered badly in the sand. It pleased me to think they would be perched there on the silver log, pointing out to sea, like a sort of soul-compass, after I was dead.

I fingered the box of razors in my pocketbook.

Then I thought how stupid I was. I had the razors, but no warm bath.

I considered renting a room. There must be a boarding-house among all those summer places. But I had no luggage. That would create suspicion. Besides, in a boardinghouse other people are always wanting to use the bathroom. I'd hardly have time to do it and step into the tub when somebody would be pounding at the door.

The gulls on their wooden stilts at the tip of the bar miaowed like cats. Then they flapped up, one by one, in their ash-colored jackets, circling my head and crying.

"Say, lady, you better not sit out here, the tide's coming in."

The small boy squatted a few feet away. He picked up a round purple stone and lobbed it into the water. The water swallowed it with a resonant plop. Then he scrabbled around, and I heard the dry stones clank together like money.

He skimmed a flat stone over the dull green surface, and it skipped seven times before it sliced out of sight.

"Why don't you go home?" I said.

The boy skipped another, heavier stone. It sank after the second bounce.

"Don't want to."

"Your mother's looking for you."

"She is not." He sounded worried.

"If you go home, I'll give you some candy."

The boy hitched closer. "What kind?"

But I knew without looking into my pocketbook that all I had was peanut shells.

"I'll give you some money to buy some candy."

"Ar-*thur!*"

A woman was indeed coming out on the sandbar, slipping and no doubt cursing to herself, for her lips went up and down between her clear, peremptory calls.

"Ar-*thur!*"

She shaded her eyes with one hand, as if this helped her discern us through the thickening sea dusk.

I could sense the boy's interest dwindle as the pull of his mother increased. He began to pretend he didn't know me. He kicked over a few stones, as if searching for something, and edged off.

I shivered.

The stones lay lumpish and cold under my bare feet. I thought longingly of the black shoes on the beach. A wave drew back, like a hand, then advanced and touched my foot.

The drench seemed to come off the sea floor itself, where blind white fish ferried themselves by their own light through the great polar cold. I saw sharks' teeth and whales' earbones littered about down there like gravestones.

I waited, as if the sea could make my decision for me.

A second wave collapsed over my feet, lipped with white froth, and the chill gripped my ankles with a mortal ache.

My flesh winced, in cowardice, from such a death.

I picked up my pocketbook and started back over the cold stones to where my shoes kept their vigil in the violet light.

Thirteen

"OF COURSE HIS MOTHER KILLED HIM."

I looked at the mouth of the boy Jody had wanted me to meet. His lips were thick and pink and a baby face nestled under the silk of white-blond hair. His name was Cal, which I thought must be short for something, but I couldn't think what it would be short for, unless it was California.

"How can you be sure she killed him?" I said.

Cal was supposed to be very intelligent, and Jody had said over the phone that he was cute and I would like him. I wondered, if I'd been my old self, if I would have liked him.

It was impossible to tell.

"Well, first she says No no no, and then she says Yes."

"But then she says No no again."

Cal and I lay side by side on an orange-and-green striped towel on a mucky beach across the swamps from Lynn. Jody and Mark, the boy she was pinned to, were swimming. Cal hadn't wanted to swim, he had wanted to talk, and we were arguing about this play where a young man finds out he has a brain disease, on account of his father fooling around with unclean women, and in the end his brain, which has been softening all along, snaps completely, and his mother is debating whether to kill him or not.

I had a suspicion that my mother had called Jody and begged her to ask me out, so I wouldn't sit around in my room all day with the shades drawn. I didn't want to go at first, because I thought Jody would notice the change in me, and that anybody with half an eye would see I didn't have a brain in my head.

But all during the drive north, and then east, Jody had joked and laughed and chattered and not seemed to mind that I only said, "My" or "Gosh" or "You don't say."

126

We browned hot dogs on the public grills at the beach, and by watching Jody and Mark and Cal very carefully I managed to cook my hot dog just the right amount of time and didn't burn it or drop it into the fire, the way I was afraid of doing. Then, when nobody was looking, I buried it in the sand.

After we ate, Jody and Mark ran down to the water hand-in-hand, and I lay back, staring into the sky, while Cal went on and on about this play.

The only reason I remembered this play was because it had a mad person in it, and everything I had ever read about mad people stuck in my mind, while everything else flew out.

"But it's the Yes that matters," Cal said. "It's the Yes she'll come back to in the end."

I lifted my head and squinted out at the bright blue plate of the sea—a bright blue plate with a dirty rim. A big round gray rock, like the upper half of an egg, poked out of the water about a mile from the stony headland.

"What was she going to kill him with? I forget."

I hadn't forgotten. I remembered perfectly well, but I wanted to hear what Cal would say.

"Morphia powders."

"Do you suppose they have morphia powders in America?"

Cal considered a minute. Then he said, "I wouldn't think so. They sound awfully old-fashioned."

I rolled over onto my stomach and squinted at the view in the other direction, toward Lynn. A glassy haze rippled up from the fires in the grills and the heat on the road, and through the haze, as through a curtain of clear water, I could make out a smudgy skyline of gas tanks and factory stacks and derricks and bridges.

It looked one hell of a mess.

I rolled onto my back again and made my voice casual. "If you were going to kill yourself, how would you do it?"

Cal seemed pleased. "I've often thought of that. I'd blow my brains out with a gun."

I was disappointed. It was just like a man to do it with a gun. A fat chance I had of laying my hands on a gun. And even if I did, I wouldn't have a clue as to what part of me to shoot at.

I'd already read in the papers about people who'd tried to shoot themselves, only they ended up shooting an important nerve and getting paralyzed or blasting their face off, but being saved, by surgeons and a sort of miracle, from dying outright.

The risks of a gun seemed great.

"What kind of a gun?"

"My father's shotgun. He keeps it loaded. I'd just have to walk into his study one day and," Cal pointed a finger to his temple and made a comical, screwed-up face, "click!" He widened his pale gray eyes and looked at me.

"Does your father happen to live near Boston?" I asked idly.

"Nope, in Clacton-on-Sea. He's English."

Jody and Mark ran up hand-in-hand, dripping and shaking off water drops like two loving puppies. I thought there would be too many people, so I stood up and pretended to yawn.

"I guess I'll go for a swim."

Being with Jody and Mark and Cal was beginning to weigh on my nerves, like a dull wooden block on the strings of a piano. I was afraid that at any moment my control would snap, and I would start babbling about how I couldn't read and couldn't write and how I must be just about the only person who had stayed awake for a solid month without dropping dead of exhaustion.

A smoke seemed to be going up from my nerves like the smoke from the grills and the sun-saturated road. The whole landscape—beach and headland and sea and rock—quavered in front of my eyes like a stage backcloth.

I wondered at what point in space the silly, sham blue of the sky turned black.

"You swim too, Cal."

Jody gave Cal a playful little push.

"Ohhh." Cal hid his face in the towel. "It's too cold."

I started to walk toward the water.

Somehow, in the broad, shadowless light of noon, the water looked amiable and welcoming.

I thought drowning must be the kindest way to die, and burning the worst. Some of those babies in the jars that

Buddy Willard showed me had gills, he said. They went through a stage where they were just like fish.

A little, rubbishy wavelet, full of candy wrappers and orange peel and seaweed, folded over my foot.

I heard the sand thud behind me, and Cal came up.

"Let's swim to that rock out there." I pointed at it.

"Are you crazy? That's a mile out."

"What are you?" I said. "Chicken?"

Cal took me by the elbow and jostled me into the water. When we were waist high, he pushed me under. I surfaced, splashing, my eyes seared with salt. Underneath, the water was green and semi-opaque as a hunk of quartz.

I started to swim, a modified dogpaddle, keeping my face toward the rock. Cal did a slow crawl. After a while he put his head up and treaded water.

"Can't make it." He was panting heavily.

"Okay. You go back."

I thought I would swim out until I was too tired to swim back. As I paddled on, my heartbeat boomed like a dull motor in my ears.

I am I am I am.

That morning I had tried to hang myself.

I had taken the silk cord of my mother's yellow bathrobe as soon as she left for work, and, in the amber shade of the bedroom, fashioned it into a knot that slipped up and down on itself. It took me a long time to do this, because I was poor at knots and had no idea how to make a proper one.

Then I hunted around for a place to attach the rope.

The trouble was, our house had the wrong kind of ceilings. The ceilings were low, white and smoothly plastered, without a light fixture or a wood beam in sight. I thought with longing of the house my grandmother had before she sold it to come and live with us, and then with my Aunt Libby.

My grandmother's house was built in the fine, nineteenth-century style, with lofty rooms and sturdy chandelier brackets and high closets with stout rails across them, and an attic where nobody ever went, full of trunks and parrot cages and dressmakers' dummies and overhead beams thick as a ship's timbers.

But it was an old house, and she'd sold it, and I didn't know anybody else with a house like that.

After a discouraging time of walking about with the silk cord dangling from my neck like a yellow cat's tail and finding no place to fasten it, I sat on the edge of my mother's bed and tried pulling the cord tight.

But each time I would get the cord so tight I could feel a rushing in my ears and a flush of blood in my face, my hands would weaken and let go, and I would be all right again.

Then I saw that my body had all sorts of little tricks, such as making my hands go limp at the crucial second, which would save it, time and again, whereas if I had the whole say, I would be dead in a flash.

I would simply have to ambush it with whatever sense I had left, or it would trap me in its stupid cage for fifty years without any sense at all. And when people found out my mind had gone, as they would have to, sooner or later, in spite of my mother's guarded tongue, they would persuade her to put me into an asylum where I could be cured.

Only my case was incurable.

I had bought a few paperbacks on abnormal psychology at the drugstore and compared my symptoms with the symptoms in the books, and sure enough, my symptoms tallied with the most hopeless cases.

The only thing I could read, besides the scandal sheets, were those abnormal-psychology books. It was as if some slim opening had been left, so I could learn all I needed to know about my case to end it in the proper way.

I wondered, after the hanging fiasco, if I shouldn't just give it up and turn myself over to the doctors, and then I remembered Doctor Gordon and his private shock machine. Once I was locked up they could use that on me all the time.

And I thought of how my mother and brother and friends would visit me, day after day, hoping I would be better. Then their visits would slacken off, and they would give up hope. They would grow old. They would forget me.

They would be poor, too.

They would want me to have the best of care at first, so they would sink all their money in a private hospital like Doctor Gordon's. Finally, when the money was used up, I would be moved to a state hospital, with hundreds of people like me, in a big cage in the basement.

The more hopeless you were, the further away they hid you.

Cal had turned around and was swimming in.

As I watched, he dragged himself slowly out of the neck-deep sea. Against the khaki-colored sand and the green shore wavelets, his body was bisected for a moment, like a white worm. Then it crawled completely out of the green and onto the khaki and lost itself among dozens and dozens of other worms that were wriggling or just lolling about between the sea and the sky.

I paddled my hands in the water and kicked my feet. The egg-shaped rock didn't seem to be any nearer than it had been when Cal and I had looked at it from the shore.

Then I saw it would be pointless to swim as far as the rock, because my body would take that excuse to climb out and lie in the sun, gathering strength to swim back.

The only thing to do was to drown myself then and there.

So I stopped.

I brought my hands to my breast, ducked my head, and dived, using my hands to push the water aside. The water pressed in on my eardrums and on my heart. I fanned myself down, but before I knew where I was, the water had spat me up into the sun, the world was sparkling all about me like blue and green and yellow semi-precious stones.

I dashed the water from my eyes.

I was panting, as after a strenuous exertion, but floating, without effort.

I dived, and dived again, and each time popped up like a cork.

The gray rock mocked me, bobbing on the water easy as a lifebuoy.

I knew when I was beaten.

I turned back.

The flowers nodded like bright, knowledgeable children as I trundled them down the hall.

I felt silly in my sage-green volunteer's uniform, and superfluous, unlike the white-uniformed doctors and nurses, or even the brown-uniformed scrubwomen with their mops and their buckets of grimy water, who passed me without a word.

If I had been getting paid, no matter how little, I could at least count this a proper job, but all I got for a morning of pushing round magazines and candy and flowers was a free lunch.

My mother said the cure for thinking too much about yourself was helping somebody who was worse off than you, so Teresa had arranged for me to sign on as a volunteer at our local hospital. It was difficult to be a volunteer at this hospital, because that's what all the Junior League women wanted to do, but luckily for me, a lot of them were away on vacation.

I had hoped they would send me to a ward with some really gruesome cases, who would see through my numb, dumb face to how I meant well, and be grateful. But the head of the volunteers, a society lady at our church, took one look at me and said, "You're on maternity."

So I rode the elevator up three flights to the maternity ward and reported to the head nurse. She gave me the trolley of flowers. I was supposed to put the right vases at the right beds in the right rooms.

But before I came to the door of the first room I noticed that a lot of the flowers were droopy and brown at the edges. I thought it would be discouraging for a woman who'd just had a baby to see somebody plonk down a big bouquet of dead flowers in front of her, so I steered the trolley to a washbasin in an alcove in the hall and began to pick out all the flowers that were dead.

Then I picked out all those that were dying.

There was no wastebasket in sight, so I crumpled the flowers up and laid them in the deep white basin. The basin felt cold as a tomb. I smiled. This must be how they laid the bodies away in the hospital morgue. My gesture, in its small way, echoed the larger gesture of the doctors and nurses.

I swung the door of the first room open and walked in,

dragging my trolley. A couple of nurses jumped up, and I had
a confused impression of shelves and medicine cabinets.

"What do you want?" one of the nurses demanded sternly.
I couldn't tell one from the other, they all looked just alike.

"I'm taking the flowers round."

The nurse who had spoken put a hand on my shoulder and
led me out of the room, maneuvering the trolley with her
free, expert hand. She flung open the swinging doors of the
room next to that one and bowed me in. Then she disappeared.

I could hear giggles in the distance till a door shut and cut
them off.

There were six beds in the room, and each bed had a
woman in it. The women were all sitting up and knitting or
riffling through magazines or putting their hair in pin curls
and chattering like parrots in a parrot house.

I had thought they would be sleeping, or lying quiet and
pale, so I could tiptoe round without any trouble and match
the bed numbers to the numbers inked on adhesive tape on
the vases, but before I had a chance to get my bearings, a
bright, jazzy blonde with a sharp, triangular face beckoned to
me.

I approached her, leaving the trolley in the middle of the
floor, but then she made an impatient gesture, and I saw she
wanted me to bring the trolley too.

I wheeled the trolley over to her bedside with a helpful
smile.

"Hey, where's my larkspur?" A large, flabby lady from
across the ward raked me with an eagle eye.

The sharp-faced blonde bent over the trolley. "Here are my
yellow roses," she said, "but they're all mixed up with some
lousy iris."

Other voices joined the voices of the first two women. They
sounded cross and loud and full of complaint.

I was opening my mouth to explain that I had thrown a
bunch of dead larkspur in the sink, and that some of the vases
I had weeded out looked skimpy, there were so few flowers
left, so I had joined a few of the bouquets together to fill
them out, when the swinging door flew open and a nurse
stalked in to see what the commotion was.

"Listen, nurse, I had this big bunch of larkspur Larry brought last night."

"She's loused up my yellow roses."

Unbuttoning the green uniform as I ran, I stuffed it, in passing, into the washbasin with the rubbish of dead flowers. Then I took the deserted side steps down to the street two at a time, without meeting another soul.

"Which way is the graveyard?"

The Italian in the black leather jacket stopped and pointed down an alley behind the white Methodist church. I remembered the Methodist church. I had been a Methodist for the first nine years of my life, before my father died and we moved and turned Unitarian.

My mother had been a Catholic before she was a Methodist. My grandmother and my grandfather and my Aunt Libby were all still Catholics. My Aunt Libby had broken away from the Catholic Church at the same time my mother did, but then she'd fallen in love with an Italian Catholic, so she'd gone back again.

Lately I had considered going into the Catholic Church myself. I knew the Catholics thought killing yourself was an awful sin. But perhaps, if this was so, they might have a good way to persuade me out of it.

Of course, I didn't believe in life after death or the virgin birth or the Inquisition or the infallibility of that little monkey-faced Pope or anything, but I didn't have to let the priest see this, I could just concentrate on my sin, and he would help me repent.

The only trouble was, Church, even the Catholic Church, didn't take up the whole of your life. No matter how much you knelt and prayed, you still had to eat three meals a day and have a job and live in the world.

I thought I might see how long you had to be a Catholic before you became a nun, so I asked my mother, thinking she'd know the best way to go about it.

My mother had laughed at me. "Do you think they'll take somebody like you, right off the bat? Why you've got to know all these catechisms and credos and believe in them, lock, stock and barrel. A girl with your sense!"

Still, I imagined myself going to some Boston priest—it would have to be Boston, because I didn't want any priest in my home town to know I'd thought of killing myself. Priests were terrible gossips.

I would be in black, with my dead white face, and I would throw myself at this priest's feet and say, "O Father, help me."

But that was before people had begun to look at me in a funny way, like those nurses in the hospital.

I was pretty sure the Catholics wouldn't take in any crazy nuns. My Aunt Libby's husband had made a joke once, about a nun that a nunnery sent to Teresa for a checkup. This nun kept hearing harp notes in her ears and a voice saying over and over, "Alleluia!" Only she wasn't sure, on being closely questioned, whether the voice was saying Alleluia or Arizona. The nun had been born in Arizona. I think she ended up in some asylum.

I tugged my black veil down to my chin and strode in through the wrought-iron gates. I thought it odd that in all the time my father had been buried in this graveyard, none of us had ever visited him. My mother hadn't let us come to his funeral because we were only children then, and he had died in the hospital, so the graveyard and even his death had always seemed unreal to me.

I had a great yearning, lately, to pay my father back for all the years of neglect, and start tending his grave. I had always been my father's favorite, and it seemed fitting I should take on a mourning my mother had never bothered with.

I thought that if my father hadn't died, he would have taught me all about insects, which was his specialty at the university. He would also have taught me German and Greek and Latin, which he knew, and perhaps I would be a Lutheran. My father had been a Lutheran in Wisconsin, but they were out of style in New England, so he had become a lapsed Lutheran and then, my mother said, a bitter atheist.

The graveyard disappointed me. It lay at the outskirts of the town, on low ground, like a rubbish dump, and as I walked up and down the gravel paths, I could smell the stagnant salt marshes in the distance.

The old part of the graveyard was all right, with its worn, flat stones and lichen-bitten monuments, but I soon saw my father must be buried in the modern part with dates in the nineteen forties.

The stones in the modern part were crude and cheap, and here and there a grave was rimmed with marble, like an oblong bathtub full of dirt, and rusty metal containers stuck up about where the person's navel would be, full of plastic flowers.

A fine drizzle started drifting down from the gray sky, and I grew very depressed.

I couldn't find my father anywhere.

Low, shaggy clouds scudded over that part of the horizon where the sea lay, behind the marshes and the beach shanty settlements, and raindrops darkened the black mackintosh I had bought that morning. A clammy dampness sank through to my skin.

I had asked the salesgirl, "Is it water-repellent?"

And she had said, "No raincoat is ever water-*repellent*. It's showerproofed."

And when I asked her what showerproofed was, she told me I had better buy an umbrella.

But I hadn't enough money for an umbrella. What with bus fare in and out of Boston and peanuts and newspapers and abnormal-psychology books and trips to my old home town by the sea, my New York fund was almost exhausted.

I had decided that when there was no more money in my bank account I would do it, and that morning I'd spent the last of it on the black raincoat.

Then I saw my father's gravestone.

It was crowded right up by another gravestone, head to head, the way people are crowded in a charity ward when there isn't enough space. The stone was of a mottled pink marble, like canned salmon, and all there was on it was my father's name and, under it, two dates, separated by a little dash.

At the foot of the stone I arranged the rainy armful of azaleas I had picked from a bush at the gateway of the graveyard. Then my legs folded under me, and I sat down in the sopping grass. I couldn't understand why I was crying so hard.

Then I remembered that I had never cried for my father's death.

My mother hadn't cried either. She had just smiled and said what a merciful thing it was for him he had died, because if he had lived he would have been crippled and an invalid for life, and he couldn't have stood that, he would rather have died than had that happen.

I laid my face to the smooth face of the marble and howled my loss into the cold salt rain.

I knew just how to go about it.

The minute the car tires crunched off down the drive and the sound of the motor faded, I jumped out of bed and hurried into my white blouse and green figured skirt and black raincoat. The raincoat felt damp still, from the day before, but that would soon cease to matter.

I went downstairs and picked up a pale blue envelope from the dining room table and scrawled on the back, in large, painstaking letters: *I am going for a long walk.*

I propped the message where my mother would see it the minute she came in.

Then I laughed.

I had forgotten the most important thing.

I ran upstairs and dragged a chair into my mother's closet. Then I climbed up and reached for the small green strongbox on the top shelf. I could have torn the metal cover off with my bare hands, the lock was so feeble, but I wanted to do things in a calm, orderly way.

I pulled out my mother's upper right-hand bureau drawer and slipped the blue jewelry box from its hiding place under the scented Irish linen handkerchiefs. I unpinned the little key from the dark velvet. Then I unlocked the strongbox and took out the bottle of new pills. There were more than I had hoped.

There were at least fifty.

If I had waited until my mother doled them out to me, night by night, it would have taken me fifty nights to save up enough. And in fifty nights, college would have opened, and my brother would have come back from Germany, and it would be too late.

I pinned the key back in the jewelry box among the clutter of inexpensive chains and rings, put the jewelry box back in the drawer under the handkerchiefs, returned the strongbox to the closet shelf and set the chair on the rug in the exact spot I had dragged it from.

Then I went downstairs and into the kitchen. I turned on the tap and poured myself a tall glass of water. Then I took the glass of water and the bottle of pills and went down into the cellar.

A dim, undersea light filtered through the slits of the cellar windows. Behind the oil burner, a dark gap showed in the wall at about shoulder height and ran back under the breezeway, out of sight. The breezeway had been added to the house after the cellar was dug, and built out over this secret, earth-bottomed crevice.

A few old, rotting fireplace logs blocked the hole mouth. I shoved them back a bit. Then I set the glass of water and the bottle of pills side by side on the flat surface of one of the logs and started to heave myself up.

It took me a good while to heft my body into the gap, but at last, after many tries, I managed it, and crouched at the mouth of the darkness, like a troll.

The earth seemed friendly under my bare feet, but cold. I wondered how long it had been since this particular square of soil had seen the sun.

Then, one after the other, I lugged the heavy, dust-covered logs across the hole mouth. The dark felt thick as velvet. I reached for the glass and bottle, and carefully, on my knees, with bent head, crawled to the farthest wall.

Cobwebs touched my face with the softness of moths. Wrapping my black coat round me like my own sweet shadow, I unscrewed the bottle of pills and started taking them swiftly, between gulps of water, one by one by one.

At first nothing happened, but as I approached the bottom of the bottle, red and blue lights began to flash before my eyes. The bottle slid from my fingers and I lay down.

The silence drew off, baring the pebbles and shells and all the tatty wreckage of my life. Then, at the rim of vision, it gathered itself, and in one sweeping tide, rushed me to sleep.

Fourteen

IT WAS COMPLETELY DARK.

I felt the darkness, but nothing else, and my head rose, feeling it, like the head of a worm. Someone was moaning. Then a great, hard weight smashed against my cheek like a stone wall and the moaning stopped.

The silence surged back, smoothing itself as black water smooths to its old surface calm over a dropped stone.

A cool wind rushed by. I was being transported at enormous speed down a tunnel into the earth. Then the wind stopped. There was a rumbling, as of many voices, protesting and disagreeing in the distance. Then the voices stopped.

A chisel cracked down on my eye, and a slit of light opened, like a mouth or a wound, till the darkness clamped shut on it again. I tried to roll away from the direction of the light, but hands wrapped round my limbs like mummy bands, and I couldn't move.

I began to think I must be in an underground chamber, lit by blinding lights, and that the chamber was full of people who for some reason were holding me down.

Then the chisel struck again, and the light leapt into my head, and through the thick, warm, furry dark, a voice cried,

"Mother!"

Air breathed and played over my face.

I felt the shape of a room around me, a big room with open windows. A pillow molded itself under my head, and my body floated, without pressure, between thin sheets.

Then I felt warmth, like a hand on my face. I must be lying in the sun. If I opened my eyes, I would see colors and shapes bending in upon me like nurses.

139

I opened my eyes.

It was completely dark.

Somebody was breathing beside me.

"I can't see," I said.

A cheery voice spoke out of the dark. "There are lots of blind people in the world. You'll marry a nice blind man someday."

The man with the chisel had come back.

"Why do you bother?" I said. "It's no use."

"You musn't talk like that." His fingers probed at the great, aching boss over my left eye. Then he loosened something, and a ragged gap of light appeared, like the hole in a wall. A man's hand peered round the edge of it.

"Can you see me?"

"Yes."

"Can you see anything else?"

Then I remembered. "I can't see anything." The gap narrowed and went dark. "I'm blind."

"Nonsense! Who told you that?"

"The nurse."

The man snorted. He finished taping the bandage back over my eye. "You are a very lucky girl. Your sight is perfectly intact."

"Somebody to see you."

The nurse beamed and disappeared.

My mother came smiling round the foot of the bed. She was wearing a dress with purple cartwheels on it and she looked awful.

A big tall boy followed her. At first I couldn't make out who it was, because my eye only opened a short way, but then I saw it was my brother.

"They said you wanted to see me."

My mother perched on the edge of the bed and laid a hand on my leg. She looked loving and reproachful, and I wanted her to go away.

"I didn't think I said anything."

"They said you called for me." She seemed ready to cry. Her face puckered up and quivered like a pale jelly.

"How are you?" my brother said.

I looked my mother in the eye.

"The same," I said.

"You have a visitor."

"I don't want a visitor."

The nurse bustled out and whispered to somebody in the hall. Then she came back. "He'd very much like to see you."

I looked down at the yellow legs sticking out of the unfamiliar white silk pajamas they had dressed me in. The skin shook flabbily when I moved, as if there wasn't a muscle in it, and it was covered with a short, thick stubble of black hair.

"Who is it?"

"Somebody you know."

"What's his name?"

"George Bakewell."

"I don't know any George Bakewell."

"He says he knows you."

Then the nurse went out, and a very familiar boy came in and said, "Mind if I sit on the edge of your bed?"

He was wearing a white coat, and I could see a stethoscope poking out of his pocket. I thought it must be somebody I knew dressed up as a doctor.

I had meant to cover my legs if anybody came in, but now I saw it was too late, so I let them stick out, just as they were, disgusting and ugly.

"That's me," I thought. "That's what I am."

"You remember me, don't you, Esther?"

I squinted at the boy's face through the crack of my good eye. The other eye hadn't opened yet, but the eye doctor said it would be all right in a few days.

The boy looked at me as if I were some exciting new zoo animal and he was about to burst out laughing.

"You remember me, don't you, Esther?" He spoke slowly, the way one speaks to a dull child. "I'm George Bakewell. I go to your church. You dated my roommate once at Amherst."

I thought I placed the boy's face then. It hovered dimly at

the rim of memory—the sort of face to which I would never bother to attach a name.

"What are you doing here?"

"I'm houseman at this hospital."

How could this George Bakewell have become a doctor so suddenly? I wondered. He didn't really know me, either. He just wanted to see what a girl who was crazy enough to kill herself looked like.

I turned my face to the wall.

"Get out," I said. "Get the hell out and don't come back."

"I want to see a mirror."

The nurse hummed busily as she opened one drawer after another, stuffing the new underclothes and blouses and skirts and pajamas my mother had bought me into the black patent leather overnight case.

"Why can't I see a mirror?"

I had been dressed in a sheath, striped gray and white, like mattress ticking, with a wide, shiny red belt, and they had propped me up in an armchair.

"Why can't I?"

"Because you better not." The nurse shut the lid of the overnight case with a little snap.

"Why?"

"Because you don't look very pretty."

"Oh, just let me see."

The nurse sighed and opened the top bureau drawer. She took out a large mirror in a wooden frame that matched the wood of the bureau and handed it to me.

At first I didn't see what the trouble was. It wasn't a mirror at all, but a picture.

You couldn't tell whether the person in the picture was a man or a woman, because their hair was shaved off and sprouted in bristly chicken-feather tufts all over their head. One side of the person's face was purple, and bulged out in a shapeless way, shading to green along the edges, and then to a sallow yellow. The person's mouth was pale brown, with a rose-colored sore at either corner.

The most startling thing about the face was its supernatural conglomeration of bright colors.

I smiled.

The mouth in the mirror cracked into a grin.

A minute after the crash another nurse ran in. She took one look at the broken mirror, and at me, standing over the blind, white pieces, and hustled the young nurse out of the room.

"Didn't I *tell* you," I could hear her say.

"But I only . . ."

"Didn't I *tell* you!"

I listened with mild interest. Anybody could drop a mirror. I didn't see why they should get so stirred up.

The other, older nurse came back into the room. She stood there, arms folded, staring hard at me.

"Seven years' bad luck."

"What?"

"I said," the nurse raised her voice, as if speaking to a deaf person, *"seven years' bad luck."*

The young nurse returned with a dustpan and brush and began to sweep up the glittery splinters.

"That's only a superstition," I said then.

"Huh!" The second nurse addressed herself to the nurse on her hands and knees as if I wasn't there. "At you-know-where they'll take care of *her!*"

From the back window of the ambulance I could see street after familiar street funneling off into a summery green distance. My mother sat on one side of me, and my brother on the other.

I had pretended I didn't know why they were moving me from the hospital in my home town to a city hospital, to see what they would say.

"They want you to be in a special ward," my mother said. "They don't have that sort of ward at our hospital."

"I liked it where I was."

My mother's mouth tightened. "You should have behaved better, then."

"What?"

"You shouldn't have broken that mirror. Then maybe they'd have let you stay."

But of course I knew the mirror had nothing to do with it.

I sat in bed with the covers up to my neck.

"Why can't I get up? I'm not sick."

"Ward rounds," the nurse said. "You can get up after ward rounds." She shoved the bed curtains back and revealed a fat young Italian woman in the next bed.

The Italian woman had a mass of tight black curls, starting at her forehead, that rose in a mountainous pompadour and cascaded down her back. Whenever she moved, the huge arrangement of hair moved with her, as if made of stiff black paper.

The woman looked at me and giggled. "Why are you here?" She didn't wait for an answer. "I'm here on account of my French-Canadian mother-in-law." She giggled again. "My husband knows I can't stand her, and still he said she could come and visit us, and when she came, my tongue stuck out of my head, I couldn't stop it. They ran me into Emergency and then they put me up here," she lowered her voice, "along with the nuts." Then she said, "What's the matter with you?"

I turned her my full face, with the bulging purple and green eye. "I tried to kill myself."

The woman stared at me. Then, hastily, she snatched up a movie magazine from her bed table and pretended to be reading.

The swinging door opposite my bed flew open, and a whole troop of young boys and girls in white coats came in, with an older, gray-haired man. They were all smiling with bright, artificial smiles. They grouped themselves at the foot of my bed.

"And how are you feeling this morning, Miss Greenwood?"

I tried to decide which one of them had spoken. I hate saying anything to a group of people. When I talk to a group of people I always have to single out one and talk to him, and all the while I am talking I feel the others are peering at me and taking unfair advantage. I also hate people to ask cheerfully how you are when they know you're feeling like hell and expect you to say "Fine."

"I feel lousy."

"Lousy. Hmm," somebody said, and a boy ducked his head with a little smile. Somebody else scribbled something on a clipboard. Then somebody pulled a straight, solemn face and said, "And why do you feel lousy?"

I thought some of the boys and girls in that bright group might well be friends of Buddy Willard. They would know I knew him, and they would be curious to see me, and afterward they would gossip about me among themselves. I wanted to be where nobody I knew could ever come.

"I can't sleep . . ."

They interrupted me. "But the nurse says you slept last night." I looked around the crescent of fresh, strange faces.

"I can't read." I raised my voice. "I can't eat." It occurred to me I'd been eating ravenously ever since I came to.

The people in the group had turned from me and were murmuring in low voices to each other. Finally, the gray-haired man stepped out.

"Thank you, Miss Greenwood. You will be seen by one of the staff doctors presently."

Then the group moved on to the bed of the Italian woman.

"And how are you feeling today, Mrs. . . ." somebody said, and the name sounded long and full of I's, like Mrs. Tomolillo.

Mrs. Tomolillo giggled. "Oh, I'm fine, doctor. I'm just fine." Then she lowered her voice and whispered something I couldn't hear. One or two people in the group glanced in my direction. Then somebody said, "All right, Mrs. Tomolillo," and somebody stepped out and pulled the bed curtain between us like a white wall.

I sat on one end of a wooden bench in the grassy square between the four brick walls of the hospital. My mother, in her purple cartwheel dress, sat at the other end. She had her head propped in her hand, index finger on her cheek and thumb under her chin.

Mrs. Tomolillo was sitting with some dark-haired, laughing

Italians on the next bench down. Every time my mother moved, Mrs. Tomolillo imitated her. Now Mrs. Tomolillo was sitting with her index finger on her cheek and her thumb under her chin, and her head tilted wistfully to one side.

"Don't move," I told my mother in a low voice. "That woman's imitating you."

My mother turned to glance round, but quick as a wink, Mrs. Tomolillo dropped her fat white hands in her lap and started talking vigorously to her friends.

"Why no, she's not," my mother said. "She's not even paying any attention to us."

But the minute my mother turned round to me again, Mrs. Tomolillo matched the tips of her fingers together the way my mother had just done and cast a black, mocking look at me.

The lawn was white with doctors.

All the time my mother and I had been sitting there, in the narrow cone of sun that shone down between the tall brick walls, doctors had been coming up to me and introducing themselves. "I'm Doctor Soandso, I'm Doctor Soandso."

Some of them looked so young I knew they couldn't be proper doctors, and one of them had a queer name that sounded just like Doctor Syphilis, so I began to look out for suspicious, fake names, and sure enough, a dark-haired fellow who looked very like Doctor Gordon, except that he had black skin where Doctor Gordon's skin was white, came up and said, "I'm Doctor Pancreas," and shook my hand.

After introducing themselves, the doctors all stood within listening distance, only I couldn't tell my mother that they were taking down every word we said without their hearing me, so I leaned over and whispered into her ear.

My mother drew back sharply.

"Oh, Esther, I wish you would cooperate. They say you don't cooperate. They say you won't talk to any of the doctors or make anything in Occupational Therapy...."

"I've got to get out of here," I told her meaningly. "Then I'd be all right. You got me in here," I said. "You get me out."

I thought if only I could persuade my mother to get me out of the hospital I could work on her sympathies, like that boy with brain disease in the play, and convince her what was the best thing to do.

To my surprise, my mother said, "All right, I'll try to get you out—even if only to a better place. If I try to get you out," she laid a hand on my knee, "promise you'll be good?"

I spun round and glared straight at Doctor Syphilis, who stood at my elbow taking notes on a tiny, almost invisible pad. "I promise," I said in a loud, conspicuous voice.

The Negro wheeled the food cart into the patients' dining room. The Psychiatric Ward at the hospital was very small—just two corridors in an L-shape, lined with rooms, and an alcove of beds behind the OT shop, where I was, and a little area with a table and a few seats by a window in the corner of the L, which was our lounge and dining room.

Usually it was a shrunken old white man that brought our food, but today it was a Negro. The Negro was with a woman in blue stiletto heels, and she was telling him what to do. The Negro kept grinning and chuckling in a silly way.

Then he carried a tray over to our table with three lidded tin tureens on it, and started banging the tureens down. The woman left the room, locking the door behind her. All the time the Negro was banging down the tureens and then the dinted silver and the thick, white china plates, he gawped at us with big, rolling eyes.

I could tell we were his first crazy people.

Nobody at the table made a move to take the lids off the tin tureens, and the nurse stood back to see if any of us would take the lids off before she came to do it. Usually Mrs. Tomolillo had taken the lids off and dished out everybody's food like a little mother, but then they sent her home, and nobody seemed to want to take her place.

I was starving, so I lifted the lid off the first bowl.

"That's very nice of you, Esther," the nurse said pleasantly. "Would you like to take some beans and pass them round to the others?"

I dished myself out a helping of green string beans and turned to pass the tureen to the enormous red-headed woman at my right. This was the first time the red-headed woman had been allowed up to the table. I had seen her once, at the very end of the L-shaped corridor, standing in front of an open door with bars on the square, inset windows.

She had been yelling and laughing in a rude way and slapping her thighs at the passing doctors, and the white-jacketed attendant who took care of the people in that end of the ward was leaning against the radiator, laughing himself sick.

The red-headed woman snatched the tureen from me and upended it on her plate. Beans mountained up in front of her and scattered over onto her lap and onto the floor like stiff, green straws.

"Oh, Mrs. Mole!" the nurse said in a sad voice. "I think you better eat in your room today."

And she returned most of the beans to the tureen and gave it to the person next to Mrs. Mole and led Mrs. Mole off. All the way down the hall to her room, Mrs. Mole kept turning round and making leering faces at us, and ugly, oinking noises.

The Negro had come back and was starting to collect the empty plates of people who hadn't dished out any beans yet.

"We're not done," I told him. "You can just wait."

"Mah, mah!" The Negro widened his eyes in mock wonder. He glanced round. The nurse had not yet returned from locking up Mrs. Mole. The Negro made me an insolent bow. "Miss Mucky-Muck," he said under his breath.

I lifted the lid off the second tureen and uncovered a wedge of macaroni, stone-cold and stuck together in a gluey paste. The third and last tureen was chock-full of baked beans.

Now I knew perfectly well you didn't serve two kinds of beans together at a meal. Beans and carrots, or beans and peas, maybe, but never beans and beans. The Negro was just trying to see how much we would take.

The nurse came back, and the Negro edged off at a distance. I ate as much as I could of the baked beans. Then I rose from the table, passing round to the side where the nurse couldn't see me below the waist, and behind the Negro, who was clearing the dirty plates. I drew my foot back and gave him a sharp, hard kick on the calf of the leg.

The Negro leapt away with a yelp and rolled his eyes at

me. "Oh Miz, oh Miz," he moaned, rubbing his leg. "You shouldn't of done that, you shouldn't, you reely shouldn't."

"That's what *you* get," I said, and stared him in the eye.

"Don't you want to get up today?"

"No." I huddled down more deeply in the bed and pulled the sheet up over my head. Then I lifted a corner of the sheet and peered out. The nurse was shaking down the thermometer she had just removed from my mouth.

"You *see*, it's normal." I had looked at the thermometer before she came to collect it, the way I always did. "You *see*, it's normal, what do you keep taking it for?"

I wanted to tell her that if only something were wrong with my body it would be fine, I would rather have anything wrong with my body than something wrong with my head, but the idea seemed so involved and wearisome that I didn't say anything. I only burrowed down further in the bed.

Then, through the sheet, I felt a slight, annoying pressure on my leg. I peeped out. The nurse had set her tray of thermometers on my bed while she turned her back and took the pulse of the person who lay next to me, in Mrs. Tomolillo's place.

A heavy naughtiness pricked through my veins, irritating and attractive as the hurt of a loose tooth. I yawned and stirred, as if about to turn over, and edged my foot under the box.

"Oh!" The nurse's cry sounded like a cry for help, and another nurse came running. "Look what you've done!"

I poked my head out of the covers and stared over the edge of the bed. Around the overturned enamel tray, a star of thermometer shards glittered, and balls of mercury trembled like celestial dew.

"I'm sorry," I said. "It was an accident."

The second nurse fixed me with a baleful eye. "You did it on purpose. I *saw* you."

Then she hurried off, and almost immediately two attendants came and wheeled me, bed and all, down to Mrs. Mole's old room, but not before I had scooped up a ball of mercury.

Soon after they had locked the door, I could see the

Negro's face, a molasses-colored moon, risen at the window grating, but I pretended not to notice.

I opened my fingers a crack, like a child with a secret, and smiled at the silver globe cupped in my palm. If I dropped it, it would break into a million little replicas of itself, and if I pushed them near each other, they would fuse, without a crack, into one whole again.

I smiled and smiled at the small silver ball.

I couldn't imagine what they had done with Mrs. Mole.

Fifteen

PHILOMENA GUINEA's black Cadillac eased through the tight, five o'clock traffic like a ceremonial car. Soon it would cross one of the brief bridges that arched the Charles, and I would, without thinking, open the door and plunge out through the stream of traffic to the rail of the bridge. One jump and the water would be over my head.

Idly I twisted a Kleenex to small, pill-sized pellets between my fingers and watched my chance. I sat in the middle of the back seat of the Cadillac, my mother on one side of me, and my brother on the other, both leaning slightly forward, like diagonal bars, one across each car door.

In front of me I could see the Spam-colored expanse of the chauffeur's neck, sandwiched between a blue cap and the shoulders of a blue jacket and, next to him, like a frail, exotic bird, the silver hair and emerald-feathered hat of Philomena Guinea, the famous novelist.

I wasn't quite sure why Mrs. Guinea had turned up. All I knew was that she had interested herself in my case and that at one time, at the peak of her career, she had been in an asylum as well.

My mother said that Mrs. Guinea had sent her a telegram from the Bahamas, where she read about me in a Boston paper. Mrs. Guinea had telegrammed, "Is there a boy in the case?"

If there was a boy in the case, Mrs. Guinea couldn't, of course, have anything to do with it.

But my mother had telegrammed back, "No, it is Esther's writing. She thinks she will never write again."

So Mrs. Guinea had flown back to Boston and taken me out of the cramped city hospital ward, and now she was driving me to a private hospital that had grounds and golf

courses and gardens, like a country club, where she would pay
for me, as if I had a scholarship, until the doctors she knew of
there had made me well.

My mother told me I should be grateful. She said I had
used up almost all her money, and if it weren't for Mrs.
Guinea she didn't know where I'd be. I knew where I'd be
though. I'd be in the big state hospital in the country, cheek
by jowl to this private place.

I knew I should be grateful to Mrs. Guinea, only I couldn't
feel a thing. If Mrs. Guinea had given me a ticket to Europe,
or a round-the-world cruise, it wouldn't have made one scrap
of difference to me, because wherever I sat—on the deck of a
ship or at a street café in Paris or Bangkok—I would be
sitting under the same glass bell jar, stewing in my own sour
air.

Blue sky opened its dome above the river, and the river was
dotted with sails. I readied myself, but immediately my mother and my brother each laid one hand on a door handle. The
tires hummed briefly over the grill of the bridge. Water, sails,
blue sky and suspended gulls flashed by like an improbable
postcard, and we were across.

I sank back in the gray, plush seat and closed my eyes. The
air of the bell jar wadded round me and I couldn't stir.

I had my own room again.

It reminded me of the room in Doctor Gordon's hospital—
a bed, a bureau, a closet, a table and chair. A window with a
screen, but no bars. My room was on the first floor, and the
window, a short distance above the pine-needle-padded
ground, overlooked a wooded yard ringed by a red brick wall.
If I jumped I wouldn't even bruise my knees. The inner
surface of the tall wall seemed smooth as glass.

The journey over the bridge had unnerved me.

I had missed a perfectly good chance. The river water
passed me by like an untouched drink. I suspected that even if
my mother and brother had not been there I would have
made no move to jump.

When I enrolled in the main building of the hospital, a slim young woman had come and introduced herself. "My name is Doctor Nolan. I am to be Esther's doctor."

I was surprised to have a woman. I didn't think they had woman psychiatrists. This woman was a cross between Myrna Loy and my mother. She wore a white blouse and a full skirt gathered at the waist by a wide leather belt, and stylish, crescent-shaped spectacles.

But after a nurse had led me across the lawn to the gloomy brick building called Caplan, where I would live, Doctor Nolan didn't come to see me, a whole lot of strange men came instead.

I lay on my bed under the thick white blanket, and they entered my room, one by one, and introduced themselves. I couldn't understand why there should be so many of them, or why they would want to introduce themselves, and I began to think they were testing me, to see if I noticed there were too many of them, and I grew wary.

Finally, a handsome, white-haired doctor came in and said he was the director of the hospital. Then he started talking about the Pilgrims and Indians and who had the land after them, and what rivers ran nearby, and who had built the first hospital, and how it had burned down, and who had built the next hospital, until I thought he must be waiting to see when I would interrupt him and tell him I knew all that about rivers and Pilgrims was a lot of nonsense.

But then I thought some of it might be true, so I tried to sort out what was likely to be true and what wasn't, only before I could do that, he had said good-bye.

I waited till I heard the voices of all the doctors die away. Then I threw back the white blanket and put on my shoes and walked out into the hall. Nobody stopped me, so I walked round the corner of my wing of the hall and down another, longer hall, past an open dining room.

A maid in a green uniform was setting the tables for supper. There were white linen tablecloths and glasses and paper napkins. I stored the fact that they were real glasses in the corner of my mind the way a squirrel stores a nut. At the city hospital we had drunk out of paper cups and had no knives to cut our meat. The meat had always been so overcooked we could cut it with a fork.

Finally I arrived at a big lounge with shabby furniture and a threadbare rug. A girl with a round pasty face and short black hair was sitting in an armchair, reading a magazine. She reminded me of a Girl Scout leader I'd had once. I glanced at her feet, and sure enough, she wore those flat brown leather shoes with fringed tongues lapping down over the front that are supposed to be so sporty, and the ends of the laces were knobbed with little imitation acorns.

The girl raised her eyes and smiled. "I'm Valerie. Who are you?"

I pretended I hadn't heard and walked out of the lounge to the end of the next wing. On the way, I passed a waist-high door behind which I saw some nurses.

"Where is everybody?"

"Out." The nurse was writing something over and over on little pieces of adhesive tape. I leaned across the gate of the door to see what she was writing, and it was E. Greenwood, E. Greenwood, E. Greenwood, E. Greenwood.

"Out where?"

"Oh, OT, the golf course, playing badminton."

I noticed a pile of clothes on a chair beside the nurse. They were the same clothes the nurse in the first hospital had been packing into the patent leather case when I broke the mirror. The nurses began sticking the labels onto the clothes.

I walked back to the lounge. I couldn't understand what these people were doing, playing badminton and golf. They mustn't be really sick at all, to do that.

I sat down near Valerie and observed her carefully. Yes, I thought, she might just as well be in a Girl Scout camp. She was reading her tatty copy of *Vogue* with intense interest.

"What the hell is she doing here?" I wondered. "There's nothing the matter with her."

"Do you mind if I smoke?" Doctor Nolan leaned back in the armchair next to my bed.

I said no, I liked the smell of smoke. I thought if Doctor Nolan smoked, she might stay longer. This was the first time she had come to talk with me. When she left I would simply lapse into the old blankness.

"Tell me about Doctor Gordon," Doctor Nolan said suddenly. "Did you like him?"

I gave Doctor Nolan a wary look. I thought the doctors must all be in it together, and that somewhere in this hospital, in a hidden corner, there reposed a machine exactly like Doctor Gordon's, ready to jolt me out of my skin.

"No," I said. "I didn't like him at all."

"That's interesting. Why?"

"I didn't like what he did to me."

"Did to you?"

I told Doctor Nolan about the machine, and the blue flashes, and the jolting and the noise. While I was telling her she went very still.

"That was a mistake," she said then. "It's not supposed to be like that."

I stared at her.

"If it's done properly," Doctor Nolan said, "it's like going to sleep."

"If anyone does that to me again I'll kill myself."

Doctor Nolan said firmly, "You won't have any shock treatments here. Or if you do," she amended, "I'll tell you about it beforehand, and I promise you it won't be anything like what you had before. Why," she finished, "some people even *like* them."

After Doctor Nolan had gone I found a box of matches on the windowsill. It wasn't an ordinary-size box, but an extremely tiny box. I opened it and exposed a row of little white sticks with pink tips. I tried to light one, and it crumpled in my hand.

I couldn't think why Doctor Nolan would have left me such a stupid thing. Perhaps she wanted to see if I would give it back. Carefully I stored the toy matches in the hem of my new wool bathrobe. If Doctor Nolan asked me for the matches, I would say I'd thought they were made of candy and had eaten them.

A new woman had moved into the room next to mine.

I thought she must be the only person in the building who was newer than I was, so she wouldn't know how really bad I was, the way the rest did. I thought I might go in and make friends.

The woman was lying on her bed in a purple dress that fastened at the neck with a cameo brooch and reached midway between her knees and her shoes. She had rusty hair knotted in a schoolmarmish bun, and thin, silver-rimmed spectacles attached to her breast pocket with a black elastic.

"Hello," I said conversationally, sitting down on the edge of the bed. "My name's Esther, what's your name?"

The woman didn't stir, just stared up at the ceiling. I felt hurt. I thought maybe Valerie or somebody had told her when she first came in how stupid I was.

A nurse popped her head in at the door.

"Oh, there you are," she said to me. "Visiting Miss Norris. How nice!" And she disappeared again.

I don't know how long I sat there, watching the woman in purple and wondering if her pursed pink lips would open, and if they did open, what they would say.

Finally, without speaking or looking at me, Miss Norris swung her feet in their high, black, buttoned boots over the other side of the bed and walked out of the room. I thought she might be trying to get rid of me in a subtle way. Quietly, at a little distance, I followed her down the hall.

Miss Norris reached the door of the dining room and paused. All the way to the dining room she had walked precisely, placing her feet in the very center of the cabbage roses that twined through the pattern of the carpet. She waited a moment and then, one by one, lifted her feet over the doorsill and into the dining room as though stepping over an invisible shin-high stile.

She sat down at one of the round, linen-covered tables and unfolded a napkin in her lap.

"It's not supper for an hour yet," the cook called out of the kitchen.

But Miss Norris didn't answer. She just stared straight ahead of her in a polite way.

I pulled up a chair opposite her at the table and unfolded a napkin. We didn't speak, but sat there, in a close, sisterly silence, until the gong for supper sounded down the hall.

"Lie down," the nurse said. "I'm going to give you another injection."

I rolled over on my stomach on the bed and hitched up my skirt. Then I pulled down the trousers of my silk pajamas.

"My word, what all have you got under there?"

"Pajamas. So I won't have to bother getting in and out of them all the time."

The nurse made a little clucking noise. Then she said, "Which side?" It was an old joke.

I raised my head and glanced back at my bare buttocks. They were bruised purple and green and blue from past injections. The left side looked darker than the right.

"The right."

"You name it." The nurse jabbed the needle in, and I winced, savoring the tiny hurt. Three times each day the nurses injected me, and about an hour after each injection they gave me a cup of sugary fruit juice and stood by, watching me drink it.

"Lucky you," Valerie said. "You're on insulin."

"Nothing happens."

"Oh, it will. I've had it. Tell me when you get a reaction."

But I never seemed to get any reaction. I just grew fatter and fatter. Already I filled the new, too-big clothes my mother had bought, and when I peered down at my plump stomach and my broad hips I thought it was a good thing Mrs. Guinea hadn't seen me like this, because I looked just as if I were going to have a baby.

"Have you seen my scars?"

Valerie pushed aside her black bang and indicated two pale marks, one on either side of her forehead, as if at some time she had started to sprout horns, but cut them off.

We were walking, just the two of us, with the Sports Therapist in the asylum gardens. Nowadays I was let out on walk privileges more and more often. They never let Miss Norris out at all.

Valerie said Miss Norris shouldn't be in Caplan, but in a building for worse people called Wymark.

"Do you know what these scars are?" Valerie persisted.

"No. What are they?"

"I've had a lobotomy."

I looked at Valerie in awe, appreciating for the first time her perpetual marble calm. "How do you feel?"

"Fine. I'm not angry any more. Before, I was always angry. I was in Wymark before, and now I'm in Caplan. I can go to town, now, or shopping or to a movie, along with a nurse."

"What will you do when you get out?"

"Oh, I'm not leaving," Valerie laughed. "I like it here."

"Moving day!"

"Why should I be moving?"

The nurse went on blithely opening and shutting my drawers, emptying the closet and folding my belongings into the black overnight case.

I thought they must at last be moving me to Wymark.

"Oh, you're only moving to the front of the house," the nurse said cheerfully. "You'll like it. There's lots more sun."

When we came out into the hall, I saw that Miss Norris was moving too. A nurse, young and cheerful as my own, stood in the doorway of Miss Norris's room, helping Miss Norris into a purple coat with a scrawny squirrel-fur collar.

Hour after hour I had been keeping watch by Miss Norris's bedside, refusing the diversion of OT and walks and badminton matches and even the weekly movies, which I enjoyed, and which Miss Norris never went to, simply to brood over the pale, speechless circlet of her lips.

I thought how exciting it would be if she opened her mouth and spoke, and I rushed out into the hall and announced this to the nurses. They would praise me for encouraging Miss Norris, and I would probably be allowed shopping privileges and movie privileges downtown, and my escape would be assured.

But in all my hours of vigil Miss Norris hadn't said a word.

"Where are you moving to?" I asked her now.

The nurse touched Miss Norris's elbow, and Miss Norris jerked into motion like a doll on wheels.

"She's going to Wymark," my nurse told me in a low voice. "I'm afraid Miss Norris isn't moving up like you."

I watched Miss Norris lift one foot, and then the other, over the invisible stile that barred the front doorsill.

"I've a surprise for you," the nurse said as she installed me in a sunny room in the front wing overlooking the green golf links. "Somebody you know's just come today."

"Somebody I know?"

The nurse laughed. "Don't look at me like that. It's not a policeman." Then, as I didn't say anything, she added, "She says she's an old friend of yours. She lives next door. Why don't you pay her a visit?"

I thought the nurse must be joking, and that if I knocked on the door next to mine I would hear no answer, but go in and find Miss Norris, buttoned into her purple, squirrel-collared coat and lying on the bed, her mouth blooming out of the quiet vase of her body like the bud of a rose.

Still, I went out and knocked on the neighboring door.

"Come in!" called a gay voice.

I opened the door a crack and peered into the room. The big, horsey girl in jodhpurs sitting by the window glanced up with a broad smile.

"Esther!" She sounded out of breath, as if she had been running a long, long distance and only just come to a halt. "How nice to see you. They told me you were here."

"Joan?" I said tentatively, then "Joan!" in confusion and disbelief.

Joan beamed, revealing her large, gleaming, unmistakable teeth.

"It's really me. I thought you'd be surprised."

Sixteen

JOAN'S ROOM, with its closet and bureau and table and chair and white blanket with the big blue C on it, was a mirror image of my own. It occurred to me that Joan, hearing where I was, had engaged a room at the asylum on pretense, simply as a joke. That would explain why she had told the nurse I was her friend. I had never known Joan, except at a cool distance.

"How did you get here?" I curled up on Joan's bed.

"I read about you," Joan said.

"What?"

"I read about you, and I ran away."

"How do you mean?" I said evenly.

"Well," Joan leaned back in the chintz-flowered asylum armchair, "I had a summer job working for the chapter head of some fraternity, like the Masons, you know, but not the Masons, and I felt terrible. I had these bunions, I could hardly walk—in the last days I had to wear rubber boots to work, instead of shoes, and you can imagine what *that* did to my morale. ..."

I thought either Joan must be crazy—wearing rubber boots to work—or she must be trying to see how crazy I was, believing all that. Besides, only old people ever got bunions. I decided to pretend I thought she was crazy, and that I was only humoring her along.

"I always feel lousy without shoes," I said with an ambiguous smile. "Did your feet hurt much?"

"Terribly. And my boss—he'd just separated from his wife, he couldn't come right out and get a divorce, because that wouldn't go with this fraternal order—my boss kept buzzing me in every other minute, and each time I moved my feet hurt like the devil, but the second I'd sit down at my desk again, buzz went the buzzer, and he'd have something else he wanted to get off his chest. ...."

"Why didn't you quit?"

"Oh, I did quit, more or less. I stayed off work on sick leave. I didn't go out. I didn't see anyone. I stowed the telephone in a drawer and never answered it. ...

"Then my doctor sent me to a psychiatrist at this big hospital. I had an appointment for twelve o'clock, and I was in an awful state. Finally, at half past twelve, the receptionist came out and told me the doctor had gone to lunch. She asked me if I wanted to wait, and I said yes."

"Did he come back?" The story sounded rather involved for Joan to have made up out of whole cloth, but I led her on, to see what would come of it.

"Oh yes. I was going to kill myself, mind you. I said 'If this doctor doesn't do the trick, that's the end.' Well, the receptionist led me down a long hall, and just as we got to the door she turned to me and said, 'You won't mind if there are a few students with the doctor, will you?' What could I say? 'Oh no,' I said. I walked in and found nine pairs of eyes fixed on me. Nine! Eighteen separate eyes.

"Now, if that receptionist had told me there were going to be nine people in that room, I'd have walked out on the spot. But there I was, and it was too late to do a thing about it. Well, on this particular day I happened to be wearing a fur coat. ...."

"In August?"

"Oh, it was one of those cold, wet days, and I thought, my first psychiatrist—you know. Anyway, this psychiatrist kept eyeing that fur coat the whole time I talked to him, and I could just see what he thought of my asking to pay the student's cut rate instead of the full fee. I could see the dollar signs in his eyes. Well, I told him I don't know whatall— about the bunions and the telephone in the drawer and how I wanted to kill myself—and then he asked me to wait outside while he discussed my case with the others, and when he called me back in, you know what he said?"

"What?"

"He folded his hands together and looked at me and said,

'Miss Gilling, we have decided that you would benefit by group therapy.' "

"*Group* therapy?" I thought I must sound phony as an echo chamber, but Joan didn't pay any notice.

"That's what he said. Can you imagine me wanting to kill myself, and coming round to chat about it with a whole pack of strangers, and most of them no better than myself. . . ."

"That's crazy." I was growing involved in spite of myself. "That's not even *hu*man."

"That's just what I said. I went straight home and wrote that doctor a letter. I wrote him one beautiful letter about how a man like that had no business setting himself up to help sick people. . . ."

"Did you get any answer?"

"I don't know. That was the day I read about you."

"How do you mean?"

"Oh," Joan said, "about how the police thought you were dead and all. I've got a pile of clippings somewhere." She heaved herself up, and I had a strong horsey whiff that made my nostrils prickle. Joan had been a champion horse-jumper at the annual college gymkhana, and I wondered if she had been sleeping in a stable.

Joan rummaged in her open suitcase and came up with a fistful of clippings.

"Here, have a look."

The first clipping showed a big, blown-up picture of a girl with black-shadowed eyes and black lips spread in a grin. I couldn't imagine where such a tarty picture had been taken until I noticed the Bloomingdale earrings and the Bloomingdale necklace glinting out of it with bright, white highlights, like imitation stars.

SCHOLARSHIP GIRL MISSING. MOTHER WORRIED

The article under the picture told how this girl had disappeared from her home on August 17th, wearing a green skirt and a white blouse, and had left a note saying she was taking a long walk. *When Miss Greenwood had not returned by midnight,* it said, *her mother called the town police.*

The next clipping showed a picture of my mother and brother and me grouped together in our backyard and smiling. I couldn't think who had taken that picture either, until I saw I was wearing dungarees and white sneakers and remembered that was what I wore in my spinach-picking summer, and how Dodo Conway had dropped by and taken some family snaps of the three of us one hot afternoon. *Mrs. Greenwood asked that this picture be printed in hopes that it will encourage her daughter to return home.*

SLEEPING PILLS FEARED MISSING WITH GIRL

A dark, midnight picture of about a dozen moon-faced people in a wood. I thought the people at the end of the row looked queer and unusually short until I realized they were not people, but dogs. *Bloodhounds used in search for missing girl. Police Sgt. Bill Hindly says: It doesn't look good.*

GIRL FOUND ALIVE!

The last picture showed policemen lifting a long, limp blanket roll with a featureless cabbage head into the back of an ambulance. Then it told how my mother had been down in the cellar, doing the week's laundry, when she heard faint groans coming from a disused hole. . . .

I laid the clippings on the white spread of the bed.

"You keep them," Joan said. "You ought to stick them in a scrapbook."

I folded the clippings and slipped them in my pocket.

"I read about you," Joan went on. "Not how they found you, but everything up to that, and I put all my money together and took the first plane to New York."

"Why New York?"

"Oh, I thought it would be easier to kill myself in New York."

"What did you do?"

Joan grinned sheepishly and stretched out her hands, palm

up. Like a miniature mountain range, large, reddish weals
upheaved across the white flesh of her wrists.

"How did you do that?" For the first time it occurred to me
Joan and I might have something in common.

"I shoved my fists through my roommate's window."

"What roommate?"

"My old college roommate. She was working in New York,
and I couldn't think of anyplace else to stay, and besides, I'd
hardly any money left, so I went to stay with her. My parents
found me there—she'd written them I was acting funny—and
my father flew straight down and brought me back."

"But you're all right now." I made it a statement.

Joan considered me with her bright, pebble-gray eyes. "I
guess so," she said. "Aren't you?"

I had fallen asleep after the evening meal.

I was awakened by a loud voice. *Mrs. Bannister, Mrs.
Bannister, Mrs. Bannister, Mrs. Bannister.* As I pulled out of
sleep, I found I was beating on the bedpost with my hands
and calling. The sharp, wry figure of Mrs. Bannister, the night
nurse, scurried into view.

"Here, we don't want you to break this."

She unfastened the band of my watch.

"What's the matter? What happened?"

Mrs. Bannister's face twisted into a quick smile. "You've
had a reaction."

"A reaction?"

"Yes, how do you feel?"

"Funny. Sort of light and airy."

Mrs. Bannister helped me sit up.

"You'll be better now. You'll be better in no time. Would
you like some hot milk?"

"Yes."

And when Mrs. Bannister held the cup to my lips, I fanned
the hot milk out on my tongue as it went down, tasting it
luxuriously, the way a baby tastes its mother.

"Mrs. Bannister tells me you had a reaction." Doctor Nolan
seated herself in the armchair by the window and took out a

tiny box of matches. The box looked exactly like the one I had hidden in the hem of my bathrobe, and for a moment I wondered if a nurse had discovered it there and given it back to Doctor Nolan on the quiet.

Doctor Nolan scraped a match on the side of the box. A hot yellow flame jumped into life, and I watched her suck it up into the cigarette.

"Mrs. B. says you felt better."

"I did for a while. Now I'm the same again."

"I've news for you."

I waited. Every day now, for I didn't know how many days, I had spent the mornings and afternoons and evenings wrapped up in my white blanket on the deck chair in the alcove, pretending to read. I had a dim notion that Doctor Nolan was allowing me a certain number of days and then she would say just what Doctor Gordon had said: "I'm sorry, you don't seem to have improved, I think you'd better have some shock treatment. . . ."

"Well, don't you want to hear what it is?"

"What?" I said dully, and braced myself.

"You're not to have any more visitors for a while."

I stared at Doctor Nolan in surprise. "Why that's wonderful."

"I thought you'd be pleased." She smiled.

Then I looked, and Doctor Nolan looked, at the wastebasket beside my bureau. Out of the wastebasket poked the blood-red buds of a dozen long-stemmed roses.

That afternoon my mother had come to visit me.

My mother was only one in a long stream of visitors—my former employer, the lady Christian Scientist, who walked on the lawn with me and talked about the mist going up from the earth in the Bible, and the mist being error, and my whole trouble being that I believed in the mist, and the minute I stopped believing in it, it would disappear and I would see I had always been well, and the English teacher I had in high school who came and tried to teach me how to play Scrabble, because he thought it might revive my old interest in words, and Philomena Guinea herself, who wasn't at all satisfied with what the doctors were doing and kept telling them so.

I hated these visits.

I would be sitting in my alcove or in my room, and a smiling nurse would pop in and announce one or another of the visitors. Once they'd even brought the minister of the Unitarian church, whom I'd never really liked at all. He was terribly nervous the whole time, and I could tell he thought I was crazy as a loon, because I told him I believed in hell, and that certain people, like me, had to live in hell before they died, to make up for missing out on it after death, since they didn't believe in life after death, and what each person believed happened to him when he died.

I hated these visits, because I kept feeling the visitors measuring my fat and stringy hair against what I had been and what they wanted me to be, and I knew they went away utterly confounded.

I thought if they left me alone I might have some peace.

My mother was the worst. She never scolded me, but kept begging me, with a sorrowful face, to tell her what she had done wrong. She said she was sure the doctors thought she had done something wrong because they asked her a lot of questions about my toilet training, and I had been perfectly trained at a very early age and given her no trouble whatsoever.

That afternoon my mother had brought me the roses.

"Save them for my funeral," I'd said.

My mother's face puckered, and she looked ready to cry.

"But Esther, don't you remember what day it is today?"

"No."

I thought it might be Saint Valentine's day.

"It's your *birth*day."

And that was when I had dumped the roses in the wastebasket.

"That was a silly thing for her to do," I said to Doctor Nolan.

Doctor Nolan nodded. She seemed to know what I meant.

"I hate her," I said, and waited for the blow to fall.

But Doctor Nolan only smiled at me as if something had pleased her very, very much, and said, "I suppose you do."

Seventeen

"YOU'RE A LUCKY GIRL TODAY."

The young nurse cleared my breakfast tray away and left me wrapped in my white blanket like a passenger taking the sea air on the deck of a ship.

"Why am I lucky?"

"Well, I'm not sure if you're supposed to know yet, but today, you're moving to Belsize." The nurse looked at me expectantly.

"Belsize," I said. "I can't go there."

"Why not?"

"I'm not ready. I'm not well enough."

"Of course, you're well enough. Don't worry, they wouldn't be moving you if you weren't well enough."

After the nurse left, I tried to puzzle out this new move on Doctor Nolan's part. What was she trying to prove? I hadn't changed. Nothing had changed. And Belsize was the best house of all. From Belsize people went back to work and back to school and back to their homes.

Joan would be at Belsize. Joan with her physics books and her golf clubs and her badminton rackets and her breathy voice. Joan, marking the gulf between me and the nearly well ones. Ever since Joan left Caplan I'd followed her progress through the asylum grapevine.

Joan had walk privileges, Joan had shopping privileges, Joan had town privileges. I gathered all my news of Joan into a little, bitter heap, though I received it with surface gladness. Joan was the beaming double of my old best self, specially designed to follow and torment me.

Perhaps Joan would be gone when I got to Belsize.

At least at Belsize I could forget about shock treatments. At Caplan a lot of the women had shock treatments. I could

167

tell which ones they were, because they didn't get their breakfast trays with the rest of us. They had their shock treatments while we breakfasted in our rooms, and then they came into the lounge, quiet and extinguished, led like children by the nurses, and ate their breakfasts there.

Each morning, when I heard the nurse knock with my tray, an immense relief flooded through me, because I knew I was out of danger for that day. I didn't see how Doctor Nolan could tell you went to sleep during a shock treatment if she'd never had a shock treatment herself. How did she know the person didn't just *look* as if he was asleep, while all the time, inside, he was feeling the blue volts and the noise?

Piano music sounded from the end of the hall.

At supper I sat quietly, listening to the chatter of the Belsize women. They were all fashionably dressed and carefully made up, and several of them were married. Some of them had been shopping downtown, and others had been out visiting friends, and all during supper they kept tossing back and forth these private jokes.

"I'd call Jack," a woman named DeeDee said, "only I'm afraid he wouldn't be home. I know just where I could call him, though, and he'd be in, all right."

The short, spry blonde woman at my table laughed. "I almost had Doctor Loring where I wanted him today." She widened her starey blue eyes like a little doll. "I wouldn't mind trading old Percy in for a new model."

At the opposite end of the room, Joan was wolfing her Spam and broiled tomato with great appetite. She seemed perfectly at home among these women and treated me coolly, with a slight sneer, like a dim and inferior acquaintance.

I had gone to bed right after supper, but then I heard the piano music and pictured Joan and DeeDee and Loubelle, the blonde woman, and the rest of them, laughing and gossiping about me in the living room behind my back. They would be saying how awful it was to have people like me in Belsize and that I should be in Wymark instead.

I decided to put a lid on their nasty talk.

Draping my blanket loosely around my shoulders, like a

stole, I wandered down the hall toward the light and the gay noise.

For the rest of the evening I listened to DeeDee thump out some of her own songs on the grand piano, while the other women sat round playing bridge and chatting, just the way they would in a college dormitory, only most of them were ten years over college age.

One of them, a great, tall, gray-haired woman with a booming bass voice, named Mrs. Savage, had gone to Vassar. I could tell right away she was a society woman, because she talked about nothing but débutantes. It seemed she had two or three daughters, and that year they were all going to be débutantes, only she had loused up their débutante party by signing herself into the asylum.

DeeDee had one song she called "The Milkman" and everybody kept saying she ought to get it published, it would be a hit. First her hands would clop out a little melody on the keys, like the hoofbeats of a slow pony, and next another melody came in, like the milkman whistling, and then the two melodies went on together.

"That's very nice," I said in a conversational voice.

Joan was leaning on one corner of the piano and leafing through a new issue of some fashion magazine, and DeeDee smiled up at her as if the two of them shared a secret.

"Oh, Esther," Joan said then, holding up the magazine, "isn't this you?"

DeeDee stopped playing. "Let me see." She took the magazine, peered at the page Joan pointed to, and then glanced back at me.

"Oh no," DeeDee said. "Surely not." She looked at the magazine again, then at me. "Never!"

"Oh, but it *is* Esther, isn't it, Esther?" Joan said.

Loubelle and Mrs. Savage drifted over, and pretending I knew what it was all about, I moved to the piano with them.

The magazine photograph showed a girl in a strapless evening dress of fuzzy white stuff, grinning fit to split, with a whole lot of boys bending around her. The girl was holding a glass full of a transparent drink and seemed to have her eyes fixed over my shoulder on something that stood behind me, a little to my left. A faint breath fanned the back of my neck. I wheeled round.

The night nurse had come in, unnoticed, on her soft rubber soles.

"No kidding," she said, "is that really you?"

"No, it's not me. Joan's quite mistaken. It's somebody else."

"Oh, say it's you!" DeeDee cried.

But I pretended I didn't hear her and turned away.

Then Loubelle begged the nurse to make a fourth at bridge, and I drew up a chair to watch, although I didn't know the first thing about bridge, because I hadn't had time to pick it up at college, the way all the wealthy girls did.

I stared at the flat poker faces of the kings and jacks and queens and listened to the nurse talking about her hard life.

"You ladies don't know what it is, holding down two jobs," she said. "Nights I'm over here, watching you. . . ."

Loubelle giggled. "Oh, we're good. We're the best of the lot, and you know it."

"Oh, *you're* all right." The nurse passed round a packet of spearmint gum, then unfolded a pink strap from its tinfoil wrapper herself. "*You're* all right, it's those boobies at the state place that worry me off my feet."

"Do you work in both places then?" I asked with sudden interest.

"You bet." The nurse gave me a straight look, and I could see she thought I had no business in Belsize at all. "You wouldn't like it over there one bit, Lady Jane."

I found it strange that the nurse should call me Lady Jane when she knew what my name was perfectly well.

"Why?" I persisted.

"Oh, it's not a nice place, like this. This is a regular country club. Over there they've got nothing. No OT to talk of, no walks. . . ."

"Why haven't they got walks?"

"Not enough em-ploy-ees." The nurse scooped in a trick and Loubelle groaned. "Believe me, ladies, when I collect enough do-re-mi to buy me a car, I'm clearing out."

"Will you clear out of here, too?" Joan wanted to know.

"You bet. Only private cases from then on. When I feel like it. . . ."

But I'd stopped listening.

I felt the nurse had been instructed to show me my alternatives. Either I got better, or I fell, down, down, like a burning, then burnt-out star, from Belsize, to Caplan, to Wymark and finally, after Doctor Nolan and Mrs. Guinea had given me up, to the state place next door.

I gathered my blanket round me and pushed back my chair.

"You cold?" the nurse demanded rudely.

"Yes," I said, moving off down the hall. "I'm frozen stiff."

I woke warm and placid in my white cocoon. A shaft of pale, wintry sunlight dazzled the mirror and the glasses on the bureau and the metal doorknobs. From across the hall came the early-morning clatter of the maids in the kitchen, preparing the breakfast trays.

I heard the nurse knock on the door next to mine, at the far end of the hall. Mrs. Savage's sleepy voice boomed out, and the nurse went in to her with the jingling tray. I thought, with a mild stir of pleasure, of the steaming blue china coffee pitcher and the blue china breakfast cup and the fat blue china cream jug with the white daisies on it.

I was beginning to resign myself.

If I was going to fall, I would hang on to my small comforts, at least, as long as I possibly could.

The nurse rapped on my door and, without waiting for an answer, breezed in.

It was a new nurse—they were always changing—with a lean, sand-colored face and sandy hair, and large freckles polka-dotting her bony nose. For some reason the sight of this nurse made me sick at heart, and it was only as she strode across the room to snap up the green blind that I realized part of her strangeness came from being empty-handed.

I opened my mouth to ask for my breakfast tray, but silenced myself immediately. The nurse would be mistaking me for somebody else. New nurses often did that. Somebody in Belsize must be having shock treatments, unknown to me, and the nurse had, quite understandably, confused me with her.

I waited until the nurse had made her little circuit of my

room, patting, straightening, arranging, and taken the next
tray in to Loubelle one door farther down the hall.

Then I shoved my feet into my slippers, dragging my
blanket with me, for the morning was bright, but very cold,
and crossed quickly to the kitchen. The pink-uniformed maid
was filling a row of blue china coffee pitchers from a great,
battered kettle on the stove.

I looked with love at the lineup of waiting trays—the white
paper napkins, folded in their crisp, isosceles triangles, each
under the anchor of its silver fork, the pale domes of soft-
boiled eggs in the blue egg cups, the scalloped glass shells of
orange marmalade. All I had to do was reach out and claim
my tray, and the world would be perfectly normal.

"There's been a mistake," I told the maid, leaning over the
counter and speaking in a low, confidential tone. "The new
nurse forgot to bring me in my breakfast tray today."

I managed a bright smile, to show there were no hard
feelings.

"What's the name?"

"Greenwood. Esther Greenwood."

"Greenwood, Greenwood, Greenwood." The maid's warty
index finger slid down the list of names of the patients in
Belsize tacked upon the kitchen wall. "Greenwood, no breakfast today."

I caught the rim of the counter with both hands.

"There must be a mistake. Are you sure it's Greenwood?"

"Greenwood," the maid said decisively as the nurse came
in.

The nurse looked questioningly from me to the maid.

"Miss Greenwood wanted her tray," the maid said, avoiding
my eyes.

"Oh," the nurse smiled at me, "you'll be getting your tray
later on this morning, Miss Greenwood. You . . ."

But I didn't wait to hear what the nurse said. I strode
blindly out into the hall, not to my room, because that was
where they would come to get me, but to the alcove, greatly
inferior to the alcove at Caplan, but an alcove, nevertheless, in
a quiet corner of the hall, where Joan and Loubelle and
DeeDee and Mrs. Savage would not come.

I curled up in the far corner of the alcove with the blanket over my head. It wasn't the shock treatment that struck me, so much as the bare-faced treachery of Doctor Nolan. I liked Doctor Nolan, I loved her, I had given her my trust on a platter and told her everything, and she had promised, faithfully, to warn me ahead of time if ever I had to have another shock treatment.

If she had told me the night before I would have lain awake all night, of course, full of dread and foreboding, but by morning I would have been composed and ready. I would have gone down the hall between two nurses, past DeeDee and Loubelle and Mrs. Savage and Joan, with dignity, like a person coolly resigned to execution.

The nurse bent over me and called my name.

I pulled away and crouched farther into the corner. The nurse disappeared. I knew she would return, in a minute, with two burly men attendants, and they would bear me, howling and hitting, past the smiling audience now gathered in the lounge.

Doctor Nolan put her arm around me and hugged me like a mother.

"You said you'd *tell* me!" I shouted at her through the dishevelled blanket.

"But I *am* telling you," Doctor Nolan said. "I've come specially early to tell you, and I'm taking you over myself."

I peered at her through swollen lids. "Why didn't you tell me last night?"

"I only thought it would keep you awake. If I'd known . . ."

"You *said* you'd tell me."

"Listen, Esther," Doctor Nolan said. "I'm going over with you. I'll be there the whole time, so everything will happen right, the way I promised. I'll be there when you wake up, and I'll bring you back again."

I looked at her. She seemed very upset.

I waited a minute. Then I said, "Promise you'll be there."

"I promise."

Doctor Nolan took out a white handkerchief and wiped my face. Then she hooked her arm in my arm, like an old friend, and helped me up, and we started down the hall. My blanket tangled about my feet, so I let it drop, but Doctor Nolan didn't seem to notice. We passed Joan, coming out of her room, and I gave her a meaning, disdainful smile, and she ducked back and waited until we had gone by.

Then Doctor Nolan unlocked a door at the end of the hall and led me down a flight of stairs into the mysterious basement corridors that linked, in an elaborate network of tunnels and burrows, all the various buildings of the hospital.

The walls were bright, white lavatory tile with bald bulbs set at intervals in the black ceiling. Stretchers and wheelchairs were beached here and there against the hissing, knocking pipes that ran and branched in an intricate nervous system along the glittering walls. I hung on to Doctor Nolan's arm like death, and every so often she gave me an encouraging squeeze.

Finally, we stopped at a green door with Electrotherapy printed on it in black letters. I held back, and Doctor Nolan waited. Then I said, "Let's get it over with," and we went in.

The only people in the waiting room besides Doctor Nolan and me were a pallid man in a shabby maroon bathrobe and his accompanying nurse.

"Do you want to sit down?" Doctor Nolan pointed at a wooden bench, but my legs felt full of heaviness, and I thought how hard it would be to hoist myself from a sitting position when the shock treatment people came in.

"I'd rather stand."

At last a tall, cadaverous woman in a white smock entered the room from an inner door. I thought that she would go up and take the man in the maroon bathrobe, as he was first, so I was surprised when she came toward me.

"Good morning, Doctor Nolan," the woman said, putting her arm around my shoulders. "Is this Esther?"

"Yes, Miss Huey. Esther, this is Miss Huey, she'll take good care of you. I've told her about you."

I thought the woman must be seven feet tall. She bent over me in a kind way, and I could see that her face, with the buck teeth protruding in the center, had at one time been badly pitted with acne. It looked like maps of the craters on the moon.

"I think we can take you right away, Esther," Miss Huey

said. "Mr. Anderson won't mind waiting, will you, Mr. Anderson?"

Mr. Anderson didn't say a word, so with Miss Huey's arm around my shoulder, and Doctor Nolan following, I moved into the next room.

Through the slits of my eyes, which I didn't dare open too far, lest the full view strike me dead, I saw the high bed with its white, drumtight sheet, and the machine behind the bed, and the masked person—I couldn't tell whether it was a man or a woman—behind the machine, and other masked people flanking the bed on both sides.

Miss Huey helped me climb up and lie down on my back.

"Talk to me," I said.

Miss Huey began to talk in a low, soothing voice, smoothing the salve on my temples and fitting the small electric buttons on either side of my head. "You'll be perfectly all right, you won't feel a thing, just bite down. ..." And she set something on my tongue and in panic I bit down, and darkness wiped me out like chalk on a blackboard.

Eighteen

"ESTHER."

I woke out of a deep, drenched sleep, and the first thing I saw was Doctor Nolan's face swimming in front of me and saying, "Esther, Esther."

I rubbed my eyes with an awkward hand.

Behind Doctor Nolan I could see the body of a woman wearing a rumpled black-and-white checked robe and flung out on a cot as if dropped from a great height. But before I could take in any more, Doctor Nolan led me through a door into a fresh, blue-skied air.

All the heat and fear purged itself. I felt surprisingly at peace. The bell jar hung, suspended, a few feet above my head. I was open to the circulating air.

"It was like I told you it would be, wasn't it?" said Doctor Nolan, as we walked back to Belsize together through the crunch of brown leaves.

"Yes."

"Well, it will always be like that," she said firmly. "You will be having shock treatments three times a week—Tuesday, Thursday and Saturday."

I gulped in a long draught of air.

"For how long?"

"That depends," Doctor Nolan said, "on you and me."

I took up the silver knife and cracked off the cap of my egg. Then I put down the knife and looked at it. I tried to think what I had loved knives for, but my mind slipped from the noose of the thought and swung, like a bird, in the center of empty air.

Joan and DeeDee were sitting side by side on the piano

bench, and DeeDee was teaching Joan to play the bottom half of "Chopsticks" while she played the top.

I thought how sad it was Joan looked so horsey, with such big teeth and eyes like two gray, goggly pebbles. Why, she couldn't even keep a boy like Buddy Willard. And DeeDee's husband was obviously living with some mistress or other and turning her sour as an old fusty cat.

"I've got a let-ter," Joan chanted, poking her tousled head inside my door.

"Good for you." I kept my eyes on my book. Ever since the shock treatments had ended, after a brief series of five, and I had town privileges, Joan hung about me like a large and breathless fruitfly—as if the sweetness of recovery were something she could suck up by mere nearness. They had taken away her physics books and the piles of dusty spiral pads full of lecture notes that had ringed her room, and she was confined to grounds again.

"Don't you want to know who it's *from?*"

Joan edged into the room and sat down on my bed. I wanted to tell her to get the hell out, she gave me the creeps, only I couldn't do it.

"All right." I stuck my finger in my place and shut the book. "Who from?"

Joan slipped out a pale blue envelope from her skirt pocket and waved it teasingly.

"Well, isn't that a coincidence!" I said.

"What do you mean, a coincidence?"

I went over to my bureau, picked up a pale blue envelope and waved it at Joan like a parting handkerchief. "I got a letter too. I wonder if they're the same."

"He's better," Joan said. "He's out of the hospital."

There was a little pause.

"Are you going to marry him?"

"No," I said. "Are you?"

Joan grinned evasively. "I didn't like him much, anyway."

"Oh?"

"No, it was his family I liked."

"You mean Mr. and Mrs. Willard?"

"Yes." Joan's voice slid down my spine like a draft. "I loved them. They were so nice, so happy, nothing like my parents. I went over to see them all the time," she paused, "until you came."

"I'm sorry." Then I added, "Why didn't you go on seeing them, if you liked them so much?"

"Oh, I couldn't," Joan said. "Not with you dating Buddy. It would have looked ... I don't know, *funny*."

I considered. "I suppose so."

"Are you," Joan hesitated, "going to let him come?"

"I don't know."

At first I had thought it would be awful having Buddy come and visit me at the asylum—he would probably only come to gloat and hobnob with the other doctors. But then it seemed to me it would be a step, placing him, renouncing him, in spite of the fact that I had nobody—telling him there was no simultaneous interpreter, nobody, but that he was the wrong one, that I had stopped hanging on. "Are you?"

"Yes," Joan breathed. "Maybe he'll bring his mother. I'm going to ask him to bring his mother. ..."

"His *mother*?"

Joan pouted. "I like Mrs. Willard. Mrs. Willard's a wonderful, wonderful woman. She's been a real mother to me."

I had a picture of Mrs. Willard, with her heather-mixture tweeds and her sensible shoes and her wise, maternal maxims. Mr. Willard was her little boy, and his voice was high and clear, like a little boy's. Joan and Mrs. Willard. Joan ... and Mrs. Willard ...

I had knocked on DeeDee's door that morning, wanting to borrow some two-part sheet music. I waited a few minutes and then, hearing no answer and thinking DeeDee must be out, and I could pick up the music from her bureau, I pushed the door open and stepped into the room.

At Belsize, even at Belsize, the doors had locks, but the patients had no keys. A shut door meant privacy, and was respected, like a locked door. One knocked, and knocked again, then went away. I remembered this as I stood, my eyes half-useless after the brilliance of the hall, in the room's deep, musky dark.

As my vision cleared, I saw a shape rise from the bed. Then

somebody gave a low giggle. The shape adjusted its hair, and two pale, pebble eyes regarded me through the gloom. DeeDee lay back on the pillows, bare-legged under her green wool dressing gown, and watched me with a little mocking smile. A cigarette glowed between the fingers of her right hand.

"I just wanted . . ." I said.

"I know," said DeeDee. "The music."

"Hello, Esther," Joan said then, and her cornhusk voice made me want to puke. "Wait for me, Esther, I'll come play the bottom part with you."

Now Joan said stoutly, "I never really liked Buddy Willard. He thought he knew everything. He thought he knew everything about women. . . ."

I looked at Joan. In spite of the creepy feeling, and in spite of my old, ingrained dislike, Joan fascinated me. It was like observing a Martian, or a particularly warty toad. Her thoughts were not my thoughts, nor her feelings my feelings, but we were close enough so that her thoughts and feelings seemed a wry, black image of my own.

Sometimes I wondered if I had made Joan up. Other times I wondered if she would continue to pop in at every crisis of my life to remind me of what I had been, and what I had been through, and carry on her own separate but similar crisis under my nose.

"I don't see what women see in other women," I'd told Doctor Nolan in my interview that noon. "What does a woman see in a woman that she can't see in a man?"

Doctor Nolan paused. Then she said, "Tenderness."

That shut me up.

"I like you," Joan was saying. "I like you better than Buddy."

And as she stretched out on my bed with a silly smile, I remembered a minor scandal at our college dormitory when a fat, matronly-breasted senior, homely as a grandmother and a pious Religion major, and a tall, gawky freshman with a history of being deserted at an early hour in all sorts of ingenious ways by her blind dates, started seeing too much of each other. They were always together, and once somebody

had come upon them embracing, the story went, in the fat
girl's room.

"But what were they *doing*?" I had asked. Whenever I
thought about men and men, and women and women, I could
never really imagine what they would be actually doing.

"Oh," the spy had said, "Milly was sitting on the chair and
Theodora was lying on the bed, and Milly was stroking
Theodora's hair."

I was disappointed. I had thought I would have some
revelation of specific evil. I wondered if all women did with
other women was lie and hug.

Of course, the famous woman poet at my college lived with
another woman—a stumpy old Classical scholar with a
cropped Dutch cut. And when I had told the poet I might
well get married and have a pack of children someday, she
stared at me in horror. "But what about your *career*?" she had
cried.

My head ached. Why did I attract these weird old women?
There was the famous poet, and Philomena Guinea, and Jay
Cee, and the Christian Scientist lady and lord knows who, and
they all wanted to adopt me in some way, and, for the price
of their care and influence, have me resemble them.

"I like you."

"That's tough, Joan," I said, picking up my book. "Because
I don't like you. You make me puke, if you want to know."

And I walked out of the room, leaving Joan lying, lumpy as
an old horse, across my bed.

I waited for the doctor, wondering if I should bolt. I knew
what I was doing was illegal—in Massachusetts, anyway, because the state was cram-jam full of Catholics—but Doctor
Nolan said this doctor was an old friend of hers, and a wise
man.

"What's your appointment for?" the brisk, white-uniformed
receptionist wanted to know, ticking my name off on a notebook list.

"What do you mean, *for*?" I hadn't thought anybody but
the doctor himself would ask me that, and the communal
waiting room was full of other patients waiting for other

doctors, most of them pregnant or with babies, and I felt their eyes on my flat, virgin stomach.

The receptionist glanced up at me, and I blushed.

"A fitting, isn't it?" she said kindly. "I only wanted to make sure so I'd know what to charge you. Are you a student?"

"Ye-es."

"That will only be half-price then. Five dollars, instead of ten. Shall I bill you?"

I was about to give my home address, where I would probably be by the time the bill arrived, but then I thought of my mother opening the bill and seeing what it was for. The only other address I had was the innocuous box number which people used who didn't want to advertise the fact they lived in an asylum. But I thought the receptionist might recognize the box number, so I said, "I better pay now," and peeled five dollar notes off the roll in my pocketbook.

The five dollars was part of what Philomena Guinea had sent me as a sort of get-well present. I wondered what she would think if she knew to what use her money was being put.

Whether she knew it or not, Philomena Guinea was buying my freedom.

"What I hate is the thought of being under a man's thumb," I had told Doctor Nolan. "A man doesn't have a worry in the world, while I've got a baby hanging over my head like a big stick, to keep me in line."

"Would you act differently if you didn't have to worry about a baby?"

"Yes," I said, "but ..." and I told Doctor Nolan about the married woman lawyer and her Defense of Chastity.

Doctor Nolan waited until I was finished. Then she burst out laughing. "Propaganda!" she said, and scribbled the name and address of this doctor on a prescription pad.

I leafed nervously through an issue of *Baby Talk*. The fat, bright faces of babies beamed up at me, page after page—bald babies, chocolate-colored babies, Eisenhower-faced babies, babies rolling over for the first time, babies reaching for rattles, babies eating their first spoonful of solid food, babies doing all the little tricky things it takes to grow up, step by step, into an anxious and unsettling world.

I smelt a mingling of Pablum and sour milk and salt-cod-stinky diapers and felt sorrowful and tender. How easy having babies seemed to the women around me! Why was I so unmaternal and apart? Why couldn't I dream of devoting myself to baby after fat puling baby like Dodo Conway?

If I had to wait on a baby all day, I would go mad.

I looked at the baby in the lap of the woman opposite. I had no idea how old it was, I never did, with babies—for all I knew it could talk a blue streak and had twenty teeth behind its pursed, pink lips. It held its little wobby head up on its shoulders—it didn't seem to have a neck—and observed me with a wise, Platonic expression.

The baby's mother smiled and smiled, holding that baby as if it were the first wonder of the world. I watched the mother and the baby for some clue to their mutual satisfaction, but before I had discovered anything, the doctor called me in.

"You'd like a fitting," he said cheerfully, and I thought with relief that he wasn't the sort of doctor to ask awkward questions. I had toyed with the idea of telling him I planned to be married to a sailor as soon as his ship docked at the Charlestown Navy Yard, and the reason I didn't have an engagement ring was because we were too poor, but at the last moment I rejected that appealing story and simply said "Yes."

I climbed up on the examination table, thinking: "I am climbing to freedom, freedom from fear, freedom from marrying the wrong person, like Buddy Willard, just because of sex, freedom from the Florence Crittenden Homes where all the poor girls go who should have been fitted out like me, because what they did, they would do anyway, regardless. . . ."

As I rode back to the asylum with my box in the plain brown paper wrapper on my lap I might have been Mrs. Anybody coming back from a day in town with a Schrafft's cake for her maiden aunt or a Filene's Basement hat. Gradually the suspicion that Catholics had X-ray eyes diminished, and I grew easy. I had done well by my shopping privileges, I thought.

I was my own woman.

The next step was to find the proper sort of man.

Nineteen

"I'M GOING TO BE A PSYCHIATRIST."

Joan spoke with her usual breathy enthusiasm. We were drinking apple cider in the Belsize lounge.

"Oh," I said dryly, "that's nice."

"I've had a long talk with Doctor Quinn, and she thinks it's perfectly possible." Doctor Quinn was Joan's psychiatrist, a bright, shrewd, single lady, and I often thought if I had been assigned to Doctor Quinn I would be still in Caplan or, more probably, Wymark. Doctor Quinn had an abstract quality that appealed to Joan, but it gave me the polar chills.

Joan chattered on about Egos and Ids, and I turned my mind to something else, to the brown, unwrapped package in my bottom drawer. I never talked about Egos and Ids with Doctor Nolan. I didn't know just what I talked about really.

". . . I'm going to live out, now."

I tuned in on Joan then. "Where?" I demanded, trying to hide my envy.

Doctor Nolan said my college would take me back for the second semester, on her recommendation and Philomena Guinea's scholarship, but as the doctors vetoed my living with my mother in the interim, I was staying on at the asylum until the winter term began.

Even so, I felt it unfair of Joan to beat me through the gates.

"Where?" I persisted. "They're not letting you live on your own, are they?" Joan had only that week been given town privileges again.

"Oh no, of course not. I'm living in Cambridge with Nurse Kennedy. Her roommate's just got married, and she needs someone to share the apartment."

"Cheers." I raised my apple cider glass, and we clinked. In spite of my profound reservations, I thought I would always treasure Joan. It was as if we had been forced together by some overwhelming circumstance, like war or plague, and shared a world of our own. "When are you leaving?"

"On the first of the month."

"Nice."

Joan grew wistful. "You'll come visit me, won't you, Esther?"

"Of course."

But I thought, "Not likely."

"It hurts," I said. "Is it supposed to hurt?"

Irwin didn't say anything. Then he said, "Sometimes it hurts."

I had met Irwin on the steps of the Widener Library. I was standing at the top of the long flight, overlooking the red brick buildings that walled the snow-filled quad and preparing to catch the trolley back to the asylum, when a tall young man with a rather ugly and bespectacled, but intelligent face, came up and said, "Could you please tell me the time?"

I glanced at my watch. "Five past four."

Then the man shifted his arms around the load of books he was carrying before him like a dinner tray and revealed a bony wrist.

"Why, you've a watch yourself!"

The man looked ruefully at his watch. He lifted it and shook it by his ear. "Doesn't work." He smiled engagingly. "Where are you going?"

I was about to say, "Back to the asylum," but the man looked promising, so I changed my mind. "Home."

"Would you like some coffee first?"

I hesitated. I was due at the asylum for supper and I didn't want to be late so close to being signed out of there for good.

"A very *small* cup of coffee?"

I decided to practice my new, normal personality on this man who, in the course of my hesitations, told me his name was Irwin and that he was a very well-paid professor of

mathematics, so I said, "All right," and, matching my stride to
Irwin's, strolled down the long, ice-encrusted flight at his side.

It was only after seeing Irwin's study that I decided to
seduce him.

Irwin lived in a murky, comfortable basement apartment in
one of the rundown streets of outer Cambridge and drove me
there—for a beer, he said—after three cups of bitter coffee in
a student café. We sat in his study on stuffed brown leather
chairs, surrounded by stacks of dusty, incomprehensible books
with huge formulas inset artistically on the page like poems.

While I was sipping my first glass of beer—I have never
really cared for cold beer in midwinter, but I accepted the
glass to have something solid to hold on to—the doorbell
rang.

Irwin seemed embarrassed. "I think it may be a lady."

Irwin had a queer, old-world habit of calling women ladies.

"Fine, fine," I gestured largely. "Bring her in."

Irwin shook his head. "You would upset her."

I smiled into my amber cylinder of cold beer.

The doorbell rang again with a peremptory jab. Irwin
sighed and rose to answer it. The minute he disappeared, I
whipped into the bathroom and, concealed behind the dirty,
aluminum-colored Venetian blind, watched Irwin's monkish
face appear in the door crack.

A large, bosomy Slavic lady in a bulky sweater of natural
sheep's wool, purple slacks, high-heeled black overshoes with
Persian lamb cuffs and a matching toque, puffed white,
inaudible words into the wintry air. Irwin's voice drifted back
to me through the chilly hall.

"I'm sorry, Olga . . . I'm working, Olga . . . no, I don't think
so, Olga," all the while the lady's red mouth moved and the
words, translated to white smoke, floated up among the
branches of the naked lilac by the door. Then, finally, "Perhaps,
Olga . . . good-bye, Olga."

I admired the immense, steppelike expanse of the lady's
wool-clad bosom as she retreated a few inches from my eye,
down the creaking wooden stair, a sort of Siberian bitterness
on her vivid lips.

"I suppose you have lots and lots of affairs in Cambridge," I told Irwin cheerily, as I stuck a snail with a pin in one of Cambridge's determinedly French restaurants.

"I seem," Irwin admitted with a small, modest smile, "to get on with the ladies."

I picked up my empty snail shell and drank the herb-green juice. I had no idea if this was proper, but after months of wholesome, dull asylum diet, I was greedy for butter.

I had called Doctor Nolan from a pay phone at the restaurant and asked for permission to stay overnight in Cambridge with Joan. Of course, I had no idea whether Irwin would invite me back to his apartment after dinner or not, but I thought his dismissal of the Slavic lady—another professor's wife—looked promising.

I tipped back my head and poured down a glass of Nuits-St.-Georges.

"You do like wine," Irwin observed.

"Only Nuits-St.-Georges. I imagine him . . . with the dragon . . ."

Irwin reached for my hand.

I felt the first man I slept with must be intelligent, so I would respect him. Irwin was a full professor at twenty-six and had the pale, hairless skin of a boy genius. I also needed somebody quite experienced to make up for my lack of it, and Irwin's ladies reassured me on this head. Then, to be on the safe side, I wanted somebody I didn't know and wouldn't go on knowing—a kind of impersonal, priestlike official, as in the tales of tribal rites.

By the end of the evening I had no doubts about Irwin whatsoever.

Ever since I'd learned about the corruption of Buddy Willard my virginity weighed like a millstone around my neck. It had been of such enormous importance to me for so long that my habit was to defend it at all costs. I had been defending it for five years and I was sick of it.

It was only as Irwin swung me into his arms, back at the apartment, and carried me, wine-dazed and limp, into the pitch-black bedroom, that I murmured, "You know, Irwin, I think I ought to tell you, I'm a virgin."

Irwin laughed and flung me down on the bed.

A few minutes later an exclamation of surprise revealed that Irwin hadn't really believed me. I thought how lucky it was I had started practicing birth control during the day, because in my winey state that night I would never have bothered to perform the delicate and necessary operation. I lay, rapt and naked, on Irwin's rough blanket, waiting for the miraculous change to make itself felt.

But all I felt was a sharp, startlingly bad pain.

"It hurts," I said. "Is it supposed to hurt?"

Irwin didn't say anything. Then he said, "Sometimes it hurts."

After a little while Irwin got up and went into the bathroom, and I heard the rushing of shower water. I wasn't sure if Irwin had done what he planned to do, or if my virginity had obstructed him in some way. I wanted to ask him if I was still a virgin, but I felt too unsettled. A warm liquid was seeping out between my legs. Tentatively, I reached down and touched it.

When I held my hand up to the light streaming in from the bathroom, my fingertips looked black.

"Irwin," I said nervously, "bring me a towel."

Irwin strolled back, a bathtowel knotted around his waist, and tossed me a second, smaller towel. I pushed the towel between my legs and pulled it away almost immediately. It was half black with blood.

"I'm bleeding!" I announced, sitting up with a start.

"Oh, that often happens," Irwin reassured me. "You'll be all right."

Then the stories of blood-stained bridal sheets and capsules of red ink bestowed on already deflowered brides floated back to me. I wondered how much I would bleed, and lay down, nursing the towel. It occurred to me that the blood was my answer. I couldn't possibly be a virgin any more. I smiled into the dark. I felt part of a great tradition.

Surreptitiously, I applied a fresh section of white towel to my wound, thinking that as soon as the bleeding stopped, I would take the late trolley back to the asylum. I wanted to brood over my new condition in perfect peace. But the towel came away black and dripping.

"I . . . think I better go home," I said faintly.

"Surely not so soon."

"Yes, I think I better."

I asked if I could borrow Irwin's towel and packed it between my thighs as a bandage. Then I pulled on my sweaty clothes. Irwin offered to drive me home, but I didn't see how I could let him drive me to the asylum, so I dug in my pocketbook for Joan's address. Irwin knew the street and went out to start the car. I was too worried to tell him I was still bleeding. I kept hoping every minute that it would stop.

But as Irwin drove me through the barren, snow-banked streets I felt the warm seepage let itself through the dam of the towel and my skirt and onto the car seat.

As we slowed, cruising by house after lit house, I thought how fortunate it was I had not discarded my virginity while living at college or at home, where such concealment would have been impossible.

Joan opened the door with an expression of glad surprise. Irwin kissed my hand and told Joan to take good care of me.

I shut the door and leaned back against it, feeling the blood drain from my face in one spectacular flush.

"Why, Esther," Joan said, "what on earth's the matter?"

I wondered when Joan would notice the blood trickling down my legs and oozing, stickily, into each black patent leather shoe. I thought I could be dying from a bullet wound and Joan would still stare through me with her blank eyes, expecting me to ask for a cup of coffee and a sandwich.

"Is that nurse here?"

"No, she's on night duty at Caplan. ..."

"Good." I made a little bitter grin as another soak of blood let itself through the drenched padding and started the tedious journey into my shoes. "I mean ... bad."

"You look funny," Joan said.

"You better get a doctor."

"Why?"

"Quick."

"But ..."

Still she hadn't noticed anything.

I bent down, with a brief grunt, and slipped off one of my winter-cracked black Bloomingdale shoes. I held the shoe up, before Joan's enlarged, pebbly eyes, tilted it, and watched her take in the stream of blood that cascaded onto the beige rug.

"My God! What is it?"

"I'm hemorrhaging."

Joan half led, half dragged me to the sofa and made me lie down. Then she propped some pillows under my blood-stained feet. Then she stood back and demanded, "Who was that man?"

For one crazy minute I thought Joan would refuse to call a doctor until I confessed the whole story of my evening with Irwin and that after my confession she would still refuse, as a sort of punishment. But then I realized that she honestly took my explanation at face value, that my going to bed with Irwin was utterly incomprehensible to her, and his appearance a mere prick to her pleasure at my arrival.

"Oh somebody," I said, with a flabby gesture of dismissal. Another pulse of blood released itself and I contracted my stomach muscles in alarm. "Get a towel."

Joan went out and came back almost immediately with a pile of towels and sheets. Like a prompt nurse, she peeled back my blood-wet clothes, drew a quick breath as she arrived at the original royal red towel, and applied a fresh bandage. I lay, trying to slow the beating of my heart, as every beat pushed forth another gush of blood.

I remembered a worrisome course in the Victorian novel where woman after woman died, palely and nobly, in torrents of blood, after a difficult childbirth. Perhaps Irwin had injured me in some awful, obscure way, and all the while I lay there on Joan's sofa I was really dying.

Joan pulled up an Indian hassock and began to dial down the long list of Cambridge doctors. The first number didn't answer. Joan began to explain my case to the second number, which did answer, but then broke off and said "I see" and hung up.

"What's the trouble?"

"He'll only come for regular customers or emergencies. It's Sunday."

I tried to lift my arm and look at my watch, but my hand was a rock at my side and wouldn't budge. Sunday—the doctor's paradise! Doctors at country clubs, doctors at the seaside, doctors with mistresses, doctors with wives, doctors in church, doctors in yachts, doctors everywhere resolutely being people, not doctors.

"For God's sake," I said, "tell them I'm an emergency."

The third number didn't answer and, at the fourth, the party hung up the minute Joan mentioned it was about a period. Joan began to cry.

"Look, Joan," I said painstakingly, "call up the local hospital. Tell them it's an emergency. They'll have to take me."

Joan brightened and dialed a fifth number. The Emergency Service promised her a staff doctor would attend to me if I could come in to the ward. Then Joan called a taxi.

Joan insisted on riding with me. I clasped my fresh padding of towels with a sort of desperation as the cabby, impressed by the address Joan gave him, cut corner after corner in the dawn-pale streets and drew up with a great squeal of tires at the Emergency Ward entrance.

I left Joan to pay the driver and hurried into the empty, glaringly lit room. A nurse bustled out from behind a white screen. In a few swift words, I managed to tell her the truth about my predicament before Joan came in the door, blinking and wide-eyed as a myopic owl.

The Emergency Ward doctor strolled out then, and I climbed, with the nurse's help, on to the examining table. The nurse whispered to the doctor, and the doctor nodded and began unpacking the bloody toweling. I felt his fingers start to probe, and Joan stood, rigid as a soldier, at my side, holding my hand, for my sake or hers I couldn't tell.

"Ouch!" I winced at a particularly bad jab.

The doctor whistled.

"You're one in a million."

"What do you mean?"

"I mean it's one in a million it happens to like this."

The doctor spoke in a low, curt voice to the nurse, and she hurried to a side table and brought back some rolls of gauze and silver instruments. "I can see," the doctor bent down, "exactly where the trouble is coming from."

"But can you fix it?"

The doctor laughed. "Oh, I can fix it, all right."

I was roused by a tap on my door. It was past midnight, and the asylum quiet as death. I couldn't imagine who would still be up.

"Come in!" I switched on the bedside light.

The door clicked open, and Doctor Quinn's brisk, dark head appeared in the crack. I looked at her with surprise, because although I knew who she was, and often passed her, with a brief nod, in the asylum hall, I never spoke to her at all.

Now she said, "Miss Greenwood, may I come in a minute?"

I nodded.

Doctor Quinn stepped into the room, shutting the door quietly behind her. She was wearing one of her navy blue, immaculate suits with a plain, snow-white blouse showing in the V of the neck.

"I'm sorry to bother you, Miss Greenwood, and especially at this time of night, but I thought you might be able to help us out about Joan."

For a minute I wondered if Doctor Quinn was going to blame me for Joan's return to the asylum. I still wasn't sure how much Joan knew, after our trip to the Emergency Ward, but a few days later she had come back to live in Belsize, retaining, however, the freest of town privileges.

"I'll do what I can," I told Doctor Quinn.

Doctor Quinn sat down on the edge of my bed with a grave face. "We would like to find out where Joan is. We thought you might have an idea."

Suddenly I wanted to dissociate myself from Joan completely. "I don't know," I said coldly. "Isn't she in her room?"

It was well after the Belsize curfew hour.

"No, Joan had a permit to go to a movie in town this evening, and she's not back yet."

"Who was she with?"

"She was alone." Doctor Quinn paused. "Have you any idea where she might be likely to spend the night?"

"Surely she'll be back. Something must have held her up." But I didn't see what could have held Joan up in tame night Boston.

Doctor Quinn shook her head. "The last trolley went by an hour ago."

"Maybe she'll come back by taxi."

Doctor Quinn sighed.

"Have you tried the Kennedy girl?" I went on. "Where Joan used to live?"

Doctor Quinn nodded.

"Her family?"

"Oh, she'd never go there ... but we've tried them, too."

Doctor Quinn lingered a minute, as if she could sniff out some clue in the still room. Then she said, "Well, we'll do what we can," and left.

I turned out the light and tried to drop back to sleep, but Joan's face floated before me, bodiless and smiling, like the face of the Cheshire cat. I even thought I heard her voice, rustling and hushing through the dark, but then I realized it was only the night wind in the asylum trees. . . .

Another tap woke me in the frost-gray dawn.

This time I opened the door myself.

Facing me was Doctor Quinn. She stood at attention, like a frail drill sergeant, but her outlines seemed curiously smudged.

"I thought you should know," Doctor Quinn said. "Joan has been found."

Doctor Quinn's use of the passive slowed my blood.

"Where?"

"In the woods, by the frozen ponds. . . ."

I opened my mouth, but no words came out.

"One of the orderlies found her," Doctor Quinn continued, "just now, coming to work. . . ."

"She's not . . ."

"Dead," said Doctor Quinn. "I'm afraid she's hanged herself."

Twenty

A FRESH FALL OF SNOW blanketed the asylum grounds—not a Christmas sprinkle, but a man-high January deluge, the sort that snuffs out schools and offices and churches, and leaves, for a day or more, a pure, blank sheet in place of memo pads, date books and calendars.

In a week, if I passed my interview with the board of directors, Philomena Guinea's large black car would drive me west and deposit me at the wrought-iron gates of my college.

The heart of winter!

Massachusetts would be sunk in a marble calm. I pictured the snowflaky, Grandma Moses villages, the reaches of swampland rattling with dried cattails, the ponds where frog and hornpout dreamed in a sheath of ice, and the shivering woods.

But under the deceptively clean and level slate the topography was the same, and instead of San Francisco or Europe or Mars I would be learning the old landscape, brook and hill and tree. In one way it seemed a small thing, starting, after a six months' lapse, where I had so vehemently left off.

Everybody would know about me, of course.

Doctor Nolan had said, quite bluntly, that a lot of people would treat me gingerly, or even avoid me, like a leper with a warning bell. My mother's face floated to mind, a pale, reproachful moon, at her last and first visit to the asylum since my twentieth birthday. A daughter in an asylum! I had done that to her. Still, she had obviously decided to forgive me.

"We'll take up where we left off, Esther," she had said, with her sweet, martyr's smile. "We'll act as if all this were a bad dream."

A bad dream.

To the person in the bell jar, blank and stopped as a dead baby, the world itself is the bad dream.

A bad dream.

I remembered everything.

I remembered the cadavers and Doreen and the story of the fig tree and Marco's diamond and the sailor on the Common and Doctor Gordon's wall-eyed nurse and the broken thermometers and the Negro with his two kinds of beans and the twenty pounds I gained on insulin and the rock that bulged between sky and sea like a gray skull.

Maybe forgetfulness, like a kind of snow, should numb and cover them.

But they were part of me. They were my landscape.

"A man to see you!"

The smiling, snow-capped nurse poked her head in through the door, and for a confused second I thought I really was back in college and this spruce white furniture, this white view over trees and hills, an improvement on my old room's nicked chairs and desk and outlook over the bald quad. "A man to see you!" the girl on watch had said, on the dormitory phone.

What was there about us, in Belsize, so different from the girls playing bridge and gossiping and studying in the college to which I would return? Those girls, too, sat under bell jars of a sort.

"Come in!" I called, and Buddy Willard, khaki cap in hand, stepped into the room.

"Well, Buddy," I said.

"Well, Esther."

We stood there, looking at each other. I waited for a touch of emotion, the faintest glow. Nothing. Nothing but a great, amiable boredom. Buddy's khaki-jacketed shape seemed small and unrelated to me as the brown posts he had stood against that day a year ago, at the bottom of the ski run.

"How did you get here?" I asked finally.

"Mother's car."

"In all this snow?"

"Well," Buddy grinned, "I'm stuck outside in a drift. The hill was too much for me. Is there anyplace I can borrow a shovel?"

"We can get a shovel from one of the groundsmen."

"Good." Buddy turned to go.

"Wait, I'll come and help you."

Buddy looked at me then, and in his eyes I saw a flicker of strangeness—the same compound of curiosity and wariness I had seen in the eyes of the Christian Scientist and my old English teacher and the Unitarian minister who used to visit me.

"Oh, Buddy," I laughed. "I'm all right."

"Oh, I know, I know, Esther," Buddy said hastily.

"It's you who oughtn't to dig out cars, Buddy. Not me."

And Buddy did let me do most of the work.

The car had skidded on the glassy hill up to the asylum and backed, with one wheel over the rim of the drive, into a steep drift.

The sun, emerged from its gray shrouds of clouds, shone with a summer brilliance on the untouched slopes. Pausing in my work to overlook that pristine expanse, I felt the same profound thrill it gives me to see trees and grassland waist-high under flood water—as if the usual order of the world had shifted slightly, and entered a new phase.

I was grateful for the car and the snowdrift. It kept Buddy from asking me what I knew he was going to ask, and what he finally did ask, in a low, nervous voice, at the Belsize afternoon tea. DeeDee was eyeing us like an envious cat over the rim of her teacup. After Joan's death, DeeDee had been moved to Wymark for a while, but now she was among us once more.

"I've been wondering ..." Buddy set his cup in the saucer with an awkward clatter.

"What have you been wondering?"

"I've been wondering ... I mean, I thought you might be able to tell me something." Buddy met my eyes and I saw, for the first time, how he had changed. Instead of the old, sure smile that flashed on easily and frequently as a photographer's bulb, his face was grave, even tentative—the face of a man who often does not get what he wants.

"I'll tell you if I can, Buddy."

"Do you think there's something in me that *drives* women crazy?"

I couldn't help myself, I burst out laughing—maybe because of the seriousness of Buddy's face and the common meaning of the word "crazy" in a sentence like that.

"I mean," Buddy pushed on, "I dated Joan, and then you, and first you ... went, and then Joan ..."

With one finger I nudged a cake crumb into a drop of wet, brown tea.

"Of course you didn't do it!" I heard Doctor Nolan say. I had come to her about Joan, and it was the only time I remember her sounding angry. "Nobody did it. *She* did it." And then Doctor Nolan told me how the best of psychiatrists have suicides among their patients, and how they, if anybody, should be held responsible, but how they, on the contrary, do not hold themselves responsible. . . .

"You had nothing to do with us, Buddy."

"You're sure?"

"Absolutely."

"Well," Buddy breathed. "I'm glad of that."

And he drained his tea like a tonic medicine.

"I hear you're leaving us."

I fell into step beside Valerie in the little, nurse-supervised group. "Only if the doctors say yes. I have my interview tomorrow."

The packed snow creaked underfoot, and everywhere I could hear a musical trickle and drip as the noon sun thawed icicles and snow crusts that would glaze again before nightfall.

The shadows of the massed black pines were lavender in that bright light, and I walked with Valerie awhile, down the familiar labyrinth of shoveled asylum paths. Doctors and nurses and patients passing on adjoining paths seemed to be moving on casters, cut off at the waist by the piled snow.

"Interviews!" Valerie snorted. "They're nothing! If they're going to let you out, they let you out."

"I hope so."

In front of Caplan I said good-bye to Valerie's calm, snow-maiden face behind which so little, bad or good, could happen, and walked on alone, my breath coming in white puffs even in that sun-filled air. Valerie's last, cheerful cry had been "So long! Be seeing you."

"Not if I know it," I thought.

But I wasn't sure. I wasn't sure at all. How did I know that someday—at college, in Europe, somewhere, anywhere—the bell jar, with its stifling distortions, wouldn't descend again?

And hadn't Buddy said, as if to revenge himself for my digging out the car and his having to stand by, "I wonder who you'll marry now, Esther."

"What?" I'd said, shoveling snow up onto a mound and blinking against the stinging backshower of loose flakes.

"I wonder who you'll marry now, Esther. Now you've been," and Buddy's gesture encompassed the hill, the pines and the severe, snow-gabled buidlings breaking up the rolling landscape, "here."

And of course I didn't know who would marry me now that I'd been where I had been. I didn't know at all.

"I have a bill here, Irwin."

I spoke quietly into the mouthpiece of the asylum pay phone in the main hall of the administration building. At first I suspected the operator, at her switchboard, might be listening, but she just went on plugging and unplugging her little tubes without batting an eye.

"Yes," Irwin said.

"It's a bill for twenty dollars for emergency attention on a certain date in December and a checkup a week thereafter."

"Yes," Irwin said.

"The hospital says they are sending me the bill because there was no answer to the bill they sent to you."

"All right, all right, I'm writing a check now. I'm writing them a blank check." Irwin's voice altered subtly. "When am I going to see you?"

"Do you really want to know?"

"Very much."

"Never," I said, and hung up with a resolute click.

I wondered, briefly, if Irwin would send his check to the hospital after that, and then I thought, "Of course he will, he's a mathematics professor—he won't want to leave any loose ends."

I felt unaccountably weak-kneed and relieved.

Irwin's voice had meant nothing to me.

This was the first time, since our first and last meeting, that I had spoken with him and, I was reasonably sure, it would be the last. Irwin had absolutely no way of getting in touch with me, except by going to Nurse Kennedy's flat, and after Joan's death Nurse Kennedy had moved somewhere else and left no trace.

I was perfectly free.

Joan's parents invited me to the funeral.

I had been, Mrs. Gilling said, one of Joan's best friends.

"You don't have to go, you know," Doctor Nolan told me. "You can always write and say I said it would be better not to."

"I'll go," I said, and I did go, and all during the simple funeral service I wondered what I thought I was burying.

At the altar the coffin loomed in its snow pallor of flowers— the black shadow of something that wasn't there. The faces in the pews around me were waxen with candlelight, and pine boughs, left over from Christmas, sent up a sepulchral incense in the cold air.

Beside me, Jody's cheeks bloomed like good apples, and here and there in the little congregation I recognized other faces of other girls from college and my home town who had known Joan. DeeDee and Nurse Kennedy bent their kerchiefed heads in a front pew.

Then, behind the coffin and the flowers and the face of the minister and the faces of the mourners, I saw the rolling lawns of our town cemetery, knee-deep in snow now, with the tombstones rising out of it like smokeless chimneys.

There would be a black, six-foot-deep gap hacked in the hard ground. That shadow would marry this shadow, and the peculiar, yellowish soil of our locality seal the wound in the whiteness, and yet another snowfall erase the traces of newness in Joan's grave.

I took a deep breath and listened to the old brag of my heart.

I am, I am, I am.

The doctors were having their weekly board meeting—old business, new business, admissions, dismissals and interviews. Leafing blindly through a tatty *National Geographic* in the asylum library, I waited my turn.

Patients, with accompanying nurses, made their rounds of the stocked shelves, conversing in low tones, with the asylum librarian, an alumna of the asylum herself. Glancing at her— myopic, spinsterish, effaced—I wondered how she knew she had graduated at all, and, unlike her clients, was whole and well.

"Don't be scared," Doctor Nolan had said. "I'll be there, and the rest of the doctors you know, and some visitors, and Doctor Vining, the head of all the doctors, will ask you a few questions, and then you can go."

But in spite of Doctor Nolan's reassurances, I was scared to death.

I had hoped, at my departure, I would feel sure and knowledgeable about everything that lay ahead—after all, I had been "analyzed." Instead, all I could see were question marks.

I kept shooting impatient glances at the closed boardroom door. My stocking seams were straight, my black shoes cracked, but polished, and my red wool suit flamboyant as my plans. Something old, something new. . . .

But I wasn't getting married. There ought, I thought, to be a ritual for being born twice—patched, retreaded and approved for the road, I was trying to think of an appropriate one when Doctor Nolan appeared from nowhere and touched me on the shoulder.

"All right, Esther."

I rose and followed her to the open door.

Pausing, for a brief breath, on the threshold, I saw the silver-haired doctor who had told me about the rivers and the Pilgrims on my first day, and the pocked, cadaverous face of

Miss Huey, and eyes I thought I had recognized over white masks.

The eyes and the faces all turned themselves toward me, and guiding myself by them, as by a magical thread, I stepped into the room.

Sylvia Plath:
A Biographical
Note
by Lois Ames

**With eight previously unpublished
drawings by Sylvia Plath**

THE BELL JAR was first published in London in January 1963 by William Heinemann Limited, under the pseudonym Victoria Lucas. Sylvia Plath had adopted the pen name for publication of her first novel because she questioned its literary value and did not believe it was a "serious work"; she was also worried about the pain publication might cause to the many people close to her whose personalities she had distorted and lightly disguised in the book.

The central themes of Sylvia Plath's early life are the basis for *The Bell Jar*. She was born in 1932 in Massachusetts and spent her early childhood years in Winthrop, a seaside town close to Boston. Her mother's parents were Austrian; her father, a distinguished professor of biology at Boston University (and an internationally known authority on bees), had emigrated to the States from Poland as an adolescent; she had one brother, two and a half years younger. A radical change occurred in Sylvia's life when she was eight: in November 1940, her father died after a long, difficult illness, and the mother and grandparents moved the family inland to the town of Wellesley, a conservative upper-middle-class suburb of Boston. While the grandmother assumed the care of the household, Mrs. Plath taught students in the medical-secretarial training program at Boston University, commuting each day, and the grandfather worked as *maître d'hôtel* at the Brookline Country Club, where he lived during the week. Sylvia and her brother attended the local public schools. "I went to public schools," she wrote later, "genuinely public. Everyone went." At an early age she began to write poems and to draw in pen and ink—and to collect prizes with her first publication of each. By the time she was seventeen, her interest in writing had become disciplined and controlled. Publication, however, did not come easily; she had submitted forty-five pieces to the magazine *Seventeen* before her first short story, "And Summer Will Not Come Again," was published in the August 1950 issue. A poem, "Bitter Strawberries," a sardonic comment on war, was accepted and published in the same month by the *Christian Science Monitor.* In her high school year book, *The Wellesleyan,* the girl who later described herself as a "rabid teenage pragmatist" was pictured:

> Warm smile . . . energetic worker . . . Bumble Boogie piano special . . . Clever with chalk and paints . . . Weekends at Williams . . . Those fully packed sandwiches . . . Future writer . . . Those rejection slips from *Seventeen* . . . Oh, for a license.

In September 1950, Sylvia entered Smith College in Northampton, Massachusetts, the largest women's college in the world. She went on scholarship—one from the Wellesley Smith Club and one endowed by Olive Higgins Prouty, the novelist and author of *Stella Dallas,* later a friend and patron. These were the years in which Sylvia wrote poetry on a precise schedule, circled words in the red-leather thesaurus which had belonged to her father, maintained a detailed journal, kept a diligent scrapbook, and studied with concentration. Highly successful as a student, she was also elected to class and college offices; she became a member of the editorial board of *The Smith Review,* went for weekends to men's colleges, and published stories and poems in *Seventeen.* But at the time she wrote in a letter: "for the few little outward successes I may seem to have, there are acres of misgivings and self-doubt." Of this period a friend later said: "It was as if Sylvia couldn't wait for life to come to her. ... She rushed out to greet it, to make things happen."

As she became increasingly conscious of herself as a woman, the conflict between the life-style of a poet/intellectual and that of a wife and mother became a central preoccupation, and she wrote: ". . . it's quite amazing how I've gone around for most of my life as in the rarefied atmosphere under a bell jar." In August 1951 she won *Mademoiselle* magazine's fiction contest with a short story, "Sunday at the Mintons," and in the following year, her junior year in college, Sylvia was awarded two Smith poetry prizes and was elected to Phi Beta Kappa and to Alpha, the Smith College honorary society for the arts. Then in the summer of 1952 she was chosen to be a guest editor in *Mademoiselle*'s College Board Contest. In her scrapbook, she described the beginning of that month in New York in the breathy style of the magazine:

> After being one of the two national winners of *Mademoiselle's* fiction contest ($500!) last August, I felt that I was coming home again when I won a guest editorship representing Smith & took a train to NYC for a salaried month working—hatted & heeled—in *Mlle's* aircon-ditioned Madison Ave. offices. . . . Fantastic, fabulous, and all other inadequate adjectives go to describe the four gala and chaotic-weeks I worked as guest managing Ed . . . living in luxury at the Barbizon, I edited, met celebrities, was fêted and feasted by a galaxy of UN delegates, simultaneous interpreters & artists . . . an almost unbelievable merry-go-round month—this Smith Cinderella met idols: Vance Bourjaily, Paul Engle, Elizabeth Bowen—wrote article via correspondence with 5 handsome young male poet teachers.

The poets were Alistair Reid, Anthony Hecht, Richard Wilbur, George Steiner, and William Burford, whose pictures were accompanied by biographical notes and comments on poets and poetry.

After 230-odd pages of advertising, the bulk of the August 1953 college issue was introduced by Sylvia as Guest Manag-

ing Editor with *"Mlle's* last word on college, '53." Under a
vapid picture of the guest editors holding hands in star forma-
tions, dressed alike in tartan skirts with matching Eton caps and
open-mouthed smiles, she wrote:

> We're stargazers this season, bewitched by an atmos-
> phere of evening blue. Foremost in the fashion constella-
> tion we spot *Mlle's* own tartan, the astronomic versatility
> of sweaters, and men, men, men—we've even taken the
> shirts off their backs! Focusing our telescope on college
> news around the globe, we debate and deliberate. Issues
> illuminated: academic freedom, the sorority controversy,
> our much labeled (and libeled) generation. From our
> favorite fields, stars of the first magnitude shed a bright
> influence on our plans for jobs and futures. Although
> horoscopes for our ultimate orbits aren't yet in, we Guest
> Eds. are counting on a favorable forecast with this send-
> off from *Mlle*, the star of the campus.

No doubt she was far more pleased with page 358—*"Mlle.*
finally published 'Mad Girl's Lovesong'—my favorite villanelle":

MAD GIRL'S LOVE SONG

A VILLANELLE
    By *Sylvia Plath*
    Smith College, '54

I shut my eyes and all the world drops dead;
I lift my lids and all is born again.
(I think I made you up inside my head.)

The stars go waltzing out in blue and red,
And arbitrary blackness gallops in:
I shut my eyes and all the world drops dead.

I dreamed that you bewitched me into bed
And sung me moon-struck, kissed me quite insane.
(I think I made you up inside my head.)

God topples from the sky, hell's fires fade:
Exit seraphim and Satan's men:
I shut my eyes and all the world drops dead.

I fancied you'd return the way you said,
But I grow old and I forget your name.
(I think I made you up inside my head.)

I should have loved a thunderbird instead;
At least when spring comes they roar back again.
I shut my eyes and all the world drops dead.
(I think I made you up inside my head.)

That summer, too, *Harper's Magazine* paid $100 for three poems which Sylvia identified as "first professional earnings." Later, assessing these bubbling achievements, she wrote, "All in all, I felt upborne on a wave of creative, social and financial success— The six month crash, however, was to come—"

These were the events which took place in her life in the summer and autumn of 1953—at the time of the electrocution of the Rosenbergs, at the time when Senator Joseph McCarthy was forcing his power, at the beginning of the Eisenhower presidency—these were the events which Sylvia Plath reconstructed in *The Bell Jar*. Years later she described the book she wanted to write:

> the pressures of the fashion magazine world which seems
> increasingly superficial and artificial, the return home to
> the dead summer world of a suburb of Boston. Here the
> cracks in her [the heroine, Esther Greenwood's] nature
> which had been held together as it were by the surround-
> ing pressures of New York widen and gape alarmingly.
> More and more her warped view of the world around—
> her own vacuous domestic life, and that of her neighbors
> —seems the one right way of looking at things.

For Sylvia then came electroshock therapy and finally her well-publicized disappearance, subsequent discovery and consequent hospitalization for psychotherapy and more shock treatment. She wrote: "A time of darkness, despair, disillusion—so black only as the inferno of the human mind can be—symbolic death, and numb shock—then the painful agony of slow rebirth and psychic regeneration."

Subsequently Sylvia returned to Smith College and recon-

quered "old broncos that threw me for a loop last year. At the
beginning of the next summer she wrote that "a semester of
reconstruction ends with an infinitely more solid if less flash-
ingly spectacular flourish than last year's." By the end of the
next academic year, she had sold more poems, earned addi-
tional prizes, and written her long paper for English honors on
the double personality in Dostoyevski's novels. In June 1955
she graduated from Smith College *summa cum laude* with the
prospect of an English Fulbright year in Newnham College at
Cambridge University. There Sylvia met the British poet Ted
Hughes, whom she married in London on June 16, 1956:
Bloomsday. Sylvia's Fulbright was renewed and, after a vacation in Spain, Ted and Sylvia lived in Cambridge for another
year. Then, in the spring of 1957, they moved to the United
States, where Sylvia was assessed by her colleagues as "one of
the two or three finest instructors ever to appear in the
English department at Smith College."

It is probable that Sylvia already had a version of *The Bell
Jar* in her trunks when she returned to the States, but she was
concentrating on poetry and on teaching. In June 1958, she
applied for a Eugene F. Saxton Memorial Fellowship to com-
plete her book of poems. The Saxton Fellowship had been
established "to honor an outstanding editor of Harper & Broth-
ers"; the trust, at the discretion of the trustees, gave outright
grants of money to writers for living expenses. Agreement of
all three trustees was necessary to make the grant, and one of
them, who called the sample poems "beyond reproach," noted
that "in looking over Mrs. Hughes' history, I see that she has
had valuable awards dropped into her lap during most of her
adult life. Perhaps it would not do her any real harm to
continue her work for a while as a teacher in a fine college.
My impulse is rejection, though I think the quality of her
work entitles her to serious consideration." In October 1958
the application was rejected with a special letter from the
secretary to the trustees, who wanted Mrs. Hughes to know
that "your application aroused more than ordinary interest.
The talent—which is marked—was not a matter for dispute
but rather the nature of the project."

Meanwhile the Hugheses had moved to a small apartment
on Beacon Hill, "living on a shoestring for a year in Boston

writing to see what we could do." Sylvia had made the difficult decision to give up teaching, and to discard an academic plan for which she had been groomed since childhood, in exchange for a less certain existence but one which she hoped would give her more time to write. However, as the year progressed, and her book of poems was repeatedly submitted and rejected under ever-changing titles, she wrote:

> Nothing stinks like a pile of unpublished writing, which remark I guess shows I still don't have a pure motive (O it's-such-fun-I-just-can't-stop-who-cares-if-it's-published-or-read) about writing. . . . I still want to see it finally ritualized in print.

In December 1959, Ted and Sylvia returned to England to live. In April 1960 their first child, Freda, was born. At last Sylvia's book of poetry, *The Colossus,* was accepted for fall publication by William Heinemann Limited. Subsequently Sylvia suffered a miscarriage, then an appendectomy, and then became pregnant again. On May 1, 1961, she again applied for a Eugene F. Saxton Fellowship; this time in order to finish a novel which she described as one-sixth completed—about fifty pages. On the application Sylvia had asked for money to cover "babysitter or nanny at about $5 a day, 6 days a week for a year, $1,560. Rent of study at about $10 a week: $520 for a year. Total: $2,080. . . . (At present I am living in a two room flat with my husband and year old baby and having to work part time to meet living expenses.)" To a friend she wrote that she was "over one third through a novel about a college girl building up for and going through a nervous breakdown." She wrote:

> I have been wanting to do this for ten years but had a terrible block about Writing A Novel. Then suddenly in beginning negotiations with a New York publisher for an American edition of my poems, the dykes broke and I stayed awake all night seized by fearsome excitement, saw how it should be done, started the next day & go

every morning to my borrowed study as to an office
& belt out more of it.

In the summer, the Hugheses moved to Devon to live in a
thatch-roofed country house, and on November 6, 1961, the
secretary to the Saxton trustees wrote that they had voted to
give her a grant in the amount of $2,080, "the sum you
suggested." Sylvia replied, "I was very happy to receive your
good letter today telling about the Saxton Fellowship. I certainly do plan to go ahead with the novel and the award
comes at a particularly helpful time to free me to do so."
On January 17, 1962, a son, Nicholas, was born. The days
were divided among the babies, housework, and writing, but
on February 10, 1962, Sylvia punctually delivered her first
quarterly report on the progress of her novel to the Saxton
trustees. "During the past three months the novel has progressed very satisfactorily, according to my drafted schedule. I
have worked through several rough drafts to a final version of
Chapters 5 through 8, completing a total of 105 pages of the
novel in all, and have outlined in detail Chapters 9 through
12." Then she gave in detail the plans for *The Bell Jar.*
Although the novel was going well, Sylvia complained to a
friend that she felt she was doing little work: "a couple of
poems I like a year looks like a lot when they come out, but
in fact are points of satisfaction separated by large vacancies."
On May 1, 1962, in the next quarterly report to the Saxton
trustees, she wrote, "The novel is getting on very well, and
according to schedule. I have completed Chapters 9 through 12
(pages 106-166) and projected in detailed outline the next lap
of the book." By June 1962 she could tell a friend: "I'm
writing again. Really writing. I'd like you to see some of my
new poems." She had begun the *Ariel* poems and was confident enough to want to show them, to have them read, to
read them aloud. These poems were different: her husband
has written that "Tulips" "was the first sign of what was on its
way. She wrote this poem without her usual studies over the
Thesaurus, and at top speed, as one might write an urgent
letter. From then on, all her poems were written this way."
On August 1, 1962, Sylvia sent her final progress report to
the Saxton trustees:

The novel is rounding out now, shaping up pretty much
as planned, and I have completed Chapters 13 through
16 (pages 167-221) and am hoping the last lap goes as
well.

After a vacation in Ireland, Sylvia and Ted decided to
separate for a while. The summer had been difficult. She had
suffered repeated attacks of flu accompanied by high fever.
Another winter in Devon seemed impossible. She began to
commute to London, where she was "getting work with the
BBC" and hunting for a flat. The manuscript of *The Bell Jar*
had been sent to the trustees of the Saxton Fellowship in the
States, and Heinemann had accepted the novel in England and
was setting it into type. A few days before Christmas, Sylvia
moved herself and the children to London, where she had
signed a five-year lease on a flat:

> . . . a small miracle happened—I'd been to Yeats' tower
> at Ballylea while in Ireland & thought it the most beauti-
> ful & peaceful place in the world; then, walking
> desolately around my beloved Primrose Hill in London
> and brooding on the hopelessness of ever finding a flat
> . . . I passed Yeats' house, with its blue plaque "Yeats
> lived here" which I'd often passed & longed to live in.
> A sign board was up—flats to rent, I flew to the agent.
> By a miracle you can only know if you've ever tried to
> flat hunt in London, I was first to apply. . . . I am here
> on a five year lease & it is utter heaven . . . and it's
> Yeats' house, which right now means a lot to me.

Sylvia took the finding of the Yeats house for a sign. She
told a friend that when she went out to look for flats that day,
she had "known" she would find it, and so, with that
confirmation, she began to make plans with energetic assur-
ance. She was working on a new novel, and the *Ariel* poems
were continuing to flow. She told another friend that she
thought of *The Bell Jar* "as an autobiographical apprentice
work which I had to write in order to free myself from the
past." But the new novel, about more recent events in her
life, she regarded as strong, powerful and urgent.

When *The Bell Jar* was published, in January 1963, Sylvia

was distressed by the reviews, although another reader, not the author and not under the same sorts of stress, might have interpreted the critics' views of the novel far differently. Lawrence Lerner in the *Listener* wrote, "There are criticisms of America that the neurotic can make as well as anyone, perhaps better, and Miss Lucas makes them brilliantly." The *Times Literary Supplement* observed that the author "can certainly write," and went on to say that "if she can learn to shape as well as she imagines, she may write an extremely good book." In the *New Statesman,* Robert Taubman called *The Bell Jar* "the first feminine novel in a Salinger mood."

In 1970, Aurelia Plath, her mother, wrote a letter to Sylvia's editor at Harper & Row in New York about the anticipated publication of the first American edition of *The Bell Jar*:

> I realize that no explanation of the *why* of personal suffering that this publication here [publication of *The Bell Jar* in the United States] will create in the lives of several people nor any appeal on any other grounds is going to stop this, so I shall waste neither my time nor yours in pointing out the inevitable repercussions. . . . I do want to tell you of one of the last conversations I had with my daughter in early July, 1962, just before her personal world fell apart. Sylvia had told me of the pressure she was under in fulfilling her obligation to the Eugene Saxton Fund. As you know, she had been given a grant by this fund to enable her to write a novel. In the space of time allotted, she had a miscarriage, an appendectomy, and had given birth to her second child, Nicholas.
>
> "What I've done," I remember her saying, "is to throw together events from my own life, fictionalizing to add color—it's a pot boiler really, but I think it will show how isolated a person feels when he is suffering a breakdown. . . . I've tried to picture my world and the people in it as seen through the distorting lens of a bell jar." Then she went on to say, "My second book will show that same world as seen through the eyes of health." Practically every character in *The Bell Jar* represents someone—often in caricature—whom Sylvia loved; each person had given freely of time, thought,

affection, and, in one case, financial help during those
agonizing six months of breakdown in 1953 . . . as this
book stands by itself, it represents the basest ingratitude.
That was not the basis of Sylvia's personality; it was the
reason she became so frightened when, at the time of
publication, the book was widely read and showed signs
of becoming a success. Sylvia wrote her brother that
"this must never be published in the United States."
The very title *The Bell Jar* should imply what Sylvia
told me and that is what the astute reader should
infer. . . .

It was the coldest winter in London since 1813-14. Light
and heat went off at unannounced intervals. Pipes froze. She
had applied, and her name was on the list, but a telephone had
not yet been installed. Each morning before the children woke
at eight, Sylvia worked on the *Ariel* poems. Here the sense of
human experience as horrid and ungovernable, the sense of all
relationships as puppetlike and meaningless, had come to
dominate her imagination. Yet she wrote with intensity, convinced that what she was now writing could be said by no one
else. Always there was the need to be practical, to find time
for the deliberate expression of anguish. Sylvia wrote, "I feel
like a very efficient tool or weapon, used and in demand from
moment to moment. . . ." She had seen a doctor who had
prescribed sedatives and had arranged for her to consult a
psychotherapist. She wrote for an appointment and had also
written to her former psychiatrist in Boston. A recurrent
problem of sinus infection developed. She had fired her *au
pair* girl and was waiting for a replacement "to help with the
babes mornings so I can write . . . nights are no good, I'm
so flat by then that all I can cope with is music & brandy
& water."

In spite of the help of friends and anticipation of spring
(she was to return to the house in Devon around May Day),
she was despairing and ill. But the poems continued to come,
even in the last week of her life—several extraordinary
poems. To those around her it appeared that she had not
given up. Frequently she seemed bright, cheerful, full of
hope.

However, on the morning of February 11, 1963, she ended

her life. Who can explain *why?* As Sylvia had written earlier in the last optimistic pages of *The Bell Jar:*

> How did I know that someday—at college, in Europe, somewhere, anywhere—the bell jar, with its stifling distortions, wouldn't descend again?

—that bell jar out of which she had once struggled brilliantly, successfully, apparently completely, but of which she could write with the clarity of one who has endured: "to the person in The Bell Jar, blank and stopped as a dead baby, the world itself is the bad dream."